Dear Reader,

This problem I've got sure has me riled up. I'm your basic, good-natured, red-blooded American male. And I'm a good ol' Alabama boy, to boot. But I guess I've been too long without a woman, and I went and let my libido catch me off guard.

You see, I've fallen for the beautiful young divorcée who just moved in next door. After thirty-six years of bachelorhood, I've finally found the woman of my dreams. All I want to do is spend the rest of my life with my love.

And all I have to do is convince her that I'm the man for her. Before you know it, I'll be sharing that two-hundred-year-old farmhouse with her. And her son... her daughter... her mother... her ex-mother-in-law.... And the resident ghost.

So now you see my problem. By the time you get to the end of the book, you'll know how it all turns out.

Tucker Highsmith

D1005558

Alabama

JACKIE WEGER
Full House

Alabama

Harlequin Books

TORONTO • NEW YORK • LONDON
AMSTERDAM • PARIS • SYDNEY • HAMBURG
STOCKHOLM • ATHENS • TOKYO • MILAN
MADRID • WARSAW • BUDAPEST • AUCKLAND

HARLEQUIN ENTERPRISES LTD.
225 Duncan Mill Road, Don Mills,
Ontario, Canada M3B 3K9

FULL HOUSE

Copyright © 1989 by Jackie Weger

ISBN: 0-373-45151-2

Published Harlequin Enterprises, Ltd. 1989, 1993

Chapter One

This was it. She had followed the hand-drawn map without error. Justine let her hands slide from the steering wheel to rest in her lap. The house stood amid ancient trees and knee-high weeds. One glance told her that far from the glowing description in the letter the agent had sent, this place was only going to add to her burdens. Damn it! And he had made it sound so grand. Spacious great room, huge kitchen, wraparound porch in Alabama's rich delta land. Just needs a little elbow grease. Elbow grease! Wrecking ball was more like it.

There were four other occupants in the station wagon: her mother, her mother-in-law, and her children, Pip and Judy Ann. No one was saying a word. Not good, Justine thought with growing trepidation. But she didn't dare voice her own disappointment lest she open herself up to a litany of "I told you so's."

Judy Ann leaned over into the front seat. "Listen, Mommy, let's just go back to Virginia and live where we did. I don't like it here."

Justine forced a smile. "We can't do that, sweetie. This is our new home."

"I don't like it!"

"Give it a chance, darling. We haven't even gotten out of the car! Look! There's a squirrel. Go make friends."

"I've seen squirrels before."

"Not in your own front yard, you haven't. Don't turn pouty on me yet, sweetie. Give it a few hours. Okay?"

Weeks ago, when life had her up against a rough wall, Justine heard about this house and felt she had been given a sign. She'd had a premonition that the move and the house would be the central focus of a new start for all of them; that things were finally going to change for the better. She gave an inward shrug. It wasn't the first time she had read a situation wrong. Or a person. If there had been a laugh left in her now, Justine would've bellowed at her own stupidity. The only thing left to her was to make the best of a poor situation. At least, she thought, she was getting darn good at that. "Well, everybody out," she said brightly.

"Who did you say told you about this place?"

Justine gave a small laugh. "I could've predicted you'd ask that, Mother. I really could."

"Well, who, then?"

"Just a friend I worked with once. Her grandparents used to lease it during hunting season. She spent Christmas with them one year. She said . . ."

"You must have done something terrible to her," interjected Agnes, who was sitting in the back seat very much under protest.

Justine sighed with the forbearance she had learned over time. Agnes Hale had been part and parcel of her household for more than twelve years and very often required as much attention as the children. As the family's senior member, Agnes felt her place was in the front seat at all times. That Pauline had beat her to it today left no room for appeasement. Sitting ramrod straight between the children, Agnes had been derisive and nitpicking since they'd driven away from the motel earlier that morning.

"The house can't be as awful as it appears, Mother Hale."

"It looks pretty bad from here," said eleven-year-old Pip.

"It looks spooky to me," added Judy Ann.

"It's just all the shade around the house," said Justine soothingly, knowing the eight-year-old was easily upset. Judy Ann was a child who needed a secure anchor in life; she thrived on sameness. Changes in routine frightened her. Justine had found it necessary to present a calm facade in front of Judy Ann even when she herself pulsed with insecurity and anxiety. Like now, she thought with inward chagrin.

"Look at those grand old trees, darling. It's lovely here. And that porch—it wraps all the way around the house, just as the agent said. Imagine sitting there on summer evenings in rocking chairs, watching the sun go down—"

"Imagine the chiggers and mosquitos, maybe even bats."

Justine held her tongue. Agnes had never in her life seen a bat outside the horror movies she was addicted to on late-night television.

"Now Agnes," cooed Pauline in defense of her only daughter. "Justine is doing the best she can under the circumstances. Let's not fault her too soon. If this property is the best she could do, we'll manage here."

"My mother, my champion," Justine said, knowing full well her mother's support was thinly given, wouldn't last and was voiced chiefly to antagonize Agnes. "How about all of you hold off on the criticism until we've seen the interior, then you can let loose. I was told there are lovely fireplaces in every room."

"We didn't mean to criticize you, dear." Pauline cut a look at her archenemy. "Did we, Agnes?"

"I certainly didn't. I can't speak for you, of course."

Justine opened her door to let in a breeze, then began rummaging through her purse.

"Don't tell me," said Pauline. "You've lost the key."

"I wasn't sent a key, Mother. I'm looking for the two little bombs I made last night. I thought I'd let you and Mother Hale each have one. Just a little something to occupy your time." She found a cigarette and lit it, inhaling deeply.

Agnes poked her daughter-in-law's shoulder with her walking cane. "You know, Justine, I think it's precisely those kinds of remarks that made Philip leave you. Not to mention your smoking. Such a filthy habit.''

Pauline smirked. "He left you, too, Agnes."

"Well, of course. A man has to cut the umbilical cord sometime!"

"Aged forty is *cutting* it a bit thin, don't you think?"

"Enough!" Justine said, grinding the cigarette out in the ashtray. "Everybody out! Right this minute, and not another word. Pip, you let down the tailgate and unload the suitcases. Judy Ann, go with Mother Hale to the porch steps. Both of you can sit there in the shade. Mother, you come with me. We'll inspect the house. We need to have an idea of the layout to tell the movers where to put the furniture."

"If they can find the place," said Agnes, sotto voce, refusing to budge. She hugged to her thin chest the straw bag in which she kept her treasures: contest newsletters, postcards, stamps, pens and pencils.

Justine dispensed one of her looks. "They had the same map we did."

"Sorry," the old woman uttered with a little toss of her head, which had the effect of making the apology meaningless.

Ignoring the sense of dismay that was overtaking her, Justine got out of the car and stretched.

"Just smell that Alabama air! It's going to be good for us here. I can feel it. Think positive everybody. Look how big that house is. We can each have our own room. Why, it seems to go on forever."

"I don't want my own room," said Judy Ann. "I wanna sleep with Gram like I always have."

"Well, okay," Justine said to keep the peace. "But only until the newness wears off the house."

"Newness wore off that house about two hundred years ago," said Pauline, delivering the opinion with a delicate sniff of disapproval.

"I don't mind that it's old, Mother. It's nice to know there're a few things in this world that last. There's a

stained-glass transom over the door. That's unusual, don't
you think?''

"You don't want to know what's running through my
mind right now, so don't ask me what I think."

"But, you'll tell me . . . all in good time?"

Pauline issued an aristocratic snort. "Philip ruined you.
You used to be such a sweet child."

"I used to be a lot of things. The past is finished. Let's
leave it alone."

"You can't go on forever keeping your emotions bottled
up, you know.''

"Mother, my emotions of the moment are focused to
cope with the present."

Justine turned away and faced the house. The agent's
letter had made her think of a once elegant home, fallen on
bad times sort of like herself. Not that she had ever been
elegant in the exact sense of that word. But she sure knew
about falling on hard times. And the greatest appeal about
the old house had been the price of the lease. It was cheap
enough that she could assure all of them a roof over their
heads for at least a year, which was the time she had allowed to make a name for herself in her chosen field.

Thinking of work, the goals she had set, made Justine's
stomach tighten. She could do it. She had to! She brushed
the inner dread aside before it overwhelmed her, and gave
her attention to details of the house.

The porches leaned, the roof was patched, the front door
lacked a screen. Its windows were wide and tall, bracketed
on each side by faded green shutters. Had she arrived at
dusk she might have thought it sinister because of the way
it was secluded so, in shade and shrub and weed. But it was
a brightly lit June morning: birds chattered, flies buzzed
and squirrels abounded. Now that she was out of the car
and looking at it head on, the house, for all its exterior
faults, looked as if it were welcoming them.

Pauline locked her arm through her daughter's as they
walked up the crooked stone path.

"Now, Justine. Philip's leaving was not your fault. You
shouldn't think that. Just be thankful he cut a deuce while

you're still young. If you're pleasing and appealing, you can always get another husband."

"Oh, I'm sure I can, Mother. Just think what I have to offer. A smart-aleck eleven-year-old son, a frightened eight-year-old daughter... stretch marks. My mother lives with me, not to mention my ex-mother-in-law. I'll just tell the first man who throws himself at me that I got Agnes in the divorce settlement and you as my inheritance. He'd be so thrilled, he'd swoon."

"Men don't swoon dear. That was Victorian women. I only meant you ought to lose five pounds. Don't be such a cynic. If a new man comes into your life, why, Agnes and I will just have to fade into the woodwork, won't we?"

"You and Agnes fading?" Justine laughed. "That'll be the day."

"I do expect that my stay with you will only be temporary, until—"

"I've heard that before. Agnes said it more than twelve years ago."

"Put her in a nursing home."

"Mother! I couldn't do that. To either of you... ever."

"Of course, not me. I still have my wits about me."

"So does Agnes."

"That's debatable."

"Mother... you *promised*."

"I said I would be kind to her face. I didn't make any promises about behind her back."

Justine sucked in a breath. It was fruitless to continue the conversation. Her mother had tunnel vision when it came to Agnes.

They climbed the porch steps. Pauline tried the doorknob. "Locked."

Justine cupped her hands and peered through a window pane into a wide hall. "I'm sure the key must be around somewhere."

"Are you sure you weren't supposed to pick up the key from the estate agent?"

"Positive. Maybe the back door's open. I'll go around."

The windows along the side of the house were huge with many panes and the look of French doors, but no handles were evident. Justine pushed, but the only thing they gave back was a full-color reflection of herself. She stepped away for a better view.

She brushed hair the color of ripened wheat from her forehead then touched under her eyes with her fingertips. No lines to speak of yet, she noted. A miracle, considering her disrupted life and the hassles of the past months. Young! Thirty-six didn't feel young. Anyway, every woman knew aging started in the arms.

She held her arms out. That's where the flab started. You could almost judge a woman's age by how long she wore her sleeves. No matter how ageless the face, after the age of thirty, one could add a year for every inch of sleeve. Justine flapped her arms, studying the tender undersides in the glass. Small miracles still abounded. Her's didn't jiggle...yet.

Another reflection suddenly mingled with her own. It was brown-haired, dark-eyed, with features sharpened one notch past handsome, and it wore a mustache. The reflection was grinning.

Mortified, Justine lowered her arms and spun about.

The man was standing in a bed of blooming jonquils as if he had just sprung up through the earth among them; an aberration of nature. His expression was that of a somnolent wolf, yet she was conscious that in that one lazy glance he was assessing her clothes, calculating her age and weight and had probably guessed what she ate for breakfast.

"Don't stop on account of me," he said, and went back to grinning.

"Who're you?" she managed. "The local Peeping Tom?"

A gleam leaped into his eyes. "Come now. Be nice. And if you're wondering, you'll do."

"I wasn't wondering. I was—never mind what I was doing. This is private property. You're trespassing, unless—" Her heart sank. "Are you the estate agent?"

"Nope. Your nearest neighbor. That is, I am if you're Mrs. Justine Hale." He held up a set of keys and dangled them. "For the house. Jim Kessler dropped them by, asked me to see that you got them. I heard car doors slam. Figured it was you."

"And, you are?" Justine demanded on a wobbly note while her brain registered and absorbed the information her eyes were sending.

He was made of rough material, a man who used brawn to do his job. She suspected his work kept him out of doors. He was well tanned for so early in the summer. A ditch-digger. A farmer. Most assuredly a jackass, sneaking up on her like that. And she could tell right off, he was the kind of man she didn't like. He had the look of a man who hoarded superiority like a Scrooge hoards pennies.

Still, the admiring way he was looking at her kept her sharp, standing straight, tummy in and shoulders back.

"Tucker Highsmith," he answered, and it was a real drawl, so that Justine knew at once that he was generations and genes full of Alabama. He gave a mock bow. "At your service...."

Justine latched on to his innuendo and wondered just how much of her background the estate agent had passed on to Tucker Highsmith. She had not said much, beyond the fact of how many members her family numbered, but Kessler *had* called her references. Who knew what one of them had let slip? Divorcées, as she had learned to her dismay, were considered fair game for a roving eye.

Poker stiff, she said, "Thank you for bringing the keys." Stepping to the edge of the porch, she held out her hand. He dropped them into her palm. They were huge and old-fashioned.

"Justine! Oh, there you are," Pauline said, as she came round the house. She beamed a smile at Tucker. "Why, hello there."

"Mother, this is Tucker Highsmith, our neighbor. He's brought our keys. My mother, Mrs. Gates," Justine said.

"Just call me Pauline, everyone does."

Tucker smiled warmly. "Nice to meet you."

"And so nice to meet you."

Justine grabbed her mother's arm and ushered her away without a backward glance. "That was disgusting, Mother. You practically drooled."

"I did not! He's quite attractive. I love men who don't part their hair, when they have any, that is. Goodness, Mr. Highsmith didn't look the kind of man one trifles with, did he? He reminds me of somebody, but I can't think who."

"You can't judge a man by the way he parts his hair. And, you've never met a man of Tucker Highsmith's ilk in your life, unless it was a gardener."

"Oh, no dear, our gardeners were always ethnic. Gardening is a talent. As far as how I judge a man, by his hair or otherwise, I did pretty well sizing up your father. He never left me to go off to some godforsaken island just so he could shave his head and wear saffron robes like—"

"That's enough, Mother."

"Well, I did try to talk you out of marrying Philip, didn't I? He was always so stodgy."

"I loved him, Mother. Can't you understand that?"

"Actually, no. I always thought you married him because he was the first man you slept with."

"I don't believe we're having this conversation."

"There you go again, Justine. Making me feel guilty. I feel such a headache coming on."

"You timed it just right. There's the moving van. Do you think you can hold off on headaches until we get settled?"

Pauline sighed. "One can only hope."

"I don't have the luxury of hope. I have to deal in realities."

"Mr. Highsmith looked real enough to me. He isn't married, you know."

"What are you now, a seer?" She handed her mother the keys. "Go unlock the door. I'll direct the movers."

"His shirt had laundry creases. No woman in her right mind sends wash 'n' wear shirts to a commercial laundry. So he's single."

"Mother," said Justine, vexed, "I'm still reeling from the effects of one failed marriage. I'm not interested in putting myself through that a second time."

"Yes, but you *thought* you were happily married. And people who've been happily married always—"

"Save your convoluted philosophy for the children, Mother. They understand it better than I do."

"Justine, dear," Pauline said, placing a restraining hand on her daughter's arm. "You need a man. I never thought I'd live to see the day I'd believe in that old adage, but in your case it's true. You're better at life when coupled."

"Coupled?"

"You know what I mean. I just want you to know, I won't stand in your way. In fact, I intend to encourage you."

Justine turned away quickly. Hot tears came up behind her eyes. Even her own mother was doing it! Thinking, suggesting, that she could not make it in life without a man.

It was true that she had always leaned heavily on Philip. But he had encouraged her to depend entirely upon him, he wanted it, insisted! Now, of course she saw through that. It was his way of proving to himself that he was a man above others.

In the end all he had proved was that he couldn't bear up under the responsibility—a classic case of biting off more than he could chew. He overloaded. His circuits went haywire. He was hoisted on his own petard as it were. When he had crumbled, her entire world had crumbled along with his.

Thinking of Philip caused a churning of hurt and anger in Justine's stomach.

If only it had been another woman!

Or even another man!

She could've battled that and won!

But how does one fight a man who has decided to abandon his family in favor of becoming a monk so he could wear saffron robes, chant "om" and go live in Southeast Asia?

There wasn't a single article in any magazine that told a woman how to cope with that! Impotency, herpes, how to argue effectively—all topics well covered. One thing those women's rags never delved into was revenge. How could they miss that a woman needed that, craved it! Justine sniffed. She got back at them. She had canceled all of her subscriptions. The satisfaction had lasted only moments.

For months, while her world collapsed, she had tried not to think or feel, pretending a strength and calm she had not really possessed. She was still pretending.

She knew the score. She was only accountable to her dreams in the dark lonely recesses of the bed she no longer shared with anyone.

Pauline's words threaded their way far into Justine's brain: "You're better at life when coupled."

Deep down in her soul Justine knew she was a woman who thrived on loving and being loved; a woman who longed to be held close, enclosed in strong arms, partnered in life and safe from the outer world. But a stubbornness that was entirely Justine Hale kept her from admitting it to herself. Or anyone else.

As she lifted her hand to greet the movers, the image of Tucker Highsmith's lazy sardonic grin crossed her mind's eye. She blinked, erasing his features.

LOTTIE ROBERTS was beside herself with excitement.

Inside the old house she flitted from one window to the next, anxious for the new tenants to come inside and unpack. It was always wonderful to peek in drawers, handle the untold and modern treasures people brought with them. She hoped they had a television. She adored television.

The previous tenants used to eat lunch accompanied by the *Tennessee Ernie Ford Show*. To this day she could still hum a few bars of "Sixteen Tons." And in the afternoon she had watched *Edge of Night* and *Dark Shadows*.

She liked electric can openers, too. Tucker Highsmith had one. The whirring sound reminded her of *The Green Hornet* on radio. *The Green Hornet* used to give her goose bumps.

At least, she imagined she erupted in goose bumps. It was terrible not to have any flesh. She had form, but it wasn't anything a body could actually see. Not that she hadn't attempted to extend herself. She had, dozens of times. She had tried everything she could think of from mustard packs and herb teas to strengthening jelly... until the barley ran out.

Thus far, nothing had worked.

Not even the family Bible had been of help and she had spent hundreds of hours scouring it, especially John 11:1-12 to see how Lazarus had done it.

Unfortunately Lazarus had had help of a higher nature. Being in the situation she was, sort of betwixt and between, Lottie didn't think it behooved her to draw attention to herself from that quarter.

Not that she thought, even for a minute, that she'd sinned enough to be thrust into Eternal Fire, but you never knew. There had been that incident with the Union soldier, howsomever, she hadn't realized God was on their side until the North had won the war and by then it was too late to undo the deed.

Of course, she never missed saying her prayers, God-fearing woman that she was. She just never *asked* for anything; most especially for an end to her condition, seeing as with Him it could go either way. Early on, she'd figured it best just to manage getting back on her own.

Anyway, doing for herself had always been her long suit. She reckoned that being strong willed was simply bred into her.

That had always been a thing said of her. Folks from miles around used to joke about it. "You got a mule that won't pull a plow," they said, "let it spend a day with Lottie Roberts. Once the fool animal sees what true balkiness is, it'll be so shamed, it'll harness itself to the plow and bellow for the farmer to step into the traces."

Lottie was counting on her will and determination to see her through. Only thing was, once extended and fleshed out again, she would have to know enough of the modern world to get by.

Some modern things frightened her. Automobiles, for instance. You had to be closed up in them and they went so fast. She'd gone off with a tenant once, in a 1917 Oakland, if she recollected right. She had felt certain she was going to be killed twice over. Her heart, or the region where she imagined her heart to be—had lunged and pounded so hard she'd thought the rattling might give her presence away.

She had been building up her courage to try it again when another war started and the tenant had gone off to fight.

Like her own Elmer, the tenant had never returned. Lottie sighed. She missed Elmer something fierce.

Oh, it had been so long since the old house had had tenants. And this bunch looked a mixed bag. Surely among them was one who would be her friend.

The front door was pushed open with a bang and a boy came barreling into the house. He raced down the hall, banging doors open.

Lottie bristled and shot up to the ceiling, out of harm's way.

That's one scamp needs manners taught! she observed.

Next through the door was a slender, elegantly clad woman with silver hair shaped into a perfectly rendered chignon. Lottie surmised the woman was about her own age. Well, not her age now, she corrected, but before.

A blond-haired girl hesitated on the threshold until she was given a push by an elderly woman with a cane. Lottie gasped.

The old lady was dressed in various shades of purple and mauve and had tightly permed curls. Purple permed curls.

Lottie had never seen hair like it. Trailing cobwebs she moved down from the ceiling and whirled about the old woman for a better look. She wanted to touch the hair, but didn't dare. The woman hobbled into the parlor and sat in a fiddleback chair.

Lottie plopped down on the matching stool and stared. She spared a glance for a younger woman who came in and began inspecting the room, but it was the purple hair that kept her enthralled.

"I swear! It's cold in here," complained Agnes. "And look," she shuddered pointing at Lottie. "Dust and spider webs are literally falling from the ceiling!"

"You don't exercise enough, Mother Hale," suggested Justine. "I think it's quite pleasant. And the agent was right about spaciousness—this room is huge."

Agnes snorted. "I guess I know cold when I feel cold. Pip, dear," she said, as he came racing into the room, "open those French doors and let in some of that nice warm breeze."

"Mom," he said breathlessly. "There's no bathroom."

"Of course there's a bathroom."

It's on a corner of the back porch, said Lottie, trying to be helpful. *It's a good bathroom,* she volunteered. *The same tenant who owned the Oakland installed it.*

No one paid Lottie any mind. That was another problem with being in the state she was in, she thought with a twinge of disgust. No one could hear her, either. The only way she had of getting a body's attention was to mingle with the other's aura and sort of make suggestions. Sometimes that worked and sometimes not.

"I looked in every room, Mom. Ask Judy Ann, if you don't believe me."

"There're all sorts of nooks and crannies in the house, darling, you just missed it, is all."

"He didn't," announced Pauline, arriving on Pip's heels. "I couldn't find it myself. I'm in a terrible fix, too."

"Are you?" said Agnes, smiling wickedly, voice full of sly hope. "Diarrhea?"

Lips pursed, Pauline scowled at Agnes.

"Please, you two," Justine pleaded. "Save your energy for unpacking. They're bringing in the beds. Mother, can you hold on? I'll locate the pot in a minute."

"No, I can't hold on. I begged you to stop at that last gas station, remember? But no—"

Justine held up her hand. "All right. It's your bedstead they're bringing in, Mother Hale. Tell them which room."

Agnes beamed and moved with alacrity, cane bouncing. Pauline protested. "She'll pick the finest room for herself!"

"Which is it to be, Mother, mover guidance or an accident in your pants?"

"The bathroom. But I must say, you've become exceedingly vulgar."

"I don't know how else to protect myself."

"From what?"

"If you have to ask . . ." warned Justine, patience growing thin as a taut wire.

"If only your father were alive," began Pauline, but the fierce gleam in her daughter's eyes caused her to stop in mid-sentence.

Lottie had taken in the whole of the conversation, observing Pauline's air of disdain and Agnes's peevishness. The outcome settled it in her mind that the one called Justine suffered a peck of trouble at the hands of the two old biddies.

Since the house was Lottie's own, she thought it did behoove her to rise to hostess duties. She left her perch on the stool and hovered near Justine.

With Pauline following, Justine went off down the wide hall. She couldn't say how she knew the bathroom was on the back porch. She just seemed to know. She put it down to an obscure, perverse intuition.

"Oh, dear!" said Pauline.

"At least it's not in the backyard."

It used to be, said Lottie. *Miserable that was, too, on a cold blustery day.*

"Look at the tub," Pauline insisted. "A bear could bathe in it."

The huge, high-sided affair was constructed of iron and porcelain, draped with cobwebs and years of dust. Its bottom was filled with windblown debris of leaves and moss.

Pauline took a tentative step closer.

"It looks like a bear *has* bathed in it! And that toilet . . ." she said of the monstrosity of iron, her voice trailing off in justifiable dismay.

"It's nothing a little Comet cleanser won't cure," Justine said succinctly and closed the door upon her mother's expression of distaste.

Seeing the set of Justine's mouth as she turned, Lottie surmised that the bathroom was not considered up to snuff. That had been the complaint from more than one prospective tenant. Lottie couldn't understand it. All one had to do was turn a valve and water shot out. Some folk were downright unappreciative, she thought. Mayhap they ought to spend washday at the working end of a pump handle. A spigot would look mighty good after that!

Justine lingered a moment on the back porch, part of which was enclosed by tattered strips of latticed wood. She had a view to the rear of the yard where a number of sheds leaned precariously into one another, casualties of the elements . . . of life. She, too, was a casualty, Justine thought. But unlike the sheds she had no other support to lean upon. And she was supposed to be the glue that held them all together. Dear God, but she had never felt so vulnerable, so lost, so unable to cope.

"We're bringing in the fridge, ma'am," one of the movers called out to her. "The other lady said you'd tell us where to put it."

"Yes, I'll be right there."

She gave a last brief glance at the backyard. She could see no other dwellings. How nearby, she wondered, did her neighbor Tucker Highsmith live?

Then, catching her train of thought, Justine moved purposefully back into the house.

Chapter Two

Tucker sat stiffly at his typewriter and for the fifth time painstakingly began to peck out the recipe for potato pie with a *creme fraiche*. He made another typo.

Damn! He couldn't concentrate. The image of Justine Hale filled the page. A one-time aberration, he concluded and tried again. He misspelled *fraiche*.

Okay, pal, he told himself. That's it. Take a breather, have a go at Justine Hale, then forget you ever saw her. Remember, there was a *Mrs*. attached to her name.

Which meant that she was married and very much off limits.

It was only that she intrigued him, beguiled him. He had caught sight of her as she rounded the corner of the porch. He didn't know what had made him stop in mid-step. The way she carried herself? The sudden intense look on her face that bespoke of vulnerability seldom expressed? The long, slender length of her? He couldn't name the attraction.

During the minutes he had observed her, before drawing attention to himself, he had watched her questioning herself—in body language. Curiously, he'd understood. He had felt drawn to her on the instant.

But it was more than her looks. It was in her eyes. They were a deep green; wondrous eyes that seemed to illuminate her face. When she had turned to face him he had looked into their depths. She had touched him in a way that he had not been touched in years.

He had sensed in her haughty deportment a cover for the vulnerability he'd seen. That knowledge had made him speculative, appraising and far too bold. But, hell! He'd had his own vulnerabilities to camouflage. His legs had suddenly needed support and he'd had to lock his knees.

But an affair with a married woman? He wouldn't even come close to considering it.

Yes, he would.

He argued the point with himself for five minutes.

On the downside he concluded Justine Hale probably wore a girdle under her shorts. That's why she looked so trim. Her hair color had to be out of a bottle and undoubtedly she'd puffed up her bosoms with falsies to make them appear enticing. He knew from experience that women pulled sly tricks to make themselves alluring, even when they didn't mean to go beyond teasing.

Well, he had Justine Hale's number. She could lure from here to hallelujah for all the good it'd do.

He rolled a fresh sheet of paper into the typewriter. The memory of a pair of green eyes mesmerized him.

"Ah, hell!"

"You still working on those field reports, son?"

Tucker stopped typing and carefully disposed of the rejected pages.

"I'm trying. If they'd make a man-sized keyboard, I'd be finished by now."

Tucker had concocted the lie about the field reports so that he could work on the book while his dad was visiting. Writing a cookbook was a secret he kept from everyone. Mostly because he couldn't quite come to terms with it himself.

He was redneck through and through. He knew it, and wore the label as proudly as he displayed the Rebel flag above his bed. He couldn't help it that he was Southern bred with the generations-held notion that the kitchen was a woman's place.

The only accounting he could give for himself concerning the art of cooking was that it had been forced on him. The premature death of his mother had sent his dad into a tailspin. The old man had spent more years since then drunk than sober. It had been learn to cook or go without. One thing led to another until he'd become pretty damned good at it.

But hell! Writing a cookbook? Oh, he knew that a few famous chefs had written cookbooks, especially foreign ones. And every time he saw them on television they were kissing each other on the cheek.

If any guy he knew tried anything like that, he'd end up in the hospital.

To his way of thinking it was okay to throw a slab of ribs on the grill, fry fish on a riverbank, whip up a pot of chili or fry eggs. The married guys in his set even admitted to opening a can of soup or boiling hotdogs for the kids when the wife was out of sorts.

But admitting to cooking fancy sauces and writing them down? Tucker's ire rose just thinking of the name calling and innuendo that would invoke.

Not that anyone would accuse him of being effeminate. At least not to his face, or he'd break the heckler's jaw. He just couldn't see any advantage in telling anybody. It'd be like telling his most secret wish.

Secret wishes seldom came true. Voiced, they just made a man sound silly or sissy or both. Holding firm to that conviction, Tucker covered the typewriter, swiveled around on the stool and scrutinized his father. Perspiration beaded the old man's face.

"Did the sun chase you in?"

"Nope. I like working up a good sweat. I weeded the tomatoes. The beans are coming on good. You'll have a mess within the week. That is, if the chickens don't beat you to 'em."

"Thanks. The garden gets ahead of me. Don't know why I keep putting one in year in and year out."

But of course he did. It was so his dad would have something he believed useful to do when he visited.

"If I lived here...all the time, I mean," Wheeler advanced, "I could keep it up."

"Ah, Dad," Tucker said gently, "that's out of the question right now."

Wheeler Highsmith sighed low. "I know. But I wish it. It's okay to wish it, ain't it?"

"Wishing doesn't hurt a thing," Tucker said, knowing his reply was contrary to his own philosophy.

Wheeler shuffled over to the table and sat down. His hands trembled. "Is it okay if I have a pipe, now?"

Tucker retrieved pipe and tobacco tin off a high shelf and handed them over. He watched his father fill the pipe, tamp the tobacco, check the draw. The palsied hands shook as Wheeler struck the match.

"I do love a good pipe," the old man said upon exhaling. "It's the one thing I crave they won't let me have at the nursing home."

"Can you blame them? It's what got you there in the first place."

Wheeler chuckled. "Caused some kinda ruckus, didn't I?"

"Being careless with lighted pipes," Tucker said reproachfully, "burning your house down around you and having the court order you to live under supervision is a bit more than 'a ruckus.' "

"Guess so," said Wheeler dryly, "but it wasn't much of a house to begin with. What about the new neighbors? Promising?"

"Nothing special." Tucker shrugged, then heard himself saying, "I thought when you took your nap I'd go see if I could lend a hand. Just to be neighborly."

Wheeler blew a smoke ring, watching it rise to the dark-beamed ceiling.

"She pretty?"

Tucker felt a sudden discomfort. "I suppose, if you like her type. Married, though."

"Whoa! Stay away from that, boy. You'll get yourself shot."

"No advice, Dad. I'm a grown man now."

"And on your way to gettin' old, like me."

Tucker shook his head. "You're trying to lay a guilt trip on me again."

Wheeler put on a display of innocence. "I ain't. I tried it before and it didn't work."

He gave his dad a half smile. "You're learning all kinds of little tricks in that old folks' home, aren't you?"

"Ain't learned none that work—yet."

"Maybe the one you just pulled did. You want to stay over another night? I'll clear it with old Iron Bottom."

"Unless she has somebody else to pick on, she'll say no just outta spite. She can't go a day without being mean."

"C'mon...she adores you."

"Her kinda lovin' I can do without. Do I get lunch, or do I have to bed down on an empty stomach?"

"Lunch. What do you say to a fresh egg-and-cheese omelet?"

"With spring onions?"

"You got it."

"And a cold beer?" said Wheeler, all hope. "Weedin's thirsty work."

"We'll share one."

"Fair enough." Like a child who knows the rewards of good behavior while under watchful eyes, Wheeler scraped spent ashes from his pipe and laid it with care in the ashtray. "I'll just go get this grit out from under my nails."

Tucker watched his father shuffle off, back still straight, still proud.

Before the woman they both loved had died, Wheeler had been the best father a boy could wish for. Helena's death had devastated father and son alike; but while Tucker had toughened, his father had weakened, becoming a shell of his former self.

Tucker had determined never to love like that. Never to become so dependent upon a woman he couldn't exist without her.

Just thinking of a commitment of that magnitude brought him as close as he would ever allow himself to a feeling of fright. He didn't want to become the man his father had, pride notwithstanding.

Wheeler had no control over his life. He hated the nursing home. Tucker hated that the old man had to stay there, but he couldn't afford the court-ordered supervision Wheeler required. He made a good enough salary as a telephone lineman, but after his own expenses, there wasn't enough left to provide the exorbitant cost of hiring full-time help.

He hoped the cookbook, if he could get it written and if he could get it published, would provide the funds to bring his dad home. Wheeler had a few good years left yet. Tucker wanted him content.

As he cracked eggs and measured spices and cream, his thoughts moved full circle, back to Justine.

Until his dad was happy he couldn't afford to get involved with a woman, either.

The muscles in his nether regions tightened, reminding him how long he'd been without the solace of a woman.

Well, he could get involved, he just couldn't consider marriage, having a family of his own.

A face materialized in his mind's eye. It was an intelligent face, composed of uneven planes and angles, anchored with extraordinary green eyes.

Justine Hale, he thought, you had the whole world to choose from. Why'd you have to move into mine?

SHE SAT ON THE STEPS and watched the moving van depart. It had Virginia plates, a reminder of her past life. Justine sighed. It had been a good life, too... once.

The van picked up speed. A trail of red dust obscured the tags; obscured her final link with a kind of life she'd never know again.

She would be in shock yet, she supposed, if reality had not slapped her in the face.

She had learned all too quickly that a single-income household could not live as if there were still two incomes. In spite of her share of the profit from the sale of the house, her bank balance had seemed to shrivel like a grape in the sun.

Only moments ago she had debated how much to tip the movers. Six months ago she would've been far too generous. Financial reality was that she could no longer afford generosity. It was a humbling experience.

More than humbling had been her efforts to borrow money against her share of the house until it sold. That had scared her.

The credit application had been the first she had filled out since leaving the courtroom. *Single. Separated. Married. Widowed. Divorced.* It had taken all the strength she could muster to mark the box, *Divorced.*

She had become a statistic, labeled as abandoned and unloved. She had two children to raise, and no credit of her own. The loan had been turned down.

Sadly her circle of friends had shriveled, too.

If divorce could happen to Justine, they said, it could happen to anybody. They didn't like being reminded. Invitations dwindled into nothing.

So now they didn't have to be reminded, Justine thought. She was eight hundred miles away.

She reached for her purse, extracted a cigarette. Except for the occasional puff, she had stopped smoking years before, when she'd become pregnant with Pip. She'd only taken the habit up again when Philip had started talking about becoming a monk. It was a terrible habit, but she had convinced herself that cigarettes were cheaper than doctors and buckets of Valium. Once her life was back on track, she'd quit again. Right now she needed something to hold her ragged nerves together. Nicotine was it.

The smell of tobacco wafting into the great room through the opened windows lured Lottie onto the porch. *I used to smoke a bit, myself,* she said conversationally. *I do miss having a pipe of an evening. We used to grow the finest golden tobacco hereabouts. Elmer had a special way of curing the leaves. Mild, our tobacco was. A man came up every year from New Orleans to buy it. Said it made a cigar to rival that from the islands. Got a good price, too.*

Course, once the war started, nobody came. The last crop just cured until it rotted. A terrible waste, that was, too.

The heavy scent of smoke hung about her like an invisible fog. Lottie inhaled and noted precisely where in the purse Justine placed her cigarettes.

Oh, for the day she'd be flesh and bone again, she thought. She longed for so much. Not riches, just the simple, everyday pleasures of life.

Before the new tenants had arrived, the balance of eternity stretched before her like a vacuous gauntlet, its torture being the promise of hours linked by boredom. Now that was all changed.

Lottie wished there was a way to let Justine know how welcome she was in her home. The expression on Justine's face was sad. There was a line of perspiration on her brow. *You're too young to appear so downhearted,* Lottie advised. *Why, when I got word that Elmer had been killed, I went straight out to the fields and worked past sundown. Slept good that night, too. So get up. Get busy. That always worked for me.*

"Justine!"

"I'm on the porch, Mother Hale."

Agnes emerged, her mouth turned down in annoyance. "There aren't any clothes closets. Not one!"

"Well, the house is older than I thought if it predates closets. We'll just have to use chests of drawers and chifforobes. I'm sure there are pantries with shelves."

The elder woman wasn't to be appeased. "I don't think I'm going to like it here, Justine."

"Oh, Mother Hale, not you, too? Look out there. Don't you think that's a setting straight out of *Gone with the Wind?* It's going to be good here for the children—for all of us—I know it is."

"But we aren't going to live in the yard, are we? We're so isolated. Suppose one of us gets hurt?"

Justine almost mentioned Tucker Highsmith, but he was a man: who could depend on one of them? "Try to think positive."

"The only thing I'm positive about is that our lives have turned topsy-turvy. You never laugh anymore, Justine. You used to laugh all the time." Agnes averted her eyes and lowered her voice. "You don't miss Philip at all, do you?"

Justine winced. "Yes, I miss him. But he's on the other side of the world. So missing him doesn't do me much good." It went unsaid that Philip apparently did not miss any of them. His only communication since Easter had been but a single card posted from some forsaken little island whose name she couldn't even pronounce. He hadn't said, "Wish you were here."

"You blame me for his going, don't you?"

"Actually I don't. Philip did what he thought was best for him. Now I'm doing what I think is best for us. I'm sorry you don't agree."

Agnes's thin lips trembled. "Well, I'm scared. I'm old, I ache and I'm infirm..."

Old! exclaimed Lottie. *Old! Why, you don't know what old is. How'd you like to be a hundred and fifty-nine! As for being infirm, trade places with me. Hah! Try out my condition and see where it gets you.*

"Justine, are you whispering?"

Lottie froze. Had she almost gotten through? She forgot to flutter and dropped down to the steps and sat there, pondering possibilities.

Justine smiled. "Maybe you're reading my mind. I'm scared, too, Mother Hale. You don't have a corner on fear."

The words spoken, Justine thought, *I may be less than sure of myself, but I'm far from willing to surrender.* She decided then and there the image she was going to present was one of strength, not weakness.

She slipped her arm through Agnes's. "C'mon, let's go back in the house. We have more important things to do than engage in self-pity."

"Justine!"

"Oh, Mother! What now?"

"This room," Pauline said, flailing her arms to indicate the great room when Justine stood on the threshold. "I'll do it up. The wallpaper has gone past fading into death, but ignoring that . . ."

"Let's do ignore it for the moment. Later on we can budget some paint."

"Budget?"

Until recently that was a word that had not been in Pauline's vocabulary. Justine watched her mother struggle with its implication and then give up the struggle.

"My peach sofa can go over there, the pickled-wood pedestal table behind it. And, I think the dhurrie rugs. We can frame the fireplace with your father's collection of Japanese Buddhist sculpture."

"No buddhas, Mother. They're too monkish."

For an instant Pauline looked blank. "Oh, of course. How tactless of me. The furniture in here will have to go, especially that chair and stool. It looks carved by a one-armed woodsmith."

Lottie swept into the room and plopped down in the chair.

The chair stays, she said, glaring at Pauline. *This is my chair.* She had painstakingly created the needlepoint for the footstool. She'd spent two lifetimes in that chair. It was her anchor to the past and the present. It was made of cypress and the first thing Elmer had built for her after they were married. Lottie quivered. She'd give in on the wallpaper, but the chair stayed. *That's my final word!* she huffed, watching to see if anyone heard.

Justine was trying to see the room completed through her mother's eyes. All she saw was dirt and dust and cobwebs. "Keep in mind Pip, Judy Ann and jelly. The television has to go in here."

"They can learn to keep their feet off the furniture. You did. We can eat our meals in the dining room, like civilized people. Being suddenly poor doesn't mean we lack manners."

"I've decided on the dining room for my office."

Pauline's elegant jaw dropped. "That means we'll have to take all of our meals in the kitchen!"

"You'll get used to it, Mother. Anyway, where we eat is the least of my worries."

"We'll have to find a place for my writing desk," put in Agnes. "Someplace that gets good light, so I can read the fine print on entry blanks."

"You and your contests," Pauline said waspishly. "What have you ever won other than that plastic camera that didn't work? The money you spend on postage . . ."

"You never know. I might win a million dollars. That'd stick in your craw, wouldn't it? And anyway, it's my money I spend on postage—out of my social security check. For a widow in the throes of bankruptcy, Pauline, you're awfully snooty about money."

"How impertinent of you, Agnes. It's ill-mannered to speak of another's ill fortune."

Agnes tossed her head; purple curls bounced. "I like being impertinent. It's good for my constitution. Like it or not, I'm putting my desk in here."

"Justine, are you going to allow her to speak to me like that?"

"Mother, you have a perfectly good tongue, which you've been using to great advantage. What I won't allow is the two of you to continue to drag me into your quarrels. Settle it yourselves. It's all I can do to referee battles between Pip and Judy Ann. But if you'd like my opinion of what would go nicely in here, may I suggest dueling pistols? Loaded. Now, if you will both excuse me, I'm going to change into some jeans, then see about lunch."

"I'll be along to help in a minute," said Agnes, falsely contrite.

"So will I," said Pauline, not to be outshone.

If it was me, said Lottie as she accompanied Justine to the kitchen, *I'd serve those two up a saucer of cream and be done with it, that catty they are.*

Chapter Three

"Mom, why don't we just go find a McDonald's?"

Judy Ann seconded Pip's suggestion with enthusiasm.

"Listen, you two, we can't drive miles and miles for pizza or hamburgers for every meal. Besides the expense, we're in the country now. Keep looking, try those boxes over there in the corner."

"You should've told Daddy he couldn't divorce us and leave us poor," accused Judy Ann.

"Dear heart, we're not truly poor. We're on a budget. It's just that the money we have has to last."

Pip frowned. "For how long? Into the next century?"

Justine turned her green-eyed gaze on her son. "You know what I think... the art of sarcasm must be genetic. You sounded just like your father." Or either of your grandmothers, she amended ruefully.

"If Dad ever sends for me, I'm going."

"If he ever sends for you *and* buys your ticket, I'll help you pack."

Justine was instantly contrite. Pip's threat was an empty one. They both knew it.

"I'm sorry for that remark."

"Why did Dad leave, Mom?"

"I don't know exactly. I wasn't to blame, nor were either of you. It was something eating inside him."

Judy Ann climbed on a box and dangled her legs. "He went 'cause he didn't like us anymore. Daddies who love their kids don't shave their heads and wear yellow night-gowns. Melissa's mother said so. She said Daddy was crazy."

"Your father is not crazy. He..."

Justine threw up her hands in a defeated gesture. Damn Philip for slinking off without giving the children an explanation. It was the least he could've done. The onerous task was left to her. Even under the most ordinary of situations it was hard to explain adult actions to youngsters. *Do as I say, not as I do.* Kids were smarter than that now. They wanted truths. She wasn't a psychologist, so how was she to explain Philip's actions when even he couldn't put them into words beyond shouting and screaming that he had to leave. Had to! Recalling their last verbal battle, after which he had slammed out of the house, filled her with a desperate sadness. It took her a few seconds to shake loose from the lingering aftereffects of recall.

"Mom," Judy Ann said, voice raised slightly, "you look like you're about to cry."

Justine's eyes lost their glazed look and she blinked back tears rapidly. "I'm not about to cry. I was lost in thought there for a minute. Listen, why don't we talk about your dad another time?"

She turned to Pip. "You're the man in the family now. I don't need you puttering around here half-cocked, so other than our whole world crashing down upon us, why're you so irritable? We talked about this move. It was going to be an adventure. We decided we'd take the bad parts with the good. You were all for it."

A large part of the reason Pip had been anxious to leave Virginia, Justine knew, was the embarrassment he had suffered among his peers. Being abandoned by one's father, who went to the other side of the world to play at becoming a monk, was outside the realm of adolescent understanding. It was beyond adult understanding! Here it was months later and she could still visualize with clarity her own friends' gaping astonishment.

The boy shifted his gaze to a point beyond her shoulder and said with unaccustomed dignity, "You never notice anything anymore, Mom. I'm going through puberty."

Justine was speechless for a full half minute.

"You're not. You're only eleven."

"I am." It was almost a plea. "I have hair under my arms. That's how it starts. My gym teacher told me."

A thousand pictures ran through Justine's mind. Pip as a chubby baby. Pip riding his tricycle, his bike. Performing handstands on his skateboard.

His gym teacher told him.... It came upon her full force that now she had to be father as well as mother to her offspring. But Pip couldn't be growing up. Not yet. It was too soon.

"You're sure it's hair, not a thread off your shirt or something?"

His grin was slight and lopsided. "I've been using deodorant for four days. Dad left it behind."

"Have you?" She wanted to cry. Her throat tightened. "That's...wonderful. Do guys in the throes of puberty still hug their moms?"

"I guess," he said, doing the deed with keen embarrassment and speed.

What would a man do when confronted with a son's burgeoning sexuality, wondered Justine. She looked at Pip's feet. No wonder he'd been outgrowing his shoes at a pair every two months.

"Once we're settled we'll have a celebration. Dinner, candles, maybe even some champagne punch. What do you say?"

"Aw, Mom. It's no big deal. I'm just growing up."

Judy Ann slid off the box and sidled up to her brother. She gazed at him with utter awe. "You can make babies now."

His face flamed. "Yuk! You're sick!" He shoved her and sent her sprawling.

"Mommy!"

"Pip! Apologize to your sister! No matter what your gonads are doing, that's no way to act."

"It's true, Mommy. When the health lady came to school to talk to us, she said puberty for girls was gettin' breasts and periods—for boys it meant they could make babies. I remember!"

Justine helped Judy Ann to her feet and dragged a reluctant "sorry" from Pip. "We'll discuss this later—separately. Let's find that box of food. We'll all be in better spirits once we've eaten."

"I could hear the yelling at the other end of the house," announced Agnes, emerging into the kitchen with an incorporeal Lottie on her heels.

"We've settled the problem, Mother Hale. Do you recall which box you packed the canned goods in?"

Lottie wasn't so easily distracted. She took in the expressions on the children's faces. *Hooey!* she exclaimed, deciding on spite and spoiled. If she were running the household, the boy wouldn't be standing there sullen or the girl sulky. She'd have them set on their chores and no debate.

"I don't," Agnes was saying. "The movers were on top of me. I recall that."

Lottie sniffed. *There's a box with food in it,* she said. *Though, truth tellin', it don't smell too fresh.* She went to look.

Surreptitiously she parted newsprint. The carton was filled with dishes stained with egg yolk, bits of bacon, jelly and used coffee beans ground into mush. Lottie gaped.

It was beyond her experience to imagine carting unwashed china from one county into the next. In her day a thing like that didn't at all reflect well on the woman who ran a household. Why, even during the War, folks kept up.

She scowled at Justine who by her lights had admitted to being chatelaine. The whole lot of them needed a firm hand, she decided. There wasn't a level-head among them. What was needed was a woman of her own constitution, one strong of back and mind.

Lottie smothered a sigh. She'd have to renew efforts to get herself extended. She just *had* to find a way.

Purple skirts flowing, cane swinging, Agnes elbowed Lottie off center.

Watch it! Lottie said tartly and alighted on the sink. Amorphous arms crossed, she proceeded to lecture, in no uncertain terms, how she expected the new tenants to keep house, lest every four- and six-legged insect God had ever created think it was invited to dine in her kitchen.

"I hate to tell you this," Pauline said as she rounded the corner, "but the movers didn't put up the beds."

Justine sagged. "They were supposed to!"

"If your father were alive, he'd telephone their home office and insist they send someone out to do the job right. I suppose we could stay in a motel tonight."

"We can?" Justine's voice was close to scathing. "How much money do you have in your purse right this minute, Mother?"

"You know I never discuss money."

Agnes arched an eyebrow. "You do—as long as it belongs to someone else."

"Stay out of this, Mother Hale." Justine parked her hands on her slender hips. "Well, Mother...how much?"

Pauline flinched. "I—I'm not sure.... Three dollars...about. But you know I'm more used to carrying credit cards. If the lawyers hadn't taken—"

Agnes smirked. "You could have considerably more than three dollars, Pauline, if you'd admit to being at least sixty-two and apply for social security."

"Age doesn't have anything to do with it. That's government money. Evan said never touch government money. Why, he'd turn over in his grave."

Not so, said Lottie, following the conversation with acute interest. Souls that got a decent burial spared the devil and stayed peacefully put. Leastways, all the ones she knew had.

"Six and two is eight," said Judy Ann proudly. "Like me."

Justine beamed. "That's good, darling. You're a smartie."

Speaking to Judy Ann, but aiming an opprobrious smile at Pauline, Agnes crooned, "Do you know eight times eight, dear?"

"I'll settle this," said Justine. "We'll sleep on mattresses tonight."

Agnes's expression went from scorn to dismay. "I couldn't." She straightened, then leaned against the great old double-tubbed sink. "I'd never be able to get up off the floor. My arthritis wouldn't let me. Anyway it's too drafty in this old house to sleep on the floor. I'd come down with pneumonia. I'm cold right now."

"It's the first week in June," Pauline said pointedly.

"It could be the first week in August for all I care. Why don't any of you believe me when I say I'm cold!"

Pauline smiled wickedly. "Because you're imagining it?"

"I'm not!" As if to prove her point, Agnes shivered involuntarily.

Lottie leaned forward and put words directly into her ear. *Do those dishes before you go to coming down with ailments, y'hear?* Agnes didn't.

Deaf as worms, you are, the whole lot of you!

Lottie was suddenly drained of energy, weary; as tired as if she'd been plowing behind a pair of mules. The sensation surprised her, considering she had no bones to ache or muscles to pull. Much as she hated to leave the new tenants on their own, she knew she needed a rest. She dragged herself off the sink, made her way out of the kitchen, into the long dim pantry and to the door set flush in the wall at the back. She crept behind the door and up the steep stairwell into the topmost part of the house.

"Mother Hale, if you're running hot and cold, maybe you're coming down with the flu. Take one of the lawn chairs and sit in the sunshine for a few minutes. See if that takes the chill off."

"What you need, Agnes dear," Pauline added, "is to check yourself into a nice modern nursing home."

"Couldn't you two stop picking on each other?" begged Justine, though deep down she knew remonstrating with them was a waste of time. Each was convinced her way was right, and no amount of persuasion seemed to make them willing to reverse positions or endeavor to understand the other. She was feeling increasingly helpless in the face of their ongoing verbal battles, mostly because she always seemed to be caught in the middle.

"Can grandmas get divorced?" asked Judy Ann.

"That's stupid," said Pip.

"It's not. If you can't get divorced, then fussin' doesn't matter. Does it, Mommy?"

Nonplussed, Justine glared over her daughter's head at the grandmothers.

"I didn't start it," said Pauline.

"Neither did I," Agnes shot back.

"There's a man lookin' in the back door," said Pip.

FILLING THE DOORWAY, hands on hips, his stance proclaiming to her how certain he was of the effects of his charm, stood Tucker Highsmith. The easy, natural way about him that had communicated itself to Justine that morning was still in place.

"You didn't give me a chance when I brought over the keys," he said without preamble, "I just wanted to offer you a neighborly hand . . . if you need it."

"We don't," she said firmly.

"Oh, yes, we do," insisted Pauline, sweeping past her daughter to graciously wave Tucker into the kitchen. "As it happens the movers didn't put up our beds."

"I told you, Mother, I'll do that tomorrow."

"The man wants to be neighborly, so let him," said Agnes, concerned with her own comfort and for once in wholehearted agreement with Pauline.

Justine clenched her fists. Of all the times for the grandmothers to suddenly see eye to eye! To protest further would make her look a fool in front of Highsmith—for the second time in the space of a few hours. She lifted a hand to indicate ill-humored acquiescence.

Pauline introduced Tucker to the children. When she got to Agnes she said, "This is Justine's former mother-in-law," placing the emphasis precisely on former.

Though for different reasons, both Justine and Agnes gave Pauline a scathing look. Pauline smiled sweetly and stepped behind Pip.

With her mother's retreat, Justine knew some small talk was demanded of her.

"Exactly where do you live that you can be so conveniently neighborly?"

There was just enough frost in her tone that Tucker understood he was not forgiven the manner of his earlier approach, nor the intrusion of the moment.

"I own the old tobacco barn that used to be a part of the estate," he said easily. He let his eyes rest intently upon her. The glossy hair was now pulled back and tied with ribbon. The style emphasized a certain stubbornness in her well-defined features. She had changed into jeans and knit shirt. Both of which were flattering to her figure. Her attributes were provided by nature, he noted, and not the subterfuge of padding and pinion. His gaze was drawn back to her eyes.

He discovered himself overtaken by a mixture of one part caution and several parts potent longing. He was, he decided, a man in trouble. "My place is out beyond the persimmon trees. You can see it if—"

Justine dismissed the way he was looking at her, ignored the fact that her heart was picking up speed.

"You live in a barn. How quaint. What other animals do you house there?"

"Justine!" Pauline said, her tone registering shock. "We've only just met the man, dear. You're being exceedingly rude."

"That's *exactly* how she used to talk to Philip," sneaked in Agnes.

Justine kept her eyes on Tucker. He was making no move to leave. He wasn't looking insulted. There was even a hint of a genuine smile on his lips beneath the mustache. Damn. He had to think her an imbecile. She deserved whatever thoughts he had of her. And she certainly wasn't setting a good example for the children. She took a breath. "I'm sorry. I was out of line. I have no objection to you putting up the beds. It's kind of you to offer to help. But I'll do my own room."

Distressed, Pauline rattled on: "Justine, you're making me look as if I were an inadequate parent in front of our new neighbor. I'm sure he thinks your father and I let you run wild. She isn't usually so high-handed, Mr. Highsmith. It's only that her patience has been so tightly stretched of late. Her divorce, the death of her father, my husband, our move..."

Oh, Mother! Justine raged silently. How can you be so unthinking? She felt as if her soul had been laid bare for inspection. Worse, Highsmith appeared to hang on to her Mother's every word.

"Don't bore the man with our life story, Mother."

"I've been accused of many things in my life," said Pauline with stiff-necked, regal dignity. "However, being a bore was never one of them."

"I'm not bored," Tucker said smoothly. "I'd like to get to know all of you."

Judy Ann thrust herself in front of Tucker. "Do you have any little girls I can play with?"

"Ah...not yet. But if I ever do, I hope she's as pretty as you."

The child preened in response to the compliment. "My dad's gone off to be a monk," she gushed.

Justine wished the floor would open up and swallow her whole.

"It's kinda like being a preacher," offered Pip.

Tucker eyed Justine to see if what he was hearing was good or bad. No doubts. Bad. "That sounds... adventuresome," he said in a carefully neutral tone. "I'd like to hear more about it sometime."

With a triumphant, quelling glance at her daughter, Pauline gestured toward Tucker.

"Come along, Mr. Highsmith. Pip, dear, you can lend us a hand."

"Just, Tucker, ma'am," he said, his own expression no less triumphant. As he squeezed by Justine, making certain that he didn't even brush her, their eyes met fleetingly: Justine's were narrowed, his full of a self-satisfied gleam.

"A *monk*?" he said softly, shaking his head.

Bright hot color blotched her neck, sped up on to her smooth cheeks. She had run out of worthy retorts. Before she could compose one mentally and get it on her tongue, his back was turned.

Her eyes followed him out of the kitchen. For the next few seconds she was full of rocketing thoughts of the man. A whirlwind of impressions raced through her mind. The most vivid were the turbulent emotions Highsmith had aroused in her, feelings she had not experienced in years. Her feminine instincts, though little used of late, told her that his interest in her went beyond being neighborly.

She didn't want that. Her life was complicated enough already. Even if her life weren't complicated, he wasn't her type.

She was gripped by a sudden internal shaking. In the deep recess of her brain a surfacing voice of intuition proclaimed Tucker Highsmith was *any* woman's type.

"Not mine!" she said vehemently. Realizing she'd spoken aloud, Justine looked quickly about and discovered Agnes and Judy Ann had also decamped in Highsmith's wake.

She gave a thought to joining them, if only to monitor the conversation. No, she wouldn't. Whatever Tucker Highsmith learned of her would not give him the advantage. She wouldn't allow it. She was in control of her destiny. Not Pauline, not Agnes, not the children.

Under her breath she called him every rogue name she could think of. Feeling much better, she resolutely pushed aside his image and continued searching for the box of food.

"TUCKER'S NEAT," said Pip for the second time in less than an hour. "He's gonna take me fishing first chance he gets. Maybe even tomorrow."

"He's got a hen with some baby chicks and I can feed them anytime I want," said Judy Ann. "So don't throw out scraps. I'm gonna find me a pail and—"

"Tucker said, Tucker did, Tucker has," complained Justine to all and sundry. "You'd think Highsmith was suddenly the only man in existence."

"Pip needs a male role model," suggested Pauline. "You don't want him to grow up effeminate, do you? I think Tucker fits the bill."

A space had been cleared around the table in the kitchen and they were eating tuna salad sandwiches on stale bread which Justine had toasted to mask its failings. Her own appetite had disappeared. She picked at bread crusts.

"It just seems disloyal that the first man to even breathe in his direction since Philip left, Pip goes gaga over."

"That could be genetic," Pauline said and took a bite of tuna. Her face fell. "This stuff is dreadful."

"I'm not gaga," protested Pip, and in the next breath said, "Tucker has a tattoo. It's a Rebel flag and when he flexes his muscles it waves. He showed me."

"A tattoo?" Justine gave her mother a look of reproach. "That's the kind of male you want your grandson to emulate?"

"The man has nice manners. I don't understand why you're so hostile toward him. He was only being kind. The South is famous for its friendliness. Tucker is a gentleman through and through. Very gallant. When that bed slat fell on my foot, he was concerned, truly concerned. I found it quite pleasant." Pauline pushed her plate aside. "When you go into town, perhaps you can find some Boursault cheese. It's wonderful on toast points."

"We're alone, with no man in the house," put in Agnes. "I think we should be careful. You certainly should not have allowed him to inspect your ankle, Pauline. We don't know anything about him. He might not be stable."

"You considered we knew him well enough to allow him to put up your bed . . . and then move it twice until it was placed to your satisfaction. If you want to discuss instability, I can name names closer to home."

Justine slapped the table with the palm of her hand. A startled silence descended. "Okay, that's enough. Listen, kids, why don't you two go outside and play, inspect your new territory. I think the movers left your bikes on the front lawn. Or if that doesn't suit, you can help unpack."

Pip vanished. Judy Ann lingered. "Where're you gonna be?" she asked.

"Right here in the kitchen. I'm not going to disappear on you, sweetie. Stop worrying."

"Daddy did."

Justine cuddled her daughter into her lap. She never seemed to have the right words ready to soothe Judy Ann's fears. "I'm not Daddy, sweetheart. I don't want to live without you. Where I go, you go. Where I live, you live. Even if you don't see me, I'm here. I love you. We all do," she added, lifting her head to include the grandmothers.

"Right!" said Pauline. "You're our special girl."

"Especially mine," said Agnes.

"See? We're all here for you. Now go play, ride your bike around that big old tree out front. I'll bet that squirrel will be so curious, he'll come right down the trunk and watch." The child slid off her lap.

"But promise you won't go anywhere without me."

"Cross my heart."

"I don't think I like Philip doing that to Judy Ann," said Agnes once the child was out of earshot.

"Ooh-la-la. Listen to that," crooned Pauline. "The overprotective mother has finally admitted a flaw in the greatest son in the world."

"I never said he was perfect."

"Only about a thousand times."

"I believe we have a house to put to rights," said Justine. "Let's get on with it, shall we?"

"I'll go make my bed," said Agnes.

"I think I'll bypass the great room for today and arrange my bedroom, too," said Pauline.

"Wonderful!" said Justine. "That leaves me with the kitchen, the hall, the other bedrooms, the bath and my office."

"I'll cook supper if that will help," volunteered Agnes.

"Don't allow it!" Pauline insisted. "We don't know where the nearest hospital is yet."

Agnes thumped her cane as she began her exit. "At least I *try*, Pauline. That's more than you can say."

Justine dropped her head onto her folded arms and began to mutter a satisfying string of expletives.

The elder women exchanged a glance, then made hasty retreats. Two seconds later Pauline poked her head around the doorjamb.

"Now, I remember who Tucker reminds me of."

Justine lifted her head. "You're wrong if you think I'm going to ask who."

"I'm telling you anyway. The Marlboro Man—if Tucker wore a Western hat—"

"He can remind you of Ghandi, Churchill and John Wayne all rolled into one, for all I care. I prefer you don't mention his name in my presence ever again."

"Your bed is put together. Why don't you take an aspirin and lie down. I'll keep an eye on the children."

"I don't need a nap and I told you I'd do my own bed. I don't like the idea of that man handling my things."

"You always were one to cut off your nose to spite your face."

"It's called having principles."

"Same thing," said Pauline. "Oh, by the by, the unmentionable person isn't married. Never has been."

"Maybe there's something wrong with him."

Pauline fingered the pearls at her neck. "He told Pip that he's thirty-six. That he's had obligations to meet that kept marriage out of the picture. To me, that makes for a right-thinking man. Your father was almost forty when we married, and there was certainly nothing wrong with him. Not in the way you mean. Which brings me to this—of late you've seen only the worst in people. Had you had that kind of attitude fifteen years ago, you wouldn't be in the predicament you're in now."

"You're deliberately rubbing salt in my wounds, Mother."

"Salt is an antiseptic, isn't it? Helps to heal?"

"Go make up your bedroom."

"I do love you, Justine. You're my only child. I want to see you happy."

"I'll get there. Eventually."

Pauline smiled slyly. "I do believe you-know-who was quite taken with you," she said on her exit, getting in the last word.

Justine inhaled, counted to nine, exhaled on ten.

"I'm capable, sane and in control," she said. Saying the words aloud convinced her.

Tucker Highsmith taken with her? In the finest sense of that word? What a lot of drivel. The man just wanted an arm piece.

"LOOK, MOMMY," Judy Ann said breathlessly, entering the kitchen on the run. "I found a bucket." She began at once to gather luncheon leftovers. "I'm gonna feed the chicks. They're so cute."

"All right. Just don't disturb Mr. Highsmith."

"I can talk to him, can't I? He likes me."

"You don't know that."

"I can tell." She puffed out her little chest importantly. "He talks to me like I'm a person."

"I talk to you like you're a person."

"No, you don't. You boss me."

"That's what mothers are for."

"He laughs. You don't laugh anymore."

Justine winced. Agnes had made that same accusation not five hours earlier. She suffered a twinge of jealousy that Judy Ann was fascinated by Highsmith, enthralled even, and had compared her to him.

"I'm going to start laughing again soon. I promise. But I need something funny to get me going. What do you say I take a break and we go ride your bike. I'll put you on the handlebars."

"The chain's off. Anyway, I want to feed the chicks."

Justine hid her disappointment with a smile. "Okay. Another time. Scoot."

Judy Ann went, then made a quick turnabout, rushing up to Justine and throwing her free arm around her neck.

"I do love you best, Mommy."

"That's the grandest news I've heard all day. I love you, too."

"Then it's okay if I talk to Tucker?"

Justine sagged slightly. *Manipulated in the name of love—again,* she thought as she followed Judy Ann onto the back porch. "Only if you see him outside..."

She watched her daughter skip down the back steps and race toward the persimmon trees, the rusty pail swinging gaily from one chubby fist.

Justine's eyes suddenly stung with hot tears. The love and attention she gave to her children was not going to be enough. They were already hungry for a surrogate father.

There was no surrogate for a husband. Either you had one or not. Dear God, but she felt so lost—so *single*! She missed the intimacy, the sharing.

At one time there had been love between her and Philip. She had to believe that. But, while she was thinking there was still hope for their marriage, he had ended it cruelly.

On his fortieth birthday.

After the successful party.

After they'd made love.

It was better that way. So he had said.

Knowing she could not permit herself to break down, Justine took control of her emotions and turned back into the house.

The disarray made her sniff. No doubt her ex-husband was at that very moment being waited upon by exotic Balinese dancing girls who wore elegant jewels in their noses and little else. He was a shirker in all respects. It was time to put him out of her mind; failing that, at least out of her daily life.

She surveyed the kitchen with a critical if not practiced eye. There was a wealth of cupboards and shelves. A pantry off to her right. It was deep and dim and had no light fixture, but it would be useful for storage.

If she went at it with a vengeance, she could have the kitchen orderly by dusk.

And if she applied the same tactic to her life, she could have it orderly by... She swiped furiously at a tear.

Her life was in much more disarray than the old kitchen. Maybe it'd take a bit longer. So what?

An exact image of Tucker flashed before her mind's eye.

She lifted her head suddenly. It was the first time since her divorce that she'd had total recall of a man.

She was recovering from disaster.

She filled one of the deep sinks with dishes. The spigot belched rusty water. She let the water run until it cleared.

She could do the same with her life, just let it run on until it cleared.

She poured in dish detergent and plunged in her hands.

Right. The analogy fit. She'd just plunge in and go with the flow.

And if the flow included Tucker Highsmith? asked a tiny interior voice.

Don't worry, it won't, Justine told it.

Highsmith had yet to reach his fortieth birthday. She wasn't about to suffer through a second man's mid-life crisis.

One in a lifetime was enough.

Chapter Four

Lottie inhaled deeply, exhaled and watched the smoke spiral upward like a spindle then waft out the dormer window.

The smoke seemed to fill the empty space in her chest, swelling inside her with a wonderfully satisfying volume. It made her feel...she searched her mind for the right word...substantial. Ah! That was the word, in the sense there was more of her than met the eye. Now, that was a truth she couldn't argue with, by tar!

She made herself more comfortable on her bed and propped nebulous elbows on the window sash.

She had filched the cigarette from Justine's purse after everyone had gone to bed last night. It was a good, mild tobacco, she thought. Not as fine a broadleaf as she and Elmer had once grown, but the taste paled in the face of discovering she could pull the smoke into herself.

She had known for years that she hadn't explored all the facets of her present state. Likely it was the stubbornness for which she had been so well known that had kept her from delving into her extra abilities. She hadn't wanted to get used to doing things spiritually, so to speak, lest she convince herself that the *essence* of being herself was better than being of bone and flesh.

Bone and flesh was better. One got noticed. And if one didn't get noticed, why one could just thwack a body up side the head. Folks paid attention then.

Puffing away, she mused on the previous night's entertainment. She'd had a wonderful time. The best night of her life in decades. She had rooted through boxes, suitcases and chifforobes; sniffed elegant soaps and scents; tried on earrings; and slipped on one of Pauline's dresses of fine silk that was a lovely shade of gray. The chifforobe mirror hadn't given back her image. Howsomever, that was of no account. She knew a good fit when she felt it.

The chest of drawers in Agnes's room had given up nothing but purple and more purple. However, she *had* discovered a pair of worn black pumps that, once polished, would do nicely. They had slipped right over her bunions, too.

The dress and shoes now reposed nearby in her cedar trunk, awaiting the *day*. She'd arrive back in style, by tar!

Just the thought of how good she'd look made Lottie smile and gaze lovingly about the attic.

All of her things were up here: her good linen, the crystal that had been her grandmother's, the hand-carved bedstead built by a furniture-maker in Mobile. Elmer's solid brass spittoon. Elmer had brought everything up after there had been talk of Union soldiers looting fine furniture and silver from homes as they swept terrifyingly across the South. And Elmer had buried all their silver and money before he himself was called up to serve. Cleverly so too, Lottie thought. To this day, it hadn't been discovered. Once she was back to normal, she'd retrieve it. Elmer had buried her wedding ring, too. She had felt naked without it all these years.

Lottie frowned.

Another item that hadn't been discovered was her bones. She didn't like to recollect how she had gotten into the state she was in, but it had happened on the steps behind the secret door. Her bones had lain there on the bottom step for she didn't know how long, with nary thought nor prayer said over them, either! Which, she considered, might be why she had remained in such a fitful condition all these years.

At first she had prayed hard and steadily to the Heavenly Supreme Being to guide friend or foe to her remains. But as she got used to her condition, and the idea of returning took hold, she said her prayers in whispers so as not to draw attention to herself from *that* quarter.

At war's end, she'd thought it a shame that no one had come to collect her bones. Now, she knew it was just as well. She would most certainly need them again. The idea of returning to normal only to discover herself with less backbone than a limp newt didn't sit well with her at all.

Eventually she had tired of having to traipse around bones everytime she'd gone downstairs and had propped them up in her solid oak rocking chair. She had spent years sitting in the chair with them—in hopes of a miracle, she supposed. So far, just sitting on them like a broody hen hadn't done any good.

Suddenly Lottie cocked her head and listened. The folks below were stirring. Best she got down there to keep an eye on things, she decided. She took one last drag off the cigarette and carefully stubbed it out in Elmer's spittoon.

CHEERFUL NOISES beckoned Justine from sleep like slow enticing music. The sounds came through the window into the room. Birds trilled and chirped, chickens clucked, wind soughed in the trees. A woodpecker's tat-ta-tat seemed to set the cadence, underlining nature's cacophony.

Pajama-clad and barefoot, she padded over to the French doors which were a feature of every outside room in the old house. She tugged them open and stepped onto the side porch. The foundation plantings on the east side of the house were of azalea. A pair of butterflies flitted among the leaves, searching for late-blooming buds.

Her world was condensed into this place, she thought. And it wasn't bad. The sky was blue, sun trickled through moss-draped limbs, and in the distance she could hear the sound of a tractor motor; a farmer in his fields.

The wind carried with it the pungent summer odor of foliage, earth and moldering leaves. A hint of smoke mingled with the old mustiness of the house.

Smoke? She sniffed. Not wood smoke, not leaves burning; it was cigarette smoke. Yet, she was the only one of her household who succumbed to that dreadful habit. She walked the length of the porch to the front of the house and spied Pip crouched among a tangle of bushes. She leaned over and parted them.

"Good morning."

Startled, he shot out of the greenery.

"Mom! You scared me."

"What're you doing hiding down there?"

"Grandma Gates sent me to find some flowers for the table."

"So?"

"It's a sissy thing to do, Mom."

"That's debatable, horticulture is big business. What else were you doing down there?"

"Nothin'!"

"Nothing...as in smoking one of my cigarettes?"

"No! Why're you accusing me? I'm not messin' up my lungs."

"Come up on the porch and let me smell your breath."

He began backing away. "No."

She pinned him with her eyes. "You were smoking, weren't you?"

"I wasn't! Why don't you believe me?"

"Because I smelled the smoke and you're here."

"Well, it wasn't me!" he yelled, voice cracking and sounding betrayed. "You blame me for everything!"

Without a backward glance he dashed off around the corner.

Justine watched him go. He looked all arms and legs and feet. Damn it! She had handled him all wrong. He was growing up. That meant confusion, rebellion and experimenting. It meant sorting the mixed messages received from adults, an idealized image of perfection, exploring the senses; especially taste and touch. Smoking, drinking, drugs, *sex!* Oh, dear God! How did a mother get a child from age ten to twenty and end up with a healthy happy human being?

Growing up was the second hardest task in the world!

The first hardest, she decided, was being a parent. Which reminded her there were two others of her kind in the house. Both of whom she'd have to speak to concerning Pip. She could see that much patience and understanding were going to be demanded of all of them.

Though she had told Pip and Judy Ann that it had not been their or her fault that Philip had left them, buried deep in her psyche was the notion that she had been at fault. She *had* failed in her marriage, *had* failed as a woman.

She was not going to fail as a mother.

With a sense of urgency that she had not hitherto experienced as a parent, Justine gathered up her clothes, scrounged a towel from her partially unpacked suitcase on the floor and hurried off to the ancient bathroom to bathe and dress.

Fifteen minutes later she was searching for Pauline and Agnes. "Where is everybody?" she called.

"Out here," came her mother's voice. Pauline stepped through the double doors into the dining room-cum-office. "We're just having our coffee, dear. Come join us."

Pauline's tone was so sugary, it was instantly suspect.

"We?" Justine asked. "Who's we?"

"Why, Agnes and myself. Who did you think? Isn't this lovely?"

Justine took in the card table draped with a pink cloth. On it sat her mother's silver coffee service, cups and saucers. The crystal bud vase nearby stood empty. Used dishes and cutlery had been stacked to one side.

"One of you cooked breakfast?" she said wonderingly.

Pauline smiled. "Agnes and I did it together."

"Once we'd figured out the stove," Agnes said. Her pasted-on smile made her thin lips appear even thinner.

Justine sat down and looked askance at her mother and her mother-in-law. Pauline, as usual, was elegantly clad in a simply designed shift that belied its cost. She was fully made up, not a gray hair out of place. Not for the first time

Justine noted that her mother had the carriage and suppleness of a much younger woman.

Agnes, on the other hand, was at the opposite end of the spectrum. She looked as if she had not only built the cross she had to bear, but had carried it around the block a few times. She was wearing her favorite purple blouse that clashed with a skirt of a different shade. The soft breeze left Pauline's carefully coifed hair alone, but it was taking Agnes's livid locks apart in frazzles.

"Medaglia d'oro," Pauline said as she poured Justine's coffee. "I had a tin in one of my suitcases."

"It's wonderfully tasty," said Agnes.

Wonderfully tasty? Justine's cat sense told her something was afoot. "All right. Out with it. What've you two done?"

Agnes went on the defensive. "Nothing."

"Well, that's not true, Agnes, dear. We had ourselves a chat."

"That's not what Justine means."

"Agnes," Pauline managed through clenched teeth. "We agreed—"

"Yes, tell me. What did you two agree on? Did the earth shake? One of you get smote by lightning?"

"My dear daughter, you're such a cynic. Agnes and I have agreed to get on with each other."

Justine had the cup almost to her mouth. She lowered it. "How did this come about?"

"I couldn't sleep last night," said Agnes. "I had the feeling that someone was in my room. I kept getting up to look."

Pauline patted Agnes on the hand. "That's neither here nor there, old dear. What we're trying to say is that both of us felt a trifle out of sorts last evening. We neither could sleep, new surroundings and all that."

"Mother, you sound awfully like defense counsel preparing an alibi for—"

"I told you she wouldn't believe us," said Agnes.

Pauline went on as if neither of them had spoken. "So we sat out on the front porch in the moonlight and talked out our differences. Not all of them mind you, but enough. And since we have, we thought you might like to go into town and buy groceries today.''

"I must be dense, but I don't get the connection between the two of you sitting down to a peace conference and my going shopping."

"Well, you've never left us alone together before for fear of...well, whatever. Now you can. We'll hold down the fort. All we could find to cook Pip and Judy for breakfast was instant oatmeal and dry toast."

"Mother, if you can convince me that you actually took a pot, filled it with water and stirred oatmeal into it, I'll take you at face value."

Pauline stiffened slightly. She shot a glance at Agnes.

"She watched," said Agnes.

"But I was in the kitchen. You know cook never allowed us in our own kitchen. It was—''

"A learning experience," Agnes finished for her.

Pauline beamed. "Right."

"Mother, for more than twelve years, I've had to keep you two apart, shuffle visits on holidays—''

"That's all in the past."

"Worse, you've been going at it like a pair of alley cats fighting over dead fish ever since you, Mother, decided to make the move with us."

"I know, dear. I behaved frightfully. I don't usually. It was just that I could bring so little—''

"Fifteen suitcases and half the moving van is so little?" murmured Agnes. Beneath Pauline's scrutiny, Agnes shriveled.

Justine had never known Agnes to retract her claws quite so quickly. It almost convinced her of the grandmothers' sincerity.

Pauline continued. "As I was saying—that dreadful law clerk inventoried everything...watched what I put in my suitcases even. Agnes and I are in the same boat now. Neither of us has any place to go if you were to decide you didn't want us here. Isn't that so, Agnes."

"Well . . .''

"Isn't it?"

"I suppose."

"There, you see. Now, you just run along to the grocer's. I've made a list...."

"I had planned to put my office together today, set up my computers. I have a September first deadline on the contract. If I blow it—"

"You won't. You're a computer whiz, your father always said so and he was seldom wrong. And anyway, it's for an insurance company, isn't it? They never do anything on time. Evan used to own stock in any number of them and he was always complaining how slow they were to pay dividends."

Justine's slowly widening smile took in both grandmothers. "Give me a minute to get used to the idea that you two have buried the hatchet outside of one another's back."

Pauline relaxed, and wore a look of supreme virtue; Agnes's expression was of more modest proportions and a lot less readable.

Out by the line of persimmon trees a rooster crowed. Justine sipped her coffee and mused on good fortune. She felt a little like crowing herself.

If the grandmothers were sincere about a truce, then she would be allowed the concentration necessary to produce the program she had contracted to write. It was a plum of a job and had come her way only by accident.

Philip had not wanted her to work after Judy Ann was born, but obstinately, she had persevered until she'd been able to sway him, though not without compromise on her part. She had been able to accept only a part-time job with a software distributor.

She had hoped to get full-time work after the divorce, but the computer industry had suffered an inopportune slump and she, being only a part-time employee, had been the first let go. Yet, her last week on the job had been fateful.

A representative of an insurance company had called asking for the name of a company in Silicon Valley. Justine had taken the call and had given the number. On her last day at work the representative had called back. Could she recommend another company? The first was too expensive. His employer, the rep had said, was relatively small, licensed to do business in only five states. He chatted a moment to give Justine an idea of what was needed, and the upshot was that the following day she had an appointment to meet with him.

Since he had mentioned the outrageous figure the Silicon Valley company had proposed to charge for the job, Justine clinched the contract by quoting a figure of only half as much. Her overhead was nil. She had the equipment and she could work at home.

She could work anywhere under the sun, as long as she had the electricity to run the computers.

Later that evening she'd suffered a crisis of confidence and had almost picked up the phone to refuse the contract. But a review of her finances had convinced her that, confidence or not, she needed the work.

A lot rode on bringing the program in on time. A lot, as in her entire future, she mused. If the job was done well and priced right, she was certain to make a name for herself in the software industry; especially if she could develop a clientele that the software giants considered too small to take on.

Silently she sent a thank you heavenward to her father, who had had the foresight to fill first his brokerage office and later his study with computers and allow her access to them even as a small child. Early on, the machines had been huge, bulky and sensitive. Now they were small, not so sensitive and much smarter.

Thinking of smart, Justine mused on the notion that the grandmothers were outsmarting *her*. Somehow.

She reminded herself she had promised to "go with the flow." And right now harmony was flowing like a flood. Who was she to dam it up?

"Just how long is this truce between the two of you supposed to last?" she asked.

"We expect to have differences," enunciated Pauline. "We've just decided to handle them in a more conservative fashion."

"What're you going to do while I'm shopping? If I go..."

"Unpack," said Agnes. "The hall is barely navigable."

"Arrange the great room," said Pauline. "I made a sketch of where things can go."

Judy Ann, hair brushed and plaited, came hurrying onto the porch carrying her shoebox of paper dolls. "I can't find my scissors."

"Go put on your sandals, sweetie," Justine said. "You can go shopping with me."

"I wanna stay here."

Justine was nonplussed. For weeks the child hadn't wanted her out of her sight; yesterday in the kitchen for example. Now, less than twenty-four hours later, she was suddenly blasé on the subject?

"I may be gone for more than a couple of hours."

"That's okay."

"The telephone's not installed yet. I won't be able to call and check on you."

Judy Ann shrugged. "I wanna stay here and play."

"Well...if you're sure," Justine said limply. "Maybe Pip would like to go. Oh. Mother, Pip was upset because you sent him to find some flowers for the table."

"The field on the other side of the house was full of wild—"

"Pip didn't think cutting flowers a manly thing to do. I'd like it if we all treated him in a more adult fashion."

"Pip's doin' puberty," said Judy Ann.

"He's what?" the grandmothers trilled in unison.

"He's growing up," warned Justine, "and very much aware of it."

"Oh," said Pauline.

"We're in for it now," said Agnes. "I remember when Philip—"

Quickly Pauline reached over and patted Agnes's arthritic hands. "Not now, dear," she said affably.

Justine studied both of them dispassionately. "It's all too easy."

"What is?"

"Never mind, I'm not staring a gift horse in the mouth. I'll just get my purse and the road maps. Judy Ann, go find your brother."

Lottie slipped into the chair Justine vacated.

Pauline passed her daughter the list she'd made "just as a reminder." Then she took up the silver pot again. "More coffee, Agnes?"

"Yes, thank you, Pauline."

Justine rolled her eyes.

Her mother said, "Was there something else, dear?"

"It's Sunday. Stores might not be open."

"They are. I believe you should look for a Delchamps. The nearest one is in a town called Spanish Fort or Fair Hope. I've forgotten which."

Justine's eyes narrowed. She was beginning to see the light from which all the sweetness flowed. "And from whom did you get this tidbit of information?"

Pauline hesitated a beat too long. "From that welcome packet the bank sent you. There were all sorts of brochures about shops, schools—"

"Good try, Mother. I don't want the man hanging around while I'm gone."

"Who?"

"Our neighbor."

"But—" Agnes began.

"But, what, Mother Hale?"

"I'm suddenly cold again. I just don't understand it. I feel like something is continually eluding my perception."

"I feel the same way," Justine said dryly.

"I'll get your sweater for you, Agnes," said Pauline and hurriedly maneuvered Justine into the house proper.

"Mother, I know you're up to some devilment."

"I'm attempting to be kind to you. I thought about it. I'm grieving only for your father, but you have two griefs. Your father and Philip... and on top of that, all the stress of changing your whole life."

"The same applies to you."

"I know, but I'm older and I've had a wonderful life. I can adjust because I can take myself back to better times. Memories, you know."

"I have a few good memories myself."

"You do?" Pauline was genuinely surprised. "With Philip?"

Justine laughed. "Mother, on that note, I think I'll leave it to you. I'm going to put on some makeup. See if you can find Pip, will you?"

"I'm certain he wants to stay here."

"You're certain?"

Pauline examined an imaginary hangnail. "I do believe that fishing trip is on. There's a creek or a river nearby."

Justine nodded and sighed. She could forbid Pip to go and unleash no telling what kind of havoc. Highsmith wasn't the man she would choose for Pip to emulate, but then, neither was Pip's own father...now. Considering the situation of the moment, any male companionship would be a boon for Pip. If necessary, she could put the skids on it later, gently.

It dawned on Justine then, that Pauline probably wanted her gone so there would be no confrontation between Justine and Highsmith when he came to collect Pip. Pauline need not have worried on that front. Before she'd drifted to sleep last night, she had given the man a moment's thought. She *had* been a tad harsh on him. If and when the opportunity arose, she meant to apologize. There was no good reason to leave him with the impression that she was a bitter and foolish divorcée. After all, they *were* neighbors.

"I don't suppose it'll hurt anything for Pip to go fishing," she said. "The attention will do him good."

"Of course it will. Now go along. Do take your time."

"Mother?"

"Yes, dear?"

Justine lifted a hand, then let it fall. "For some obscure reason, I feel bested."

"You're just not used to things going well. Now they are. Accept it."

"The same way you're suddenly accepting of Agnes?"

"I'm beginning to understand her. And we do have something in common for the first time. We're both widows."

Justine didn't think it the prudent moment to mention there had been grandchildren in common for eleven-plus years.

"Whatever the reason, Mother, I'm pleased."

"You're going to be even more pleased when I tell you that I've thought of a way to get some money for the communal purse. It came to me last night when I was trying to get used to all the creaks and thumps this old house makes at night."

"How?"

"I'll tell you after I've worked out the details."

"It isn't illegal, is it?"

"Why should you think that?"

"My suspicious nature and your ambiguity."

"Justine, go shopping. I've got to find that eyesore of a rag Agnes calls a sweater. I don't want her coming down with pneumonia. We've got work to do."

"Eyesore of a rag, Mother?"

"It slipped. I've never been fond of purple. Tell the truth, have you?"

Justine laughed. "Some truths are better left unsaid."

"I love your laugh, Justine. It's such a gay, throaty sound."

"Why, thank you, Mother."

"You still need to lose five pounds."

"Why do you keep saying that? I don't see it!"

Pauline waved in the direction of her daughter's derriere. "That's because you're always walking away from it."

"Next time," Justine said, "I'll stop while I'm ahead."

She excused herself and disappeared into her bedroom for makeup, car key and purse. On her way out she glanced over her shoulder into the armoire mirror. Maybe there was just the tiniest hint of spread there. Her mind's eye carried her five years into the future until she was visualizing hips over which she could not tug a pair of hose.

Cottage cheese, she thought. Lots of it!

"YOU JUST WANT to get close to the mother without a tad-pole hanging on a teat," grumbled Wheeler.

"Dad, I didn't tell the boy I'd take him fishing. He asked me what there was to do around here and I said, the river's nearby and I know a good fishing hole, and that I'd take him sometime. He said, maybe tomorrow and I said 'maybe' just off the top of my head."

"Kids don't hear 'maybe.' Their ears ain't situated right."

"He's got his heart set on going. Apparently he's never done any fishing. But if you don't want to take him, I'll talk to him, put it off. I'd take him myself, but the old ladies snared me when I was coming back from my run this morning. Somehow I found myself agreeing to shuffle fur-niture."

"You're just full of virtue this weekend, ain't you, son?"

Tucker grinned. "I'm always full of virtue."

"Full of somethin' else, if you ask me. Tell you what, I'll take the boy fishing if you make it worth my while."

"Hold on! You love to fish."

"This don't come under the heading of fishin', it comes under baby-sitting."

Tucker sighed. "Keep it reasonable."

"I wanna take my pipe, a couple of cold beers and you gotta agree to clean and cook any fish we catch before you haul me back to Iron Bottom's clutches tonight."

"Done," said Tucker.

Wheeler's hangdog affectation fell away. "Somehow I find myself in a right merry mood to dig worms," he said cheerfully. "What's the boy's name?"

"Pip."

"What kinda name is that?"

"Short for Philip, I think. You want me to drive you down to the river, or you want to walk?"

"We'll walk. I think I can handle a quarter mile without bringin' in the medics. Call the kid."

"He's hanging around outside."

Wheeler eyed his son. "You knowed all along I'd agree!"

"I was hoping."

"Huh! What you're hopin' ain't fit to voice. I guess you're aiming to rub elbows and no tellin' what else with the boy's mother."

"All I've done so far is rub her wrong."

Tucker did think helping out up at the house might give him a chance to get on a better footing with Justine. Perhaps, he decided wryly, he would apologize for his snide remarks—provided the opportunity arose so he could do it without sounding mealy-mouthed.

Wheeler thumped Tucker on the back. The idea of the two beers, his pipe and nobody looking over his shoulder put him in an expansive mood. "Like as not, by day's end you'll have her eatin' outta the palm of your hand. Anybody who can charm old Iron Bottom ain't got to worry about lesser folk." In the midst of adjusting his hat lower on his brow, Wheeler stopped. "Say, tell me what the two that's my age look like. Maybe one of 'em is my type."

Tucker drew his hand over his mouth to hide his smile. It had been his mother's death that had put his Dad on the road to perdition, but the years since then had softened the blow. Wheeler still had a lingering weakness for drink and tobacco. But recently he'd begun to show more interest in other people, particularly women. Unfortunately there wasn't a suitable female at the old folk's home with faculties up to Wheeler's rough, sparring nature.

With a casualness that was ground cover for mirth, Tucker mused aloud, "The one called Agnes, the ex-mother-in-law, has a face longer than a thigh bone. Pauline dresses as if the preacher is expected for breakfast, lunch and dinner and all day on Sunday."

Wheeler paused only a fraction. "Fishin' sounds better. Get my pipe. I got worms to dig."

A half hour later, having seen his dad and Pip off on the path toward the river, Tucker aimed his steps toward the big house.

He had the feeling that he was about to complicate his life.

Pauline met him at the back door. "It's so kind of you to lend us a hand, Tucker. We're very grateful."

"No problem, I'm happy to do it."

"I do hope we can work with some speed. I'd like the great room to be finished before Justine returns from doing the marketing. It'll be a nice surprise for her."

Tucker stopped in mid-stride. "Your daughter isn't here?"

"I just told you. She's gone shopping."

"I see," he said. "Did she approve of my lending you a hand?"

Pauline hesitated. "She didn't disapprove. And she was delighted that Pip could get in some fishing."

"You mentioned my dad to her?"

"I think that slipped my mind."

"Justine did know I was coming up to the house?"

Pauline smiled beatifically. "Well, the great room wouldn't come off as a surprise if I told her, now would it? She'll be so pleased. You'll see."

All Tucker could see was that he had been had. And by a sly old matriarch to boot.

Chapter Five

Some three hours later Justine no more than pulled into the yard and tapped the horn than Pip came flying out the front door.

"I caught a bucket full of fish, Mom! Real fish. We're gonna have 'em for supper. They're called mullet. We're gonna have a fish fry! We'd still be fishin' but Wheeler said we'd just have to throw 'em back. I can go on my own now, can't I? It's safe 'n' everything. Wheeler showed me the path to the—"

Justine smiled at his exuberance, the genuine joy in his face, an emotion he had not displayed since last Christmas morning. She did not want to put a damper on his joy, but she had not quite understood all that he had said. "Run all that by me again, sweetheart. Slowly."

Pip repeated himself with barely an inhaled breath.

"Who or what is Wheeler? I thought Tucker was taking you fishing."

"He couldn't. He had to help Gram."

A revelatory light suffused Justine's brain. The reason her mother had been so darned anxious to get her out of the house fell into place. Obviously Pauline had enlisted Agnes *and* Highsmith in the conspiracy.

"Wheeler is Tucker's dad," said Pip.

"His dad?" Somehow, in the periphery of her consciousness, Justine had not expected Highsmith to have a parent, to be that *human*. It put him in a different light.

"Wheeler is in old folks' storage all week," the boy enlightened, echoing the old man verbatim. "Tucker gets him out on weekends so he can fish and putter around."

Justine's mind was racing. Highsmith was sounding more and more like a devoted son. It almost gave them common ground. On the face of it, it was going to be awfully hard to maintain a forceful dislike of a man who was kind to old folks and children, not to mention helpful and attentive.

On the other hand his behavior could be a deliberate, very fortuitous facade.

"Wheeler *likes* me, Mom. He said I'm gonna make a right fair fisherman when I grow up. Next weekend he's gonna teach me how to bottom fish for flounder. But I can fish for mullet on my own. Can't I?"

"I don't—" Justine stopped herself in mid-sentence. She wanted the children to become independent, learn new things outside the hurly-burly of the city, have more nature in their lives. Pip had tumbled into it headlong. If fishing was an activity that caused him not to dwell on the past, she'd be doing him a disservice to put a halt to it. Gazing into his joy-filled face, she even felt a tiny twinge of envy. "I don't see why not."

"Thanks, Mom! I've got to go tell Wheeler. He's loaning me a pole till I get one of my own."

"Hold it! Lend a hand with these groceries first." But Pip was too fleet of foot.

"Back in a minute!" he shouted, disappearing beyond the line of persimmon trees.

"Justine, dear. you're back!" Pauline emerged onto the porch, smiling the smile of a satiated cat. Agnes and Judy Ann soon appeared behind her.

"Yes, I am," Justine said. "And, oh, what a tangled web you weave, Mother."

"She figured it out," said Agnes. "I warned you!"

Pauline's smile slipped. "Now, Justine, don't be upset. Wait until you see what we've accomplished."

"I'm not upset. Do I look upset?" She walked in silence to the tailgate of the station wagon, knowing full well if she said one word, she wouldn't be able to hold back a flood of thousands ... all irate. In spite of her mother's good intentions, Justine felt tricked. *Had been tricked.* It wasn't a good feeling.

Pocketing a screwdriver, Tucker joined the others on the porch. He had an air about him that seemed pleasantly self-assured and competent. "Those drapery rods will stay in place now," he said to Pauline, then he looked at Justine. His gaze suddenly turned reticent, cautious.

Justine's posture became stiffly erect.

Awkwardness filled the space between them.

Pauline eyed one, then the other. "There are a few finishing touches we've yet to do," she said quickly and herded Agnes and Judy Ann back into the house.

Tucker left the porch, sauntered to the auto, leaned an elbow on the roof. He watched Justine's face, thinking how achingly lovely it was. It didn't take a bolt of lightning to tell him why she was standing there so rigid or explain her frown, though even that puckered brow could not mar her beauty for him. He knew the mere fact of his presence was causing her hackles to rise. The last thing he wanted was to be a continuing source of distress to her.

"I hope you know it wasn't my idea," he said. "Pauline snared me. I couldn't say no."

The movement of his well-formed mouth flexed the strong jawline. Whatever the reason he wore a mustache, Justine thought, it wasn't to hide any defects. It fit his face, complemented the laugh lines at the corners of his eyes.

"I'm not blaming you, Mr. Highsmith. I know my mother and how devious she can be, though she hides it under what she calls 'good form.' I'm just...embarrassed. You've given us so much of your time, more than being a good neighbor calls for."

"The truth is, I wanted to make a good impression on you. On second thought, that's not exactly right. I had hoped to change the first impression you had of me, which I have the inkling was not—"

"You've done that."

"Give me a hint." A trace of a smile was beginning to appear. "Is it better or worse?"

Justine avoided his eyes. "Better, I guess."

Tucker shifted his weight, bent slightly into her space. "Good. Do you think you could give over on the 'mister' and call me Tucker?"

A small sigh rippled through her. "All right. Tucker."

"That's better."

Now was the opportunity to make amends, Justine mused. She had planned it out, word for word, on the long drive home from the market, yet the apology lodged in her throat. She wanted to make it, but too much of her wifehood had been spent saying "I'm sorry," to Philip's accusations, regardless of how unjust. *You've just lost your nerve,* a small voice at the back of her mind insisted. *Too right,* Justine thought. She didn't want the man to think she was some silly, willy-nilly divorcée with her head on backward.

She looked at her sandals, adjusted the purse strap on her shoulder, let her gaze slide off to the side. "Listen, I wanted to say—"

"I have something I want to say, too."

Reprieve! Her head came up. "You do? What about?"

"The way I came up on you when you arrived. Hiding in the bushes like an adolescent. I had you at a disadvantage. I knew you were expected. You had no notion of me. I should've left a note on the door or—"

"It wasn't your fault. I just didn't like...I felt like a clown. Foolish."

"Far from foolish. Truth is, I thought you had—have, the best looking ankles... Not just ankles—" Her extraordinary eyes were clouding up, closing him out.

"Uh-oh. I can taste the shoe leather."

Justine smiled suddenly. "How do you do that?"

"What?"

"Look so virile and masculine one minute and the next come off like a chastised little boy."

"Does it work?"

Her smile went a bit rueful. "I'm afraid so."

Don't just stand here gaping like an idiot he told himself. *Do something!* He thrust out his hand. "Friends?"

"Sure. Friends."

As her hand slid into his, a nice prickly sensation ran down the length of Tucker's spine.

"Hey! Let me help with those. Looks like you bought for an army."

"No. You've already helped more than you bargained for." Her voice dropped an octave. "It's really nice of you to take an interest in Pip. Your dad, too."

"He seems a good kid. I like his enthusiasm."

The way he was staring at her was daunting. Justine turned away, grabbed up the nearest bag of groceries.

Her actions told Tucker she had taken the conversation as far as she would allow herself. Disengage, he told himself. Get out of her space. He gestured toward the bags.

"You're certain you can manage these on your own?"

She nodded without looking at him. "Mother and the kids will help. Truly, you've done enough."

He turned to leave, but couldn't just give it up. "I promised my dad and Pip a fish fry. You'll join us? The rest of your family, too? They landed quite a few."

She shook her head. "Thank you, no. We couldn't impose on you further."

"Pip will be disappointed. It's a red-letter day when a boy catches his first fish."

There was no debate on that score in Justine's mind. Pip had literally hummed with excitement, accomplishment. "He won't be in your way?"

Damn! "Not at all. And my dad would be disappointed, too. He's got a hundred fish stories yet. Pip's an avid audience, hangs on his every word. Dad eats it up."

Justine felt slightly light-headed from being in such close proximity to Tucker and knowing that, though there was an innocent conversation on one level, they were also speaking with their bodies. She had picked up on the chemistry between them. He had, too. She could see it in his stance.

In any language he was attractive. Tall, dark-eyed. Rugged good looks. His sensitivity toward Pip surprised her, softened her. Made it too easy to imagine herself in his arms, imagine herself as the object of that sensitivity. As those images filled her mind, she realized that he was probably having the same thoughts. But it was too soon. Friends as well as lovers could inflict pain with their rejections and betrayals. She shifted to put a bag of groceries between them.

"All right," she said. "I'll let Pip join you for the fish fry."

Tucker felt if he pressed her he would lose some important advantage that he could not identify.

"Good deal. But you know you're all welcome if you change your mind about joining us," he said, and left it at that.

THE GREAT ROOM had been transformed into a living room that had much warmth and livability. So much so that one hardly noticed the faded wallpaper, the paint peeling from the ceiling, the scuffed wide-planked floors.

Two sofas, end tables, lamps and a coffee table had been arranged upon one of Pauline's Kazak carpets of a deep striking blue. The area formed a cozy conversation nook in front of the fireplace. Agnes's rolltop desk and padded chair were against the wall that shared space with the French doors. The doors were open. Through them Justine could see Judy Ann. The child was intent upon her dolls, having arranged them at the card table where she had laid out her tea set.

At the opposite end of the room, near the front wall, a television viewing nook had been created with Justine's sofa, La-Z-Boy chair and low side tables. A stack of oversized pillows leaned against the wall—floor loungers for the children.

"I thought we'd make use of the credenza as a liquor cabinet," said Pauline. She was sitting on one end of the sofa, threading hooks into a pair of pale gray drapes. An activity, Justine suspected, that Pauline had engaged in purposefully so that she did not have to meet her daughter's eyes. "And we don't need any window coverings at all on the French doors, we'll be using them so often. What do you think?"

"You've created silk out of sow's ear, for sure," Justine said.

Done more than that, Lottie said huffily, perching on an arm of the sofa. *You see my chair's gone, don't you? Agnes got to put her chair in here. I don't see why mine couldn't stay. I'm putting it back, like it or not.*

She eyed Pauline with gravity. With the exceptions of watching Elmer ride off to war on the big roan and finding herself in her present condition, Lottie had never endured such misery as she had felt watching her chair and footstool being dragged out of the room and discarded in the backyard.

To her way of thinking the chair was her measure stick. As long as the chair lasted, year in, year out, she lasted. Now it kept company with the crates and cardboard boxes that she was certain were meant for the trash heap or burn barrel.

It was true the parlor looked more beautiful than it ever had, but that didn't excuse Pauline's preemptive behavior about her chair. *Just you wait!* she threatened.

"I knew you'd be pleased. I told Tucker so."

"Look at me, Mother."

Reluctantly Pauline dragged her gaze up from the gray fabric to meet Justine's.

"You went behind my back in having Tucker up here to help you."

Pauline bristled as much as her sense of propriety allowed.

"Would you have agreed to his help otherwise? Agnes is practically crippled. And none of us have the strength to shove this heavy stuff about."

"That's true. I would not have agreed."

"Well then. The end justifies the means, doesn't it?"

"Mother, it doesn't. You tricked me and I have an idea you tricked Tucker in some way, too. You *used* him. And, you made me a part of that."

"He didn't mind."

"I mind!"

"You're such a stick-in-the-mud, sometimes, Justine. You remind me of your father."

"Dad was honest and principled."

Pauline sniffed. "Had I been his kind of honest, we wouldn't be sitting on these sofas right now. Had I told those horrid lawyers that these were in storage, they'd have refused to let me have them. They would've had them on the auction block, too. And your father's sculpture, and—"

Justine sighed. "Mother, does it ever occur to you that you change principles to suit your needs? Dad indulged you too much. You'll never change."

"Then, I'm forgiven?"

"Provided you don't do anything sneaky in the future. Discuss things with me first. I promise to keep an open mind." ·

Pauline bent her head, her attention on the drapes once again. "I notice we're using Tucker's name openly now. I think that's nice. You did apologize to him for your behavior, didn't you?"

"We exchanged apologies."

"What? Why? That young man never said or did a single thing out of the way."

"You don't know everything."

Pauline raised a perfectly plucked eyebrow, and said after a lag of five seconds, "Mothers seldom do, as you are on the brink of discovering."

"Oh my, what is that I'm hearing? Sarcasm or hope?"

Pauline lifted her chin. "Public schools. That's what made you so sassy. I warned your father, but no, the two of you had to have your way."

"You know, it's odd—you never think any part of me, any of my mannerisms came from you."

"The good ones did," Pauline said swiftly.

Justine grinned. "How nice of you to notice, Mother."

"Sass and more sass," Pauline muttered.

"Sometimes I think you forget that I'm thirty-six years old."

"Whatever your age, it doesn't erase the fact that I'm the mother and you're the daughter."

"With a mind of my own."

"Of course. Isn't that what this entire conversation has been about—your mind?"

Justine shook her head. "I give up." She stood and stretched. "I'm going to cook dinner."

Pauline brightened. "Did you get everything on the list I gave you?"

"Everything except the caviar, the Boursault cheese, the truffles, the Godiva chocolates and the prime rib."

Pauline looked stricken. "But, that's all there was on my list!"

"I know. How does meat loaf and cottage cheese sound?"

Pauline slumped back on the sofa. "I shall starve to death."

Lottie snorted at Pauline's ineffectual drama. *There are lots easier ways to pass over than starvation,* she snapped, wishing with all her heart she could be heard.

A snatch of a childish tune came her way. She looked out at Judy Ann. The girl was feeding pretend food to a rag doll that had long since seen its better days.

That's so sweet, thought Lottie. She and Elmer had longed for a child. But alas! She had remained barren.

It was in her mind that she had tried to get through to all of the adults and failed.

But children were innocent, more open, more receptive. Perhaps if she played with Judy Ann, made friends with her...

Lottie drifted onto the porch and sat gently next to the rag doll. For some minutes she observed how Judy Ann played the game. The rag doll's name was Mrs. Pratt. When it came the doll's turn again, Lottie lifted a tiny tea cup to its mouth. *Do have some tea, Mrs. Pratt,* she said. *It's all the way from China.*

Judy Ann gaped.

"Mommy! Mommy!" she shrieked in panic.

Chapter Six

Justine awoke early as usual, her dreams fading the moment she opened her eyes. The air was still, which made for an eerie silence about the house and the fields beyond. Murky morning light filtered into the bedroom.

She turned on her side and observed Judy Ann. The child had had a troublesome night, tossing and turning, whimpering during dreams, which probably accounted for Justine's own edginess. Whatever the reason, she knew she could not lay abed.

She moved off the mattress, then rearranged the blue eyelet coverlet over Judy Ann. At the moment, her daughter's face was serene. But the searing imprint of its panic-riddled expression of yesterday stayed with her.

The child had been almost incoherent, babbling that one of her dolls had lifted a tea cup on her own.

Perhaps the deeper trauma of the effects of the divorce were only now emerging. It was a terrible truth to realize that your father no longer cared for you, or even if he did, selfishly went his own way.

In small ways, Judy Ann had taken her father's departure harder than Pip. She was at that age when daughters fell in love with their fathers, learned innocent flirtation, began to experience the power of being female.

Judy Ann now had no sense of boundaries, no sense of where she fit, no sense of security. Like me, Justine thought sadly.

But knowing that about both of them did not make it easier to cope with the problem.

Oh, she thought, so much has been lost. Lost!

She padded over to the window and drew down the old yellowed shade against the pale light and slipped out through the doors onto the porch.

It was a bleak and sunless day, the sky a limitless gray. A lone cardinal, the only splash of color on the landscape, cruised above weeds dressed with dewfall.

Justine had never before been aware of such silence. It was as if the earth itself was hoarding sound, awaiting some signal from nature before bursting into life.

As she retraced her steps she took several deep breaths of the humid, leaden air. Damp or not, she thought, the air had the taste of an invigorating earthy freshness. On impulse she bent down to touch her toes. Her back crackled. Age thirty-six, she scolded herself, is too young to be falling into disrepair. If she wasn't careful, she would end up as unsteady on her feet as Agnes.

Quietly and with haste she dressed in shorts and shirt and, carrying her tennis shoes, made her way down the wide hall into the kitchen.

Finally there was a path of sorts in the hall. Boxes and crates of still-unwrapped ornaments and unending hundreds of books were ranked along the walls. Still the house was taking shape, becoming homey and comfortable. She supposed it had lost some of its strangeness by the simple virtue of having familiar furniture in place, old favorites unpacked and placed now to her convenience.

The kitchen easily accommodated the cherrywood dining ensemble. Oddly, though purchased for a more formal setting, the table and the chintz-covered chairs did not look out of place.

One wall of the kitchen was given over to open shelves. She had stacked dishes on the lower shelves. Those higher than she could normally reach she had arranged with basketware, cookbooks and the every-growing assortment of knickknacks that seemed to just collect of themselves. Beneath the shelves was a sturdy wooden cabinet, a work station in earlier years, she surmised, as it contained bins for potatoes, flour and sugar.

The only light fixture in the old kitchen was the bulb hanging on a wire from the ceiling. Justine had placed a small Tiffany lamp on the countertop near the microwave. She switched it on and the kitchen took on a welcoming glow.

The light also revealed a can of chili, opened, its contents undisturbed. The lid still clung to the magnet on the can opener.

Pip, after a midnight snack, she wondered. Impossible. He'd returned from Tucker's almost green from stuffing himself on fish and hushpuppies. Not Agnes. Chili was too spicy for her.

Pauline was the culprit. Of course. Her mother would have considered getting the can open a major accomplishment. But warming it up was probably beyond her. Or perhaps she feared the noise of rattling pots and pans and waking the rest of them. Justine sniffed the food. Waste not, want not, she decided and spooned it into a bowl and put it in the fridge.

She put coffee on to perk. She wanted a cigarette, if only to calm the creeping anxiety she felt. She decided against it. She would have one cigarette—and only one—with her coffee.

That virtuous decision made, she went into the dining room. It was dim and gloomy, her desk and the crates with her equipment loomed in shadowy disarray. She hit the light switch. The bulb was weak, seemingly throwing deeper shadows into corners. She turned the light off. She was not ready to face that task yet, not before breakfast.

Damn! But her nerves were on fire. She seldom succumbed to headaches, but the tautness at the back of her neck coupled with lack of sleep suggested one was trying to surface.

Had she been back in Virginia, she'd be out the door by now, on her way to the spa for a workout, maybe take in a class of jazzercise or a lap around the school athletic field.

Shoes in hand, she moved back down the hall and out the front door. She had no idea how far beyond the house the dirt road meandered. Surely it was as good as any athletic track. A ten-minute run, she decided, and sat down on the steps to lace up her shoes.

Swinging her arms, she walked at a brisk pace the first several yards. Sensing her tension beginning to wane, she moved into a trot.

The road narrowed until the overhead foliage began to converge in a canopy above her head. Shadows grew deeper at the verge. The only sounds were those of her feet slapping the dirt and her own breathing, loud and uneven.

A deer leaped across the road in front of her. Startled, Justine gasped and stopped in her tracks. Another deer followed the first, a doe with her fawn running nimbly at her side.

"Beautiful, aren't they?"

Justine squawked and spun about.

"Sorry, I didn't mean to scare you," said Tucker.

"For crying out loud! Where did you come from?"

"Behind you. Saw you ahead of me. I was pacing you."

"Why didn't you call out?"

"Figured you'd see me when you turned around at the dead end. Anyway, I'm not much for conversation at daybreak." He kept moving, running in place and, Justine noticed, not a bit out of breath.

She put her hand on her heart. It was racing like a metronome out of sync.

"Okay?" he asked.

"I will be," she answered, trying not to display her awareness of his lean and fit body. He wore a shirt with the sleeves torn out, a pair of cutoffs, hightop running shoes and a green sweatband on his head.

In the shadowy light his features appeared sensuous, his body powerful.

And she had left the house without running a comb through her hair. Damn! She waved her hand. "You go on."

"It's only a quarter mile to the dead end."

"I'll walk it. I'm out of shape."

He grinned. "Not by my lights. C'mon, push a little. It'll do you good." He headed down the road backward, to keep her in view. "The whole run is only two miles. If you fag out, I'll carry you back."

He offered just enough challenge for her to accept. "If I fag out, as you say, I'll just lie down by the side of the road until I'm recovered."

They ran side by side. He was a strong runner, moving powerfully like the deer and as fluidly. Pacing him, Justine felt awkward in mind and body. She was certain he was holding back in order not to out-distance her. Out of the corner of her eye she caught sight of the tattoo on his bicep. It was glistening with sweat.

Tucker was aware of her fleeting inspection, knew the exact moment she stopped thinking of him and began to concentrate on her own body, the pace she had set for herself.

He was also very much aware of the sleek figure she presented. She had more than just a pair of nice ankles. Her legs were sensational. Toward the end of the run, she was a little wobbly on them. He stayed close. The salty-sweet smell of her sweat was laced with the scent of shampoo and soap. Heady stuff for a man who'd been too long without a woman. Proceed with caution, he warned himself.

When she peeled off at the path that led up to her house, she raised her hand. "Coffee? It's perked."

He curved back to follow her. "A quick cup."

Raising a trembling arm, she indicated the table and chairs on the side porch.

As soon as she was inside the front door and out of his sight, she bent over double and gasped, sucking air into her burning lungs. "Stupid! Stupid! Stupid!" she rasped, and didn't straighten up until she had reached the bathroom, splashed water on her face, dried her face and neck and run her fingers through her tangled hair. She did several quick knee bends to alleviate the spasms in her calves.

Thus composed, she served the coffee-filled cups and condiments off a wicker tray.

Tucker took his coffee straight. After a tentative sip, he said, "Looks like we're going to have a gully-washer before the morning's out."

"I like rain. I work better when it's dreary outside. If the sun's shining I want to be out in it."

"Your mother said you do some kind of computer work."

"I write software."

"I'm impressed. You're a smart lady."

She had listened for any derision in his voice and found none. It had been a long, long while since she had favorably impressed anyone. A pleasant tremor passed through her.

"I hope I am."

"I don't doubt it for a minute."

"Considering you barely know me, I'll accept that as flattery."

"Hold on. I know more about you than you might think."

"Oh?"

"Maybe only a little about how your mind works, but I sure as hell can see what you're up against. A lot flows from that."

"What do you want me to say? That you're perceptive?" Her sarcasm was light but there all the same.

"Now you're trying to pick a fight."

Justine bit on her lower lip. "I know. I don't know why I do that."

"I'm no grass-roots philosopher, but I'd say... Ah, never mind, it's too early in the morning to spout psychology."

Justine leaned forward. "Don't tantalize me like that. Say what you were going to say."

"You'll toss me out."

"I won't. I promise."

"Your word pretty good?"

"It'll hold until you finish your coffee. Will that do?"

"I'm just a redneck country boy. What do I know?"

"How would you like to wear this coffee?"

"Violent, too? I knew you had a mean streak."

Justine made as if to get up. "I'm going into the house. Enjoy your coffee."

"Okay. Sit down. But remember, you dragged it out of me."

Justine kept silent, sipped her coffee, watching him over the rim of the cup.

"What it is . . . is, I get the sense that you drum up hostility to warn people off. Or maybe it's just to warn me off? Want to think about that for a minute?"

His eyes met hers. She felt the force of his gaze, but did not look away. "I don't need to think about it. You're right. It's just . . . I *used* to know where I fit in the scheme of things. Now, I don't. My husband left me to become a monk, for crying out loud. Tell people that and they look at me as if I have three noses or something. You made fun of it, too. Remember?"

"It does have a bit of shock value."

"I suppose."

"Ever think about hanging around to hear what else those people might say about it?"

"What could they say?"

"Maybe they'd say the guy had to be off his marbles to leave you, to forsake his kids. I'd say, it was his loss."

"Mine, too."

"Forget him. You're one hell of a good-looking woman, you know."

His words made her feel warm all over. "Thank you."

He gave her a winning smile. "You don't need to protect yourself from me. I'm harmless."

Her eyes flashed. "That's the last word I'd use to describe you."

"Tell me some of the first."

"Perceptive."

"Very cute. How about, handsome?"

She pursed her lips. "Maybe . . . in a way."

"Sexy?"

"More like . . . helpful."

"What about sexy?"

"Good-natured."

"You're not making my day, you know." He drained his cup and stood up. "Get yourself a sweatband by tomorrow. I'm gonna run your socks off in the morning."

"Oh, but I just—"

"Do unto others, I always say." He stepped off the porch. "Gotta go. Work beckons." He loped off.

"Tucker. Wait! I didn't mean to hurt your feelings."

He stopped at the line of persimmons and clutched at his chest. "I'm crushed, undone!"

Justine turned away from his antics. Sure you are, Mr. Highsmith. You look about as undone as a caliph with a harem.

She picked up the tray and carried it back to the kitchen, poured herself a second cup of coffee and, standing at the counter, lit up a cigarette.

Smiling, she stared at the column of smoke as it spiraled ceilingward. She felt better about herself than she had in months. Amazing what a bit of exercise will do. The column of smoke registered on her brain. She stubbed out the cigarette. Run my socks off? Ha! Think again, neighbor.

TUCKER SOAPED HIMSELF and sang in the shower. He was happy with himself, his life... Hell! Even his problems appeared manageable for a change.

The old man had been in a mellow mood when he'd driven him back to the nursing home last night. They had parted without his dad making a single reference to being stashed in old folks storage for the week. He'd only left Tucker with specific instructions for Pip on taking care of the fishing pole.

Somehow the boy was good for the old man. And, no somehow about it, the mother was good for himself.

Tucker felt invigorated. As if he could walk a fence or write tens of dozens recipes—if only he had the time.

He debated calling in sick, taking the day off. He had some sick leave coming. Better not, he thought. Better to save it. Now and again the old man went into depression and he had to take a day off to sit with him, or get him out of Iron Bottom's clutches, even if only for a few hours.

Anyway he'd see Justine again tomorrow morning. He'd bet his last fifty cents that she'd be waiting for him at the top of her driveway.

Gettin' a little cocky, ain't you old son? came a tiny voice at the back of his mind.

Sure am, he thought. *I like it, too.*

He closed his eyes as he shampooed his hair. Thinking of Justine, he remembered watching her tie Judy Ann's hair ribbon. Then his thoughts turned to memories of their run. He could see Justine's legs pumping. Could see her soft white inner thighs.

He felt a sudden rise in his nether regions.

Now *that* feels good, he told himself as warm soapy water cascaded over his body enhancing the sensation. But damnation. He couldn't run around like that all day.

He reached for the faucets, turned off the hot and turned on the cold.

LOTTIE ROCKED back and forth, her thoughts as dark and brooding as the morning sky. Things were not going well, she mused glumly.

In the first place she was miserable. Second, she hated herself. She couldn't comprehend how she had misjudged like that. She had only wanted to make friends, let the tenants know she was around. Why, she could be such a help! But, no. They were so unaccepting.

Hot tears came up behind her lids and streamed down her face and splashed in her bony lap. Oh, if only Elmer were here. He always knew the done thing, knew how to wring a problem out until it dried up and blew away. Times like this she felt like giving up. Just going on over to the other side without squeak nor squawk. She would find Elmer and join up with him.

An inner resistance stopped her thoughts in that direction. It seemed a shame she had come this far only to backtrack. She may not have flesh as yet, but she had fiber as stout as a length of good hemp rope. That's what made folks what they were—fiber.

Anyhow, she couldn't be certain of Elmer's whereabouts. She had no doubt about which direction she herself was going when the time came—she'd been good-hearted and God-fearing her entire life. Howsomever, Elmer had a tendency to curse a blue streak and thunder at the Lord when weather went against him, soil washed away or tobacco worms devastated tender shoots. He had favored strong drink, too. Could be he was still atoning and had been thwarted on his final upward journey.

It wouldn't do to get ahead of Elmer. He had firm ideas about a woman's place. Which had made for a fair amount of bickering between them. That forward thinking she'd been, even in those days.

Lottie shifted in the rocker.

Last night she had not dared to traipse beyond the kitchen, had taken little joy from trying out Justine's gadgets.

Recollecting how she had frightened Judy Ann put a cloud on even that small pleasure.

Mayhap, she thought unhappily, she ought to just stay in her attic for a while, let things below quiet down.

She could keep busy straightening up. She'd been neglectful of her things ever since the newcomers' arrival, hardly touching dust rag or broom. Why, she'd been so intent on learning about the new family that she had ignored all manner of dust and web. More than that, whilst she'd been below last night a possum had sneaked into the attic and left droppings from one end t'other. No doubt the flea-ridden thing was curled up in a nook somewhere sleeping, just waitin' for dark to crawl out and make mischief.

Lottie brushed away her tears and began to scurry about.

That's the ticket, she told herself. She always felt cheerful once she'd aimed her energies toward fruitful occupation.

AGNES SPOONED PRUNES onto her shredded wheat. "Isn't Judy Ann coming to the table?"

"I thought it best to give her some special attention. I made her cinnamon toast and hot chocolate and let her have it in bed."

"Does she seem better?"

Justine shrugged. "She still won't have anything to do with Mrs. Pratt—otherwise, she seems her normal self."

"Of course she's normal," put in Pauline. "She just got carried away by her imagination."

"Imagination or not, she believes Mrs. Pratt served herself tea. I'm not trying to convince her otherwise. It upsets her."

Agnes made an elaborate gesture out of placing her napkin in her lap. "Don't either of you find something odd about this house?"

"Odd? How?"

"Don't you think it strange that I always seem to be surrounded by pockets of cold air, even when it's perfectly warm outside. I mean—I have the sense the house is—" Agnes floundered "—well . . . occupied."

Pauline snorted delicately behind her hand. "It is. We're here. But keep on thinking like that Agnes, dear. You'll make it to the funny farm yet."

"I'm not crazy. I resent you even suggesting I don't have my wits about me. I have every bit as much sense as you. More! I, at least, can cook."

Justine intervened. "What happened to your truce? The big peace summit?"

Agnes cut a look at Pauline. "The truce was her idea—just to get you out of the house while that man came over to move furniture. She kept saying how useless I was—"

"In a nice way!"

"There's no nice way to tell someone she's useless."

"You went along with it!" Pauline sputtered. "Now, you tattle."

"The two of you had better get back on track," warned Justine. "I need peace and quiet in order to work. I'm not of a mind to sort your battles or dress wounds inflicted in them. Do you both understand?"

Pauline lifted her nose to a regal height. "There's no need to speak to me as if I were one of the children."

"Same here," huffed Agnes.

Justine could feel nerves beginning to bunch at the base of her skull. She massaged her neck. "Look, let's take things one at a time. Mother Hale, your arthritis has always made you more sensitive to atmospheric conditions, and you know your blood pressure is low. You haven't been taking your potassium. You're supposed to eat a banana every day. And, Mother, I remind you, we've agreed that you wouldn't go behind my back, anymore."

"I promised to try. But, Justine, you don't handle conflict well at all. I was only trying to save you grief."

"I don't handle—? Mother, did you actually give birth to me or was I a foundling?"

"Of course you're my own child. Why would you make a silly comment like that?"

"Because I had to learn to handle conflict and criticism in the cradle, that's why."

"Darling, I never criticize you. Not overtly. I only...suggest. There's a difference. And you have a wonderful glow this morning. I trust you slept well?"

The glow was from the pleasant moments spent with Tucker. A fact Justine had no intention of sharing with her mother. She reached for her lighter. "I need a cigarette."

"While we're eating, dear?"

She clenched her jaws. "I'll step outside."

"Shall we save some of this bacon for Pip?"

"Eat your fill. He's old enough to manage his own breakfast when he gets up. If you really want to be of help, Mother, how about doing the dishes."

"Of course," she said absently. Then the penny dropped. "Wha—?"

Agnes snickered. "You're welcome to use my apron, Pauline."

Before her elders could thoroughly embroil her in their bickering, Justine shook a cigarette from the pack and escaped through the screen door.

Damn it! And the day had begun so promisingly! In her mind's eye she replayed the moments spent with Tucker, recalling the smooth and fluid way he moved and their banter over coffee. He had a pleasant voice, as deep and persuasive as an actor's. He probably knew its power, too. He had employed it subtly to make her accept his every word. Still, most of his words had been nice to hear.

After a couple of puffs, she stepped down into the yard and ground the cigarette beneath her heel. Maybe she ought to cut the darn things in half, or stop altogether, or reconsider Valium, or lock herself in a closet for an hour. Only there were no closets.

The wind was beginning to gust, trees and shrubs bent under its force. Justine turned her face into the breeze. She could feel the dampness on her skin.

A movement caught her eye, a shadow in the lee of the outbuildings. The shadow materialized into a man—old, angular and thin. He looked as if he was walking around, waiting for his turn at last rites. He wore an ancient felt hat, brim turned low, and a shabby coat with the hem hanging loose.

Tucker's dad? she wondered. But Pip had said Tucker had returned him to the nursing home.

When the man had shuffled within speaking distance, he tipped his hat. "How 'do, ma'am. Name's Milo Roberts."

"Justine Hale."

"Yes'um. Knowed that."

She arched a brow. "You did?"

"Yes'um. Mr. Kessler told me. I keeps up the yard, the outbuildings, like. Mostly the yard. Gophers 'n' snakes are a plague here'bouts."

"Snakes?" Justine backed up onto a step, out of the ankle-high grass. "Mr. Kessler didn't mention there was a grounds keeper."

"Yes'um. I collect the trash, too. You jest put it in the burn barrel yonder."

"Do you live nearby, Mr. Roberts?"

"Fair close. Down the river a piece."

He didn't look capable of it, but she asked anyway. "Could I hire you to hang some curtains?"

"No'um."

"Oh."

"Outside work. That's all I do. Nuthin' in the house."

"Why not in the house?"

His desiccated old face closed up. "Don't like workin' inside."

"I see. Well, what about the back porch? The washer-dryer connections are out there and that's where we've put the machines. Could you install those for us?"

"Might could," he replied and stood there, waiting.

"Might? What would make it a sure thing?"

"Ten dollars."

"You're hired."

"Cash."

"Okay. When's a good time for you?"

"Anytime."

"Now?"

"Reckon not. Once the rain lets up."

"Tomorrow?"

"Once the rain lets up."

"Right."

"Yes'um. Nice day to you, ma'am." He doffed his hat and disappeared the way he'd come, coattails hanging.

"Thank you," Justine called to his receding back. She eyed the tall grass and shuddered. Snakes! She should've pressed the old man to mow the grass.

She spied the old chair and footstool amid the boxes they had tossed out. Darn! Her mother should not have thrown them away. Somewhere in the estate manager's file there had to be an inventory listing all of the furnishings that came with the house, meager though they were. Snakes notwithstanding, no way was she going to be charged an arm and leg for furniture that'd pass for Salvation Army chic.

She retrieved the pieces from the trash pile and hauled them onto the back porch.

"Aw, C'MON MOM. Let me go fishing."

"It's raining. Anyway, before you go alone, I want to see where your fishing hole is. Make sure it's safe. Mr. Roberts said there's a problem with snakes."

"Snakes don't bother you if you don't bother them. I learned that in Cub Scouts."

"My answer is still no. Now, go find something to do or, help me. I could use a hand untangling wires."

"That's boring."

Justine straightened up and rubbed the small of her back. "Listen, Pip, I'm not spending my life entertaining you. You've got to learn to entertain yourself. Use your imagination."

"We only get one channel on TV. All that's on is soaps."

"We'll get an antenna for better reception. One thing at a time, for heaven's sake. However, that's not what I had in mind. Read a book or work on one of your model cars. When I was your age, I loved to daydream."

"Sissy stuff. I'm almost a man."

Justine blinked. "Hair under your arms does not make you a man . . . or even almost a man. You have a long way to go, sweetie. Brain-wise and body-wise."

"You don't like me, Mom. You're always trying to put me down. It's because I look like Dad, isn't it? You don't want to be reminded."

Justine's jaw dropped. "Did you stay awake last night dreaming that up? I like you. I adore you. You're my son as much as your father's. You know what I think? You're trying to make me the villain. Pip, your father is the one who went away. Not me."

He glared at her for a few seconds then spun on his heel and dashed across the hall into his room and slammed the door. The sound reverberated throughout the house.

Justine slumped down into her desk chair and let her arms dangle over the armrests. "Shoot!"

Pauline appeared on the threshold. "What was that all about?"

"Pip's just having a bad day."

"Maybe there's something in the air. Agnes has gone to lie down. Her bones ache. Judy Ann can't be coaxed out of bed, Pip is in rebellion. Now, you look out of sorts."

"Things will be fine, Mother. Just keep a stiff upper lip."

"I didn't mean to imply that I was having a bad day, even if you are trying to turn me into kitchen help. I'm not. I have some ideas. I'd like to discuss them with you."

"Can it wait? I'm almost finished linking up."

"Couldn't you at least take a break for some tea?"

"Reluctantly. Give me fifteen minutes."

"You will comb your hair first, won't you? One always feels better when one looks her best."

"Oh, by all means, Mother. I wouldn't dare to enter your drawing room without first washing up."

"Mark my words, Justine, you and Pip are of the same cloth."

"You were eavesdropping."

"He was shouting. I'll go make that tea. Which do you prefer? Earl Grey or Darjeeling?"

"You choose. Your taste is much finer than mine."

Pauline sniffed. "I did bear a child. But come to think of it, there could've been a mix-up in the nursery."

Justine laughed. "Wishful thinking, Mother."

"If you didn't have my small ears and my lovely forehead, I would accept it as entirely probable."

"The Earl Grey," Justine said. "I feel like something nice."

Chapter Seven

Agnes emerged from her room as Justine was crossing the hall to enter her own.

"You feel better after a nap, Mother Hale?"

"I couldn't rest. There are scrabbling noises in the ceiling over my bed."

"Squirrels, probably," Justine replied in a tone of empathy. "I've seen them race along that limb that hangs near the roof. Maybe they have a nest in the attic."

Agnes tightened the sash on her purple chenille robe. "Something has a nest up there."

"Now, Mother Hale," Justine said with a soft smile. "You know there's no such thing as spirits and goblins turned loose on us mortals."

"I don't know any such thing. Remember Einstein's theory of relativity. He said just because we can only see things within our own frame of reference doesn't mean other things aren't out there. At least, he said something to that effect. It's just that if we can't see a thing, measure it in a practical manner, we tend to say something cannot exist. You went to college, Justine, you ought to know. Why're you looking at me like that?"

"You were quoting Einstein. That's a new one for you."

"Philip used to leave his textbooks lying about and since I worked so hard to pay for them, I read them, too. I may be in my seventies, but I'm not brain dead." Tears suddenly glistened in her eyes.

"You know what I was thinking? I worked as a waitress all those years to put Philip through school. Had I put myself through college, got myself that Ph.D. instead of him, I'd be better off. I could've had a fine job, been somebody. The way things turned out, I feel like I've wasted my life."

Justine put her arms around the frail and bony shoulders. "You are somebody, Agnes. And your life hasn't been a waste. You're here for me and your grandchildren. That means a lot. Really, when you think about it, that's pretty special."

"I'm a burden to you. Pauline keeps saying—"

"Mother very often doesn't think before she speaks. Don't take everything she says amiss."

"I try not to, I remind myself that Evan has only been dead a few months, that she's lost everything . . . but she makes me so mad!"

"I know," Justine crooned in an effort to remain neutral. "We're having a cup of tea, come join us."

"I think I'll just work on my contests. Has the postman come?"

"When it stops raining, I'll have Pip check."

"You don't think they lost our forwarding address?"

"I'm sure not."

"It would be lovely to win a big contest, wouldn't it?"

"It would be lovely if you won even a little one. After I check on Judy Ann, I'll tell Mother to add another cup, in case you change your mind."

Judy Ann was sprawled on the bed, connecting dots in an activity book. Mrs. Pratt, in all her rag-tag splendor, was propped on the chest of drawers.

The bedroom doors were open. Water gushed off the roof, falling in a haphazard curtain around the porch. Thick-trunked trees in the yard stood as sentries, draping moss passing for hundreds of flags heralding nature in her abundance. The grayness of it all gave Justine a sense of a primeval forest.

She picked up Mrs. Pratt and sat at the foot of the bed.

"Do you believe in magic, sweetie?"

"On television."

"There are certain kinds of magic in real life, too."

Judy Ann's gaze shifted from the book to Mrs. Pratt in her mother's lap. "Dolls aren't magic."

"Maybe they are. If you wish it hard enough."

"I was only doin' pretend. I didn't wish anything. Mrs. Pratt picked up the tea cup all by herself. She's alive."

"You and Mrs. Pratt have been friends a long time."

Judy Ann shrugged.

Justine tried another tack. "What shall we do with her?"

"She can stay in my toy box, I guess. If you put the lid down."

"Sweetie, are you scared of Mrs. Pratt?"

"I don't know what she might do!"

That tells the whole story, thought Justine. "Suppose I put Mrs. Pratt in my office, keep an eye on her? Just to make sure she's friendly. That sounds better than banishing her to the toy box."

"Maybe she doesn't like it here."

"Sure she does. We all do. You hear that, Mrs. Pratt?"

Judy Ann gave her mother a grave look, then bent her attention to the book.

Justine sighed despairingly. "I'll leave the door open, sweetheart. If you want anything, call out."

In the great room, the elders were each in their respective staked-out territory. Agnes was at her desk, her back to the room, poring over a contest newsletter. Pauline sat on a sofa in the conversation nook, fussing with the tray, adjusting the cozy on the teapot.

It was obvious that each was taking great pains to ignore the other, the tension between them being almost visible. Justine felt a sudden ache in her heart. They were both so dear to her. She would not want to lose either of them. But how to bring them together; put a halt to their bickering? If there was an answer, it escaped her.

"Ah! Justine. There you are. I was beginning to wonder if you had changed your mind about tea."

"I took a few minutes to look in on Judy Ann."

"Maybe she'd like for me to read to her later in the afternoon."

Justine hid her surprise. Her mother was far too impatient to sit still for storybooks, always had been. It had been her father who had read Justine bedtime stories. The sudden offer to cater to Judy Ann had some underlying meaning. I'm being buttered up, Justine thought, and smoothly, too.

"I'm sure she'd enjoy that," she said pleasantly. "Shall I pour?"

"No dear, you just relax." Then, in a voice matched only by saccharin, she called to Agnes. "Shall I bring you tea? I've an extra cup."

Agnes refused. Justine accepted hers, sipped from it, then leaned back and waited for the shoe to drop.

She watched her mother pour her own tea, put the cup down, smooth her wrinkle-free skirt, pick up the cup again, sip from it, put it back down on its saucer, fiddle with the tea cozy and, finally, look up and smile.

"Tea quite hits the spot doesn't it? That was one of my first accomplishments—brewing decent tea. My mother, and I wish you had met her Justine, had a firm belief that a lady should know proper tea service."

Justine smiled her answer. It must be something big, she thought. It was taking an awfully long time for Pauline to pull it out of the hat.

"That idea I had," Pauline began. "I've really been thinking about it—it's kept me up nights. I just know it'll work."

"I'm all ears," Justine encouraged.

"I knew you'd agree."

"Not so fast. What is it you think I'm so agreeable to?"

"Why, I've decided to get a job."

Justine sputtered into her tea.

Agnes lost interest in the newsletter. "I find I'm thirsty after all," she said. She hobbled across the room and sat down near Justine so that Pauline was obliged to pour. The task done, Pauline sat ramrod stiff as if facing an inquisition that upon finding her guilty would sentence her to the stake.

"I can tell you both that I will not be put off about this. I intend to get a job."

"Mother, you've never worked a day in your life. You don't have any marketable skills."

Pauline pulled a folded paper from her pocket. "You don't know that. I'm willing to work. That has to count for something. Now, I've organized a list. I have a social security card, have had for years, so that's one thing out of the way. I have a suitable wardrobe, although I may need some stockings. The tiny little thing that has to happen first is that I do need to learn how to drive."

"The tiny little thing! Mother, we only have the one car." Justine had instant visions of the station wagon wrapped around tree trunks, telephone poles, languishing in ditches and plunging over cliffs.

"I know, dear. But think how convenient it'll be for you. I can do the shopping, run errands—"

"Wreck the car."

"I won't."

"I just can't see you pounding the pavement hunting for work."

"Much less finding a job that meets with your imperial standards," put in Agnes.

"I won't be sidetracked by either of you! I'm going to set up appointments by phone—when we get one. Which will be...?"

"Tomorrow sometime, I think," said Justine.

"It's settled then. When can you teach me to drive?"

Justine leaned back and closed her eyes. Pauline was asking too much of her. There were already so many demands upon her time and emotions. It seemed that lately she did little but give parts of herself away. If it kept up she would be reduced to zero—useless to others as well as herself.

"Right now I don't have a spare hour!" Unless she were to give up running with Tucker. She couldn't make herself mention that.

Pauline slumped, seeming utterly dispirited.

"Oh, Mother, I hate to disappoint you."

"I can drive," said Agnes.

"Well, there!" said Pauline, reviving. "Agnes can teach me."

Justine suddenly felt very tired. "Mother Hale, you haven't had a driver's license since you broke your hip... that was before Philip and I married!"

"Is a license necessary to learn?" asked Pauline. "Out here in these woods? When we arrived, we drove for miles and miles on a dirt path."

"Oh.. miles on a dirt path."

"Oh...perhaps not." Justine leaned forward. "Mother, you don't know what you're letting yourself in for—"

"If Agnes is willing to teach me, I don't see why you should object."

"Though that's no small consideration, that's not what I meant. You're going to run into sexism, age discrimination—I don't think you can handle it."

"Those things are against the law. Anyway, I handled your father for better than forty years. I do have some experience."

"It's not the same."

"Why are you being so mulish? I want to be independent. Like you."

"Like me?"

"Aren't you making your own decisions, deciding where you want to live, how to spend your money? I want to do that, too. Only I have to make some money first. Besides, I like the idea of getting a job. I have so much time on my hands. I never had a hobby, unless it was shopping. I can't even do that now."

"If she had a job, she'd be out of the house most of the day," said Agnes, voicing a dubious defense on behalf of her prime antagonist.

"That's the most appealing part mentioned so far. But I have to raise my main objection—I can't be stuck out here without transportation all day. Suppose one of the children got hurt? Or Agnes got sick?"

"Can we cross that bridge when we come to it?" pleaded Pauline. "I know it won't be soon, but eventually your father's estate and the bankruptcy will be settled. The lawyers say I'll get what's left. It's bound to be enough to buy a car—used," she emphasized quickly to ward off the skepticism spreading over her daughter's face.

Justine moved out from under her mother's gaze to the porch. The storm had spent itself, the rain now little more than drizzle, and that mostly dripping from porch eaves and trees. Frogs were beginning to chirrup; a lone hen, feathers wet and bedraggled, scratched in weeds.

She was caught up in a classic case of role reversal. She could not issue a cavalier refusal. Her mother had to find her place in life as she herself was trying to do. And much as she would like to, she couldn't protect Pauline from failure, or what the working world was all about.

The rain-washed air was cool, freshening. Justine hugged herself and turned back into the house. "All right, Mother, I'll go along with it. Give it your best shot."

"I would never do less. This is important to me." She turned to Agnes. "I'm accepting your offer to teach me to drive. However—"

Agnes tucked her chin down in her attack position. "However what?"

Pauline faltered. "Dear me. What I was going to say slipped right out of my mind."

"There's a car at the top of the drive," Justine commented. "It may be the mailman. Yes," she said, moving to get a better look. "It is."

"Finally!" exclaimed Agnes. "I'll send Pip."

"Well, now that the ills of the world are solved, does anyone mind if I get back to putting my office together?"

"Why no," said Pauline. "Work as late as you like. Goodness me! I feel so energetic, I think I'll even prepare supper."

Justine paused. "You might think of heating up that chili you opened last night, put it with some wieners."

"I didn't open any chili. I loathe chili. Did you ever know cook to serve chili?" She shuddered. "Heavens! It's made from stuff that grows between cow toes."

"Mother, where did you hear that?"

"Your father told me."

"He was putting you on. Cows don't have toes. They have hooves."

"Do we have any lamb chops? I could manage lamb."

"Manage the chili, add hot dogs, chopped onion, pickle relish and mustard."

Pauline frowned. "If you say so. But once I have a job, I'm buying some real food and I'm going to hire a cook to prepare it."

Justine rolled her eyes. "I don't think I'll hold my breath."

"Daughter, you are sadly lacking in respect for your elders."

"I love you, though."

Pauline scoffed. "Small compensation."

"WAIT A MINUTE!" Justine yelped as Tucker veered right, onto a path bracketed with thick wood instead of making an about-face at the fenced-off dead end.

"I told you I was going to run your socks off. C'mon."

"I thought you meant a faster run, not longer." She held on to the sturdy wooden railing, doing knee bends in an effort to stop the quivering in her calves.

"You shoulda read my mind. Stop holding up that fence. Best part of the run is yet to come."

"I did my best part. I gave up cigarettes so I could get this far." She also had on her best pair of cuffed shorts, white with green piping, zipper at the side and a sleeveless shirt, tails tied at her waist. Her hair was plaited, loose golden wisps held off her face with a pink sweatband left over from aerobics class. She had not gone so far as to apply cosmetics, but she thought she looked presentable. Had looked presentable. Now the blouse was glued to her by rivulets of sweat.

By comparison, Tucker had yet to take an extra breath and his sweatband had yet to serve any more purpose than to emphasize features that looked to have been chiseled whole from hardwood. However, though his mustache was bristly and luxuriant as usual, his jaw was clean-shaven. Yesterday he had worn beard stubble. Perhaps he had shaved this morning for her benefit. The idea sent a quick thin sliver of delight through her body.

"A two-minute rest," he said. "Then, we'll go on."

Tucker decided he couldn't allow more than that. He couldn't be around her without being involved in some activity. She had been on his mind all yesterday and all night: miserable night rife with gnawing dreams of her.

He swung his arms to counter the urge to touch her.

Justine stopped doing knee bends to peer in the direction Tucker meant for them to run. Tall trees and underbrush flanked the path as if reluctant to allow even that narrow a passage. It looked a jungle in there, thick with vines and creepers and tree ferns. No doubt it was home to all manner of wildlife.

"Let's just go back on the road," she suggested.

His dark eyes danced and teased. "Not afraid that I might drag you off into the bushes and ravish you, are you?"

"Tucker, you're a man who has charmed my mother, charmed my children, charmed me. I don't think you're that type. I'm a city girl. I was thinking more along the line of snakes and lizards."

"A snake wouldn't dare strike at you, not while you're with me." He couldn't help himself, he leaned into her space. She smelled flowery. He liked it . . . a lot.

"Charmed by me, you say?"

She remained silent.

He looked beyond her shoulder, contriving to appear unaffected. "Just wondering."

Justine gave in. He was so appealing it was hard not to. "Yes, I'm charmed by you—a little. You're flirting with me. I liked it yesterday and I like it now. You might as well know that's as far as it'll go. I'm not into men right now."

"That's because you were married to a snake. Got bit, too."

She turned frosty. "I'm glad we see eye to eye on the subject."

"You've somehow got the idea that I like you and now you're trying to put me off. I haven't felt any chemistry between us. Have you?"

Her smile was lofty. "Not a bit."

Liar, he thought, suddenly rethinking the issue. Justine was a woman with two children to raise, a mother and an ex-mother-in-law on board—responsibilities with a capital *R*. He owned a few of those miseries himself. He liked the family well enough, *but*—and therein lay the crux of the matter.

It was enough to scare a man. Make him think twice about starting something. He looked at his watch. It was six-fifteen already. "Are we gonna run, or jaw all morning?"

To Justine's surprise he spun off back down the road.

"I thought we were going to play Hansel and Gretel," she said when she caught up to him.

"Left it too late."

She was winded by the time they reached her drive, but she managed, "Coffee?"

She was prepared today. The coffee was perked and in a thermos on the table, waiting to be poured.

"Maybe tomorrow," he said and left her with only a brief backward glance.

Justine sighed and had never meant a sigh more.

She had been looking forward to their tête-à-tête, expected it to become a pleasant morning ritual; one that she could reflect upon during odd moments as the day wore on. In her mind, sharing coffee and conversation with Tucker had taken on a special significance. That was probably because she had not mentioned it to her family. Not that she was keeping it a secret, exactly. It was only that pleasures were few and far between these days.

It was foolish, almost adolescent, wasn't it? To hoard and hold private those few moments spent with Tucker. Of course she felt the chemistry between them! Yet what good could come of encouraging it?

An affair?

Impossible. Affairs were but a temporary panacea for the misery of being lonely. Anyway, where would she find the time? Even if she did manage time, how could she face herself? The children? Her mother? Agnes?

Suppose she actually fell in love? Not that she would, but suppose?

It was one thing to take children by a previous marriage into a relationship—but a mother and ex-mother-in-law? Would a man sit still for that? Not if he had an ounce of common sense.

There was another strike against it happening. His age. Thirty-six. Which made him eminently unsuitable. If only he were even one minute past forty....

Nip it in the bud, she ordered herself, avoid temptation, avoid heartache. Don't run with him again. Be friendly, yet distant.

He was smart. He'd get the message loud and clear—especially when she wasn't waiting for him tomorrow morning at the top of the drive.

Issue settled, she decided. Solomon couldn't have done better. With an immense sense of virtue and not a little of the martyr, Justine went about her daily life.

The sun shone. Leaves washed clean of dust appeared greener, the grass higher. Milo Roberts arrived and hooked up the washing machine, though there was no outlet for the dryer. She took it in stride and directed clotheslines to be strung.

She allowed Pip to go fishing, Judy Ann played house in the yard, fed scraps to the chicks. Pauline, with Agnes at her side, spent an hour in the station wagon familiarizing herself with gears and brake and gas pedals. Wonder of wonders, when they came back into the house, they were still on speaking terms.

The telephone was installed, and the estate agent, Jim Kessler, alerted that they had arrived and settled in. Their newspaper subscriptions started arriving, and the mailman brought Agnes's social security check.

Justine booted up the computers, found them all working to her satisfaction, then spent an hour after supper arranging her desk and files and planning a work schedule.

It was one of those days when all went right, making her feel good about the world.

She went to bed feeling noble, honorable and righteous.

Her dreams were pleasant and all of Tucker Highsmith.

She awakened with the notion that she was in absolute control of her life and her emotions.

Her earlier thoughts about Tucker had been foolish. She took things too seriously these days.

The man flirted with her. So what? Men did that. It was meaningless chitchat, done solely to boost their own egos. The only reason she had taken it so to heart, made an issue out of it, was that she hadn't engaged in flirtations in years. It may have been the done thing in some marriages, but not in her own.

Heavens! She had no grandiose designs on the man, her thoughts and dreams were nothing more than flights of fancy—entertainment, really.

There was no good reason for her to stop jogging.

She did, after all, have those five pounds to trim.

Having no wish whatsoever to attempt to bedazzle, she donned her oldest sweatshirt, faded blue shorts and tied her hair back in a style she considered most unflattering.

At 5:42 ante meridiem the sky began to lighten, birds were chattering, a rooster was crowing as if he were the bugle that called up the sun.

At 5:50 a.m. Justine was at the top of the drive. Waiting.

TUCKER STARED bleary-eyed into the mirror. He'd had a bad night. Dreams of Justine had been interspersed with scenes from his youth—scenes he had not recalled in years.

He fingered the beard stubble on his jaw, but his mind was filled with images of himself as a ten-year-old.

His mother had been dead a month. The only food in the shack was a sack of potatoes. He'd peeled and boiled them while his dad holed up on the bed with a bottle of whiskey.

When the potatoes ran out, terrified that he was going to starve to death, he gathered up the peelings he had tossed out, washed them and fried them, surviving on them until his dad had sobered up enough to scrounge a few dollars.

He hadn't starved, but harking back to those years still called up the stark terror he had suffered.

He knew he was stronger for the experience. He had learned early on to look after himself, to persevere in the face of adversity. He had managed a year of college, got himself a good job, had a little money in the bank and his own home, such as it was. Not to mention fried potato peelings were *in* these days. Add a dab of sour cream and a sprinkling of chives. Hell, in the matter of food, he'd just been ahead of the times.

The image of himself as a boy faded, replaced by one of Justine. A small spark of terror stayed with him. He tried to dismiss it.

He wasn't scared of a woman. Especially her. There was no way, even given the opportunity, she was going to change his plans, the goals he had set for himself.

So what if he was taken with her? Couldn't stop thinking about her? He had seen women he couldn't have before. Hell's bells! She was just a neighbor with a good-looking pair of legs. Nothing to get excited about. It wasn't as if she had become a drug he couldn't do without. What a hoot! He hadn't even *touched* her.

Better to stop all this willful thinking before he made a grave mistake.

Women hated to be stood up. That's how he'd handle it. He'd take the back path, jog along the river instead. Leave her standing at the mailbox high 'n' dry with a case of the furies. That'd be the end of it.

Feeling as if he had culled a millstone from around his neck, Tucker brushed his teeth but stopped short of shaving since he wasn't out to impress anybody.

Before he set off, he scooped up a pail of corn and scattered it for the hens. Then he loped down the track toward the river. He had only gone a few yards when an unacceptable idea slowed his pace to a walk.

For crying out loud! He was running from a woman! Like a weak-kneed ninny with his tail between his legs.

It was an image of himself that Tucker Highsmith could not countenance. His rebel-warrior self-image was already stretched thin by the knowledge that he was involved—to his way of thinking—in the very feminine action of gathering recipes and putting them in a book.

Two dents in his self-esteem were more than he could bear.

The truth of the matter was that he had let his libido catch him off guard, then do his thinking for him. He had a lock on it now, grit to withstand seduction of any sort. Justine Hale could stand buck naked before him and he wouldn't be stirred. Not a chance.

The oddly fluttering sensation in his chest he put down to indigestion. Too many spicy foods.

He reversed his direction.

Chapter Eight

Tucker signaled her to fall in as he jogged past. His expression was as hard and dark as slate. Justine's cheery good-morning died on her lips.

"Get up on the wrong side of the bed?" she asked.

"Save your breath. We're going the distance today. That is, if you think you can keep up."

It was a frontal attack, roughly done and to Justine's way of thinking, wholly unjust. All she had said yesterday was that she wasn't into men. Had he dwelled on that? Taken it so personally that his ego was bent out of shape? Game playing! Damn it! She couldn't juggle him along with all else.

"I'll try," she said. "If I fall behind, you go on. Don't wait for me."

"Suits me."

Justine let him pull ahead. He was being downright nasty. With no good reason. A few yards farther on and he missed her at his side.

"Fagged out already?" he called over his shoulder.

That did it. "I think I'll pass today."

"Can't handle it?"

He was challenging her as if she were guilty of some infraction of the rules, *his* rules.

"Guess not," she said, mustering a superficial smile.

He hesitated long enough to track her once from head to toe. As if suddenly he did not wish her to see what might lie in his eyes, he turned and went on down the road.

She walked back to the house.

Deep down she expected Tucker to follow.

He didn't.

She was disappointed. *Keep it in perspective,* an inner voice cautioned. Considering the upsets in her life during the past year, it was little more than the irritation of a pesky fly.

She had wanted it nipped. It was nipped.

She opened the thermos and poured herself coffee. There was nothing that said she couldn't enjoy the morning, the hour or so she had to herself before others in the household awakened. It was just as pleasant without Tucker as with him.

No, it wasn't.

He made her feel alive.

When he looked at her, she felt a woman again. He made her forget that she was a discard.

But what was the point of thinking about him? She had decided against him at the very outset. Events had proved that decision wise. The only thing left to her was to come to terms with her future as a woman—what her life might be like without the chance of ever remarrying.

The craving for a cigarette overtook her.

The craving to be loved and wanted, to be held dear came on just as strong. In that context she no longer thought so much about Philip as the center of her existence. What she did miss, what she mourned most was the cushion, the shelter of being married and the sharing of life's burdens. Oh, give it up, she told herself. Things are the way they are. Accept it.

She took her second refill and sat on the front porch steps.

The shade was thicker there, the dome of trees hugging the house seeming to create a hush. It fit her mood.

She stared into her cup and forced every single thought out of her brain. It was a trick she had learned in college to make her brain a clean slate upon which to cram for exams.

Bit by bit Tucker's image crossed her mind's eye. His dark hair, brushed back from his face, yet curling somewhat about his ears and at the nape, filled the slate. The nose, straight and narrow between dark eyes that could glare with unnamed fury or light with disarming humor, held her attention.

She began the technique again, trying to obliterate his image. It hung on as if nailed in place.

What a fool you are, Justine! If the man knew how much he was in your thoughts, he would think you ridiculous.

She thought herself ridiculous! Becoming obsessed with a man she hardly knew was outside all boundaries of good sense.

The bottom step squeaked. Her introspection faded, her eyes lighting on the size-eleven, Nike-clad foot. Her gaze traveled upward until she was looking at his face.

"You give up too easily," he said.

"I didn't know I was being tested. Anyway, I promised myself to avoid negative vibes. You were bristling with them."

"Okay. Guilty as charged." He looked as if it cost him everything he owned in the world to say it.

"Why?"

"Why?" He sat down on the step beside her. "I'll tell you why. You're driving me crazy. I haven't had a decent night's sleep since you moved in. I don't know what it is with you. I've seen hundreds of attractive women—not one of them ever caused me a sleepless night."

"We make too much noise? The kids are disturbing you? You're the one who encourages them to visit you every afternoon after work."

"Coyness doesn't suit you. You know what I mean."

She was afraid she did. He was dispensing with trivialities, insisting that she do the same. An airy sensation in her stomach made her sit up straighter. "On the off chance that I do know what you're talking about, what do you suggest?"

He shrugged, shifting uncomfortably. "Nothing. You gonna drink that coffee?"

She passed it to him. "Nothing?"

"Some relationships are all chemical—"

"I told you I don't feel—"

"I have a hunch you do." The coffee was lukewarm. He drank it down in a couple of swallows.

She stared at his hands holding the cup: masculine hands with blunt, trimmed nails. She had an urge to trace the prominent veins running the length of his arm. Despite her denials it was too easy to imagine herself folded into his arms; those hands moving over her body, caressing her breasts, her thighs, the parts of her that made her wholly woman. Her throat tightened so that when she spoke the words were barely audible.

"There's no law that says we have to get involved. We're not at all suited."

"Believe me, I agree with that on more than one front. I'm just a country boy, one year of college under my belt, I work for the telephone company." He was supervisor of a crew that laid cable to commercial buildings now, but early on he had worked residential properties. He had seen all manner of houses, all manner of furnishings. Justine's furniture bespoke an affluence far beyond his own. That gave a cautious man pause. He went on doggedly. "I can't dance more than a two-step—"

"What does dancing—"

"I've got my dad to look after—"

There was a panic inside her body, an excruciating awareness of him, his nearness. Their arms were almost touching. Attempting to put the conversation back on more neutral territory, she interrupted.

"Maybe we're on the same wavelength because I have my mother and Agnes—that puts us in the same boat. You're just misreading the signals. You know the old saying 'Misery loves company.' It's the wave of the future—children caring for their elderly parents. We're part of that. Maybe—"

"What a bunch of crock. C'mon, give me credit where credit's due. I've got eyes and ears." He looked at the slow rise and fall of her breasts and had the idea that she would be astonishing in bed—lovely and surprising and ardent. He tried to split his senses, keep that image to himself and failed abysmally.

Justine felt her panic rising. "If you think I've led you on, you're wrong."

"I'm not blaming you," he said hoarsely. "It's the law of nature that's worrying me. I'm having a damned hard time of it just sitting here next to you without reaching for you."

"Oh."

"Yeah. Oh." He couldn't believe he was blurting out what was on his mind. That was another thing she was doing—loosening his tongue. He was beginning to feel he could tell her anything. Even about the book! He was all at once drawn to the long line of her throat, the shape of her mouth.

He drew closer to her, hesitated a fraction, then he touched his mouth to hers. Briefly, but it was enough.

A vein pounded in his temple. "See what I mean? I felt that in my gut."

Numbed, all her senses thrown into chaos, Justine sat utterly still.

Someone called her name. It took a few seconds before she realized the voice was not Tucker's.

She started, then leaped guiltily to her feet. Agnes stood just inside the screen door, clutching her robe closed with her gnarled fingers.

"I thought I heard voices. What're you doing?" She eyed Tucker with open disapproval, her mouth drawn down at the corners. "What's he doing here at this time of morning? It's hardly light."

"We—" Justine wavered and appealed to Tucker with her eyes.

He didn't help her. Merely judged the hearing distance between Agnes and themselves and lowered his voice. "I want you, but it is too fast, too..." He left the rest unsaid, raising his voice for Agnes's benefit. "I was just leaving."

He thrust the cup at Justine and retreated before he did some dangerous, stupid thing like ask her for a date or feel her out on what she thought about tattooed rednecks who aspired to write cookbooks. And in front of an audience yet!

Free floating, legs rubbery, Justine sidled through the screen door held open by Agnes. She felt robbed by the interruption and tried to keep her exasperation in check.

"It's too early for you to be up and about, Mother Hale. Why don't you try for another hour or two of sleep."

"Justine, are you seeing that man on the sly?"

On the sly? Her mouth opened with the shock of such an accusation. "No. Though, if I want to see him, I'm free to do it." A trace of anger crept into her voice. "I'm single. And it wasn't my doing."

"Are you implying—"

"I'm not implying anything. Don't you see? I'm trying to put our lives together. I need your support, not innuendo."

"I'm...I'm sorry. I was only curious."

"Please go back to bed. I'd like to get some work done this morning before the whole house is roused."

"Perhaps I ought to start looking for my own place."

"Don't talk silly. Your home is with us. You're family."

"I'm not blind. That man finds you attractive. I think you like him, too."

The old woman was begging for reassurance. Justine did her best to give it. "Agnes, should I ever get involved with a man, and I say ever because right now it's the farthest thing from my mind, you would still have a home with me, with us."

"That's what you say, but what man would want a reminder of your past hanging about?"

"What would you call Pip and Judy Ann?"

"That's different."

"I have no intention of playing games with my children's lives or yours. Now, please, I do need to get to work."

"All right. But if ever you want me to go, you have only to ask." She went back to her room and closed the door with a soft swish.

Justine went into her office, opened the French doors, sat at her desk, booted up and spent a melancholy half hour staring at the blinking cursor on the computer screen.

She couldn't stop thinking about that moment when he had put his mouth to hers. For those few moments she'd been suspended, finding herself on the brink of believing that all things were possible.

But of course they weren't. Loneliness was a potent illness, its cure, addictive. Tucker was not the cure. She was going to have to get past this.

One of the unspoken reasons for taking the lease-purchase on this house so far away from all she had known was to remove herself from temptation. She was determined not to become like some of her divorced friends who scurried to every dinner party in hopes of an available strong shoulder to lean on, or hung out in singles bars just to avoid one lonely night, or sat by the phone and waited for a call that seldom came and when it did, was only to set up an hour in some seedy motel.

No, that scene was not for her.

She was high-minded. Work was going to salvage her life. *High-minded?* An inner voice laughed.

She heard Tucker's truck rev up, caught a glimpse of it on the lane as it went past the persimmon trees.

So, get to work! she ordered herself. Get busy. Forget Tucker Highsmith. He was laying the groundwork. He just wanted someone to sleep with. That's what the conversational minuet was all about. Couldn't do more than a two-step. Pooh! The man had danced a verbal circle around her! Punctuated it with a kiss. For one brief moment she had hoped for the kiss to go on, become deeper. The only excuse she could offer was that she had no previous experience with any man even remotely like Tucker.

SHE LEANED BACK in her chair and massaged the back of her neck. Four solid hours of work. And well-done, too. The program was taking shape, and with far less difficulty than she had imagined. Her computer skills were up to the job. It was a good feeling.

She put her fingers back on the keyboard. The screen suddenly went blank. "No!" she yelped.

Pip stuck his head into the office. "The TV went off."

"Justine!" called Pauline. "The toaster just died."

"Something's the matter with the washer. It's stopped right in the middle of a spin cycle," informed Agnes.

Justine tried a light switch. "The electricity has gone off. I've lost a whole morning's worth of work!"

Pauline went through the rest of the rooms in the house. "All the lights work in the bedrooms."

"Let's find the breaker box," said Justine.

There was no such thing as a modern-day circuit breaker box. They located a fuse cabinet in the bathroom. None of them knew how to change the fuses, and even if one of them had known, there weren't any extras.

"Don't touch it, Justine. You might get electrocuted."

"Couldn't we unscrew the ones meant for bedrooms and put them—"

"How do you know which are blown?"

Defeated, Justine put in a call to Mr. Kessler. "It's an old house," he told her in his high, thin voice. "It's not wired two-twenty. You can't run a half-dozen different appliances at once."

"Why didn't you mention that before?"

"Well, little lady, you didn't ask. Tell you what—I'll run some fuses out and show you how to change them."

"When?" She had an entire morning's worth of work to reconstruct. She felt jinxed.

"Today. Later this afternoon."

She thanked him and rang off.

"Well," Pauline said, "Agnes and I might as well get to my driving lesson."

Justine was filled with a negative energy. It would be a useless waste of time to sit and stare at the computer while she waited for the estate agent.

She cornered the kids.

"Why don't we three go for a walk? Pip, you can show us your fishing hole."

"Wheeler says if a woman gets her smell on the place the fish won't bite."

"That's drivel. But if you want to keep it your secret place, fine with me. It's time we investigated the storage buildings out back anyway. There may be a lawnmower. You can cut the grass."

"All right. I'll show it to you, but you can't get too close."

Judy Ann gathered scraps to feed the chickens.

Milo Roberts was in the backyard. Justine peered at the line of holes he was digging.

"You must be after a whole nest of gophers," she said by way of greeting.

Frowning, he held the shovel poised over a deep hole. "Yes'um."

"You do fill those up again, don't you? If someone were to step into one, they'd likely break an ankle."

"Yes'um."

He seemed disinclined to be sociable. An eccentric old man, Justine thought, hurrying the children along. When she glanced back over her shoulder, Milo was watching them. She lifted her hand.

Judy Ann insisted on taking the short cut onto Tucker's property.

"No, sweetheart. He isn't home. We shouldn't—"

"He doesn't care, Mommy. He said so. He said I could feed the chickens anytime I like. How can I feed them if we don't go where they are?"

That excuse was all Justine needed to linger at the edge of the yard to study the renovated tobacco barn.

One entire downstairs wall had been given over to windows capped with brown-and-white striped awnings. She could see through to the opposite yard, the view made possible by a sliding glass door in the back wall. It seemed large and cheerily sunlit.

Just looking at where he lived, ate, slept made her feel light-headed and weightless; made her heart thud like a trapped bird.

Judy Ann took her hand. "C'mon, I want to show you the baby chicks. And the garden. I want a garden, too, Mommy. You'll have to buy me some seeds. I can grow all our food."

Pip retrieved a fishing pole lying along the side of an outbuilding and, from beneath an old square of damp canvas, a can of bait.

"No sense wasting a trip to the river," he said.

Justine envied them their familiarity with the place, their apparent easy friendship with its owner.

Consciously she avoided the idea that she might be falling in love with Tucker, while another part of her was infused with a hopeless yearning.

She couldn't let Tucker into her heart. She couldn't! She needed more time—time to sort everything out, time to make it on her own, to be her own person. She had to know, answer the question for herself, see if she could break the boundaries into success, support herself and the children. Independence. She would never give that up again. The cost of losing it was too high.

"Hurry up, Mom!"

Displaying a counterfeit show of gaiety, Justine ran to catch up with her children. Together they followed the path to the river.

LOTTIE HAD IDEAS going six ways to a dozen, trying with all her might to focus on just one that would do her some good. Distractions were everywhere.

The one bothering her most at the moment was that mule-faced Milo Roberts! From her perch at the window she could see him poking about. Dig, dig, dig, that's all he did. In all the years he'd been looking, he had never even come close.

There had been lonely times when watching Milo search for her money and silver had been her only entertainment. Things were different now. She wished he'd go away.

He was so many cousins removed from Elmer he could hardly count himself a Roberts, but he did it anyway, no doubt thinking that gave him the right to go poking about for things that didn't belong to him. It galled her to think her house and land had been handed down to him. 'Course, he was sly about it, never once telling a tenant.

She remembered clearly the day Milo had first arrived in the house. He had brought a newspaper with him that announced in bold black that President Franklin D. Roosevelt, the thirty-second president of the United States, had died.

She had sat right down in her chair and wept. Not for the thirty-second president of the United States, but because the last president she had known of was the seventeenth, Andrew Johnson.

Before that, it had seemed she'd only been in her condition a few months, at most a year. She just had not given it any thought. On her side of infinity there was simply no reference for Time. She had counted up the years. Best she could figure was that, by then, she had been between and betwixt for close on eighty-six years!

The shock of it had made her creep up to the attic and stay there for she didn't know how long. Minutes or days.

When she had felt up to stirring again, she had discovered Milo was tearing out the floors, taking the fireplaces apart brick by brick. He was doing it so methodically she finally figured out he was looking for her silver and the money Elmer had hidden.

She'd been so incensed she had got into his space and stayed there. She hid his clothes, his wallet, his keys, his pipe, night after night. To her way of thinking, if he wanted to search for something, let it be his own things.

She had gone through the house at odd moments, turning on the radio, cranking the small black Victrola to play the disk until the tune "In the Mood" sounded tinny.

It had worked. He had moved out and he hadn't set foot in the house since.

She missed having the Victrola.

Somewhere below a door slammed. Lottie stretched to lean farther out the window.

The station wagon was occupied. She watched it jerk forward, brake, reverse. Pauline was at the wheel. She caught a glimpse of purple on the passenger side—Agnes, then.

She regarded the unlikely duo with a sort of maternal affection and not a little envy. The useless old biddies! They took their solid, physical reality for granted, having no idea whatsoever of that privileged state.

The auto gathered minimal speed and moved down the dirt road toward the dead end.

Lottie heaved a giant sigh.

It was so awful to have been prematurely forced adrift, trapped in an inexplicable gray landscape of empty space where there was no movement or sound.

She visualized living downstairs, herself an integral part of the household, caught up in ordinary tasks. Why she could have a kitchen garden again! Run some chickens . . .

Oh, how she longed to get back into a world filled with noise and light and color; with clocks and calendars.

The longing reminded her that she had not been down among the family for several hours. A thread of panic seized her. Maybe it had been days, or even *weeks*.

She stiffened. Her chair! How could she have forgotten something so monumental. Lor! That mule-faced Milo could've burned it by now!

Lottie paused at the screen door and spotted her chair on the back porch. It was piled high with used linen. She deplored its being put to such an ignoble use and debated whether to return it to its proper place at once or scout the empty house. The chair was safe enough for the moment. Poking and prying won out. With the others out of the way she could do it at her leisure without caution.

For shame! she exclaimed upon noting the kitchen sink stacked with dirty dishes. Pip's room was a disaster: socks and small clothes lay where he had stepped out of them. Toys and books were piled haphazardly in corners. The pair of oriental carved statues Justine refused to have in the great room sat as sentinels on either side of the headboard of the unmade bed. A baseball cap perched on one, the other was draped with a discarded towel. Lottie itched to set the room to rights. Clucking unhappily she moved on to the other bedrooms.

Agnes and Pauline, she noted, had at least made their beds. But dust lay thick on every surface. And such fine furniture, too.

In Pauline's room she discovered a trove of frothy material heaped upon a ladder-backed chair. Closer inspection revealed undergarments of the finest material and textures. Awed, Lottie fingered them. A pair of stockings caught her eye. She held them up to afternoon sunlight pouring into the room. So fine and delicate were the stockings, she could see right through them. Lor! They felt like pure silk. Why, in her whole life she had never owned a pair of stockings so fine, so sheer. They were as delicate as a newly woven spiderweb.

To think Pauline cared so little that she just tossed them aside. Lottie sniffed. Probably she cared so little she wouldn't even miss them. Or the navy-blue slip with the ever so tiny straps. Lottie folded the lot carefully, deciding the sensible thing to do was to pack them tidily in her trunk where they would be cared for, revered, until...

Oh, for the day to arrive when she was restored! She felt like praying, but caught herself before the telling words could leave her lips.

It wasn't truly stealing, she told herself as she tucked the silks atop the gray dress. Her simple dream had to come true one way or another. She was just helping it along. Imagine getting back over to the side of Time only to discover herself as naked as the day she was born! The idea made her shudder with mortification. The only intelligent thing to do was to plan against all possibilities. If stealing was the only way, why even perfectly honest folk like herself had no choice. Anyway, of all the clothes she had left, only her corset appeared to have withstood time. Moths and dry rot had taken its toll of all else.

Downstairs, the house was still empty and silent. Lottie heaved another great sigh. She was so lonesome for companionship, she'd even be willing to sit through one of Pauline's and Agnes's catty repartees.

She consoled herself for a while by rooting through kitchen cabinets, reading labels on cans and boxes of food. Tiring of that, she went to sit on the front porch steps, watching for the station wagon to return.

Chapter Nine

"We really appreciate you coming out," Justine said to Jim Kessler. She felt more than a little awkward about standing in the bathroom with him. However, being the kind of person who needed a hands-on approach to learn, she had no choice if she wanted to know the nuts and bolts of exchanging fuses. Kessler seemed not at all disturbed. She watched over his shoulder as he unscrewed and checked the fuses.

"Hated I couldn't be here to welcome you and give you the keys, granddaughter's birthday y'see. Took Tucker up on his offer to see you got 'em." He looked back at her over his shoulder. "Didn't know you was going to be a houseful a beauties, though, else I'd of passed that cake right up."

Lottie, perched on the edge of the tub, rolled her eyes. The sly-tongued old goat always did fancy women. Had any man ever spoke thataway to her, Elmer would of poked him with a pitchfork where it'd do the most good.

"Thank you," Justine murmured.

As unobtrusively as the space permitted she put a bit more distance between herself and the estate agent. She thought he looked like a character right off the page of an Erskine Caldwell novel. He was bald, bony-chested and gaunt to the point of emaciation. His suit was an elderly, blue seersucker, the cuffs of which were far short of his ankles, revealing black cotton socks held up by old-

fashioned garters. The band on his floppy straw hat
matched his blue polka-dotted bow tie. One of his shoes
had been cut out to accommodate a bunion at the side of
his big toe.

"Here you go," he said, leaning into the light to display
the blown fuse. "See that there tiny spit of metal? It's
broke. Means the fuse is shot." He pulled several others
from his pocket. "See these? Metal's in one piece. That's
how you tell which is good and which ain't. Best you keep
a supply handy."

Lottie squeezed between them. She needed the lesson on
modern inventions as badly as Justine. Things were far
more simple in her day. Candles and oil lamps had been
sufficient.

Kessler turned back to the box and screwed in a new fuse.
The hair on the back of his neck stood straight out. "Hey!
Hey!" he choked. "Hey!"

He yanked his hand, leaped back into Lottie and stood
stunned for a moment. "The dern thing shocked the heck
outta me." He stared at his fingers then, misreading Justine's expression of dismay, said "Do pardon my language."

"Are you hurt?"

"Naw. Fingers are prickling a bit. Felt the current down
to my toes for a second there. Must be a loose wire some-
wheres."

"Can you fix it?"

"I reckon so. If I don't kill myself."

"We could call an electrician."

"No, we can't. Costs an arm 'n' a leg to git folks this far
out. I'll just check my toolbox in the car. Reckon I have a
rubber-handled screwdriver that'll do the trick."

Lottie was sitting on the floor, between the old iron toilet and the tub, where the jolt of current had knocked her.
She had felt the buzz of it the instant Kessler had bumped
into her. It had just flowed over her like water. She had felt
a sudden warmth, as if she actually had flesh. She could
hardly countenance it, but for an instant she had felt *earthly*
again.

She held out her hands before her face. Why...she could almost see the shape of them. Lor! Her legs were forming! Oh, no! This wasn't how she'd planned. She couldn't just appear out of nowhere, and stark naked, to boot! That would ruin everything!

Heart thudding, ears ringing, she made herself as small as she could. Her brain held but a single thought: escape to the attic and get on her bones before the whole of her dream went amiss and no undoing it.

Kessler left the bathroom, Justine on his heels.

Lottie raced out behind them, noted the kitchen was un-occupied—thank the Lord for small favors—dashed into the pantry and ran headlong into Agnes.

Pardon me, she said, then stopped. Oh, dear.

Agnes swivelled her head. A can of beans slipped from her hand. "Who's there," she whispered. "I know you're there."

Of all the times to get through to somebody! Lottie wailed. She huddled in the deep, shadowy recess of the pantry, not daring to open the hidden door. And by gar, she wasn't going to do anything as unseemly as passing through it, either. Suppose she was suddenly restored altogether and got stuck within its thick timbers? Lor! That would be courtin' calamity.

Peering into the dark end of the pantry, Agnes took a few steps toward the hidden door. She stopped suddenly, shivered, then retreated, walking backward.

"Agnes?"

"Agggh!"

Pauline stared at her stricken expression. "Good heavens. What's wrong with you? You're pale as a sheet."

"I—" Agnes bit her tongue. If she said what she had seen, or thought she had seen, Pauline would accuse her of being mad as a hatter. Then Pauline would get her way. Justine would put her in a nut house. "I dropped a can on my foot," she said breathlessly. "Hurts like the devil."

"Oh, you poor dear. Come sit down."

"I think I'll go lie down," Agnes said.

"You're not too badly hurt are you? I don't want us to miss a driving lesson."

Agnes snapped her head around. "Don't worry. If the car can take your abuse, I most assuredly can!"

"That was uncalled for. I shudder to think what my poor Justine has had to suffer with you all these years."

"I've been more help to her than you have! She knows it, too."

"What do I know?" asked Justine, entering the kitchen.

"Nothing," said Agnes.

"Exactly," said Pauline.

Lottie did not wait to hear the end of the argument. She slipped behind the door, hurried up the stairs and fitted herself on her bones. *Made it,* she gasped, and closed her eyes with relief.

Her eyes flew open. Lor! She didn't want to miss a bit of it. She could barely contain her excitement. Imagine! Any minute now...

But even as she watched, anticipating the wonder of restoration, her hands and legs faded into nothing again.

She stared bleakly at her bones, panic penciled into her expression. So close, she had come so close. Oh, if only it was safe to pray. She'd plead, she'd get down on her knees and stay there until she keeled over. She reached for the family Bible and opened it on the bed. She'd read a bit for solace. That always used to help when she was distraught.

She lingered over her favorite scriptures, but she couldn't rid herself of the idea that perhaps she had lost herself for good and always and that the self she had known would not be coming back. Ever.

That can't be, she cried. *It has to happen. Has to!*

She just had to think it out.

"YOU'VE SETTLED IN better'n most, I'd say," Kessler said as he took in the arranged elegance surrounding himself. "The old house has taken on a glow. Terrible waste these past years, having it empty, except for the odd summer or huntin' season now and again. Impossible to get folks out in the country anymore. Old houses like this ain't much

more than white elephants, less'n they're in some histori-
cal district t' other.''

"So far it suits us fine."

"Maybe you'll be wanting to buy it, then? As I said, the
owner would make it a bargain."

Justine smiled faintly. "We do have the length of the
lease to decide..."

"Quite right," he said and spread his thin smile to include Pauline as she arrived with tea.

"I always heard a watched pot never boils," she said. "I
think it's true. I do hope the electricity stays on now."

"I 'spect you'll blow a fuse now and again. No help fer
it, all the gadgets you got. Just got to keep a supply in, buy
'em at the grocery store." He crossed his legs, hiked his
pants at the knee. "Tea. Ain't this nice," he purred, eyeing Pauline. "Bet you can cook up a storm, too."

She spied the hole in Kessler's shoe and frowned. "I'm
afraid tea and lamb chops are my only culinary accomplishments," she answered and cut a look at Justine which
said, "Get me out of this." She poured, served, then sat
stiff as a board, refusing to be drawn into conversation.

After Kessler took his reluctant leave without an invitation to dine, she pounced on Justine.

"You terrible child. You saw what he was doing. You just
sat there and let him run on. Why, I thought I wouldn't be
able to bear it, the way that horrid tie kept bobbing on his
Adam's apple. I do believe he was actually flirting with
me."

"You wanted independence, Mother. You want out in the
real world, you're going to have to learn to handle all sorts
of people. I found him rather old-fashioned and nice, myself. He looked hungry. Maybe we should've invited him to
supper."

"We most assuredly don't see eye to eye on men. Speaking of which, how are you and Tucker getting on? Agnes
said he was here this morning."

"He stopped by for a minute."

"And?"

"We're nothing more than neighbors, Mother. The man stopped in to say hello. Don't make a federal case out of it."

"The children adore him."

Justine stiffened. "They're vulnerable right now. They'd like anybody who pays them the least bit of attention."

"I was only making an observation. You don't have to be so argumentative. Or protest so passionately."

Justine opened her mouth to say something, then stopped and looked away, unable to trust herself. The feelings inside might come out shrieking, words that once said, could not be retracted.

"If you want to invite a man to dine, consider calling on Tucker one evening," Pauline continued. "He's been such a help, and I much prefer his company to Mr. Kessler's."

"Perhaps later on," Justine said, regaining herself. "I want to try to get some work done now. I've lost too much time as it is. Pip's still fishing, but can you keep an eye on Judy Ann?"

"Of course."

After dinner Justine continued to work toward reconstructing her lost program. She blotted out the sound of the television, sharp words between Agnes and Pauline and the children's protests at bedtime, and managed good-nights without losing her train of thought.

When she finally shut down the computer, moths were flying in through the open French doors and flitting about the desk lamp. She shook a cigarette out of a pack and took it out to the porch to smoke. It was her third one of the day. Tomorrow, she promised herself, she'd cut back to two.

Bits and pieces of the evening intruded on her solitude. Pip's version of a fish story, Agnes's odd quietness at dinner. Pouting, Justine surmised, or showing a twinge of envy concerning Pauline's hope of finding a job. Agnes needed something outside of entering contests and watching television to occupy her time.

Oh, bag it, Justine told herself, one worry only led to another.

It was a beautiful night: the sky was inky, the stars twinkling, a slice of golden moon cast a surprising amount of light that illumined the moss-draped oaks. She shifted her gaze to the persimmon trees. She could just see light spilling from Tucker's windows. So, he was still up. She wondered what he was doing; what he'd say if she walked over and knocked on his door. Not that she had any intention of doing that, ever. But for a few seconds she indulged in an imaginary conversation with him.

An owl hooted. It was a singularly lonely sound.

I'm afraid, Justine thought. I'm the kind of woman who wants to have a man as a focal point in her life.

But she had done that once and come up a failure.

All that lip service she paid to being independent, making it on her own—she was just parroting talk-show guests, quotes in magazines and books—liars all, she scoffed. Herself included. She didn't want to be alone for the rest of her life.

A good marriage was a barrier, a safety net, protection. Two people *were* stronger than one. Despite what feminists said, divorce left one feeling like a second-class citizen. Why didn't they tell you how to cope with how scary that was instead of mouthing platitudes? Why didn't they warn of how difficult it was to sleep when a woman was suddenly alone in a bed that she had shared for years?

I need a soul mate, Justine thought. The acceptance of that was as frightening as admitting to herself that she was deeply and utterly afraid of the future.

She glanced once more toward Tucker's house. Impossible, she thought wistfully: Tucker had many wonderful qualities, but that didn't make him her soul mate. She'd rather face her fears alone than tie herself to the wrong man, again.

Finished with her cigarette, she stubbed it out, pulled the doors closed on the night, switched off lights and trod quietly across the darkened hall to her room.

LOTTIE STOPPED PACING the hall. *Finally!* she exclaimed. She could take care of her chair now that Justine had gone off to bed.

She had decided that if she could just sit in her chair and dwell on her situation, she could find the answer to her dilemma. She knew exactly where she'd place it—near the television set.

She thought it prudent to move the chair while the house did its night settling. That way the creaks and groans would cover whatever unintentional noise she made.

Justine put down the first series of thumps to the squirrels inhabiting the attic. She plumped up her pillow and turned over in bed. She had it to herself again, since Judy Ann had returned to the room she shared with Agnes.

The thumping changed to a dragging sound. Agnes must be up, she thought drowsily, interpreting the sound as that of the cane and shuffling slippered feet. She dozed, but the shuffling noises kept penetrating her subconscious, as did memories of Agnes's behavior at supper. Was the old lady ill and keeping it to herself out of some misguided fear of being thought too much trouble?

Damn. She'd better check, or be ready to spend a restless night wondering if Agnes was okay. Reluctantly she threw back the coverlet, switched on the bedside lamp and shrugged into her robe.

Light suddenly spilled from Justine's bedroom into the hall.

Drat! Lottie muttered watching the other doors along the hall open one after another. She stood rigid in deep shadow, the old fiddle-backed chair clutched to her bosom.

"Did you hear it, too, Mom?"

"Pip! What're you doing up?"

"I heard a noise by my door."

"Your grandmother, I heard her cane."

"It wasn't me," whispered Agnes, peeking around her door.

Tying the sash of her robe, Pauline emerged from her room. "What in the world is all the racket about?"

"Nothing, Mother. Go back to bed."

Pauline looked to her left, her right. "Everybody's up. Something must be going on."

"Judy Ann?" Justine asked of Agnes.

"Standing right behind me," said Agnes, sounding much more forceful now that Pauline was looking at her.

Lottie felt the chair slipping from her grasp. She thrust out a hand to catch a rung, but the chair passed through her disincarnate limb and crashed to the floor.

Five pairs of eyes suddenly swiveled in her direction. They were filled with disbelief and sudden consternation.

Lottie pressed against the wall. Hooey! She was caught fair, and no doubt about it.

Pauline took a step toward her.

"It's that dreadful old chair I threw out. How did it get—"

Dreadful old chair! It's my chair, you uppity old snout. Keep back. Lottie grasped the fiddle-back. Head high, dignity asserted, she began dragging it toward the place she'd selected for it.

Pauline dropped her arms. "Dear me," she croaked weakly.

"The chair's movin' by itself!" squeaked Pip, falling in and following behind it.

Justine grabbed him by his pajama shirt, yanking him to her side. "Stay back."

The chair moved past Agnes and Judy Ann. Agnes stared for a long second, tugged Judy Ann into her arms, then slammed her door closed.

The chair kept up its wobbly pace until it disappeared into the great room.

Justine's chest felt suddenly tight. "I've heard of things like this happening. It's called kinetic energy."

"Yeah," said Pip, his voice quavering. "Like in the movies. Remember *Poltergeist*?"

Pauline moved closer to her daughter. "Maybe we ought to call the police."

It wasn't an idea Justine relished. "How would we explain—"

"Well, we'd just . . ." Pauline leaned heavily against the wall. "I don't know. You could say we were being burgled. Let's go to a hotel."

"Let's get Tucker," said Pip. "He's not afraid of anything!"

"Yes," breathed Pauline. "Do. Let's all go get Tucker."

"No." Justine's mind was racing. "There's some scientific basis for kinetics. Pip is going through puberty. That could be it."

"Hey! I didn't move that chair. I wasn't even thinking about chairs. I was dreaming about fish! Stop blaming me!"

Pauline moved past Justine into the lighted bedroom. "Come along, Pip. You and I will get Tucker."

"Wait a minute, Mother. That's not a good idea, either."

"You have a better one? I'm not sleeping in a house that has furniture moving about on its own. It's unheard of."

"I'm sure there's a reasonable explanation."

"Like what?"

"It's supernatural," suggested Pip, his tone belying a shiver of thrill as well as fear. "Maybe you ought to call a priest, Mom. He can come and—"

"There is nothing supernatural in this house!"

"I wish we had a gun with silver bullets, or a stake."

Pauline crawled to the middle of Justine's bed and sat there. "I don't care what you say it isn't. I left my room so quickly, I failed to turn on the light. If you refuse to get Tucker, I'll finish out the night in here. Pip, dear, get up here beside me. We can protect each other."

There was enough edge in her mother's tone to make Justine scrutinize her closely. Pauline's lips were rimmed in white; her entire body trembled.

"Look," she said, "we can't let our imaginations run wild. There must be a perfectly logical reason—"

Pauline was at once indignant. "You might try that line on Agnes or one of the children, but not on me! I didn't imagine a chair suspended above the floor, nor did I imagine it trotting off on its own!"

At that moment Justine would have willingly given up everything to be back in Virginia, married to Philip—running to answer his summons for a fresh shirt, clean socks, or even being chastised for her flaws—to have life simple again.

"It might attack us if we go to sleep," said Pip.

"A chair is nothing more than wood and fabric, for Pete's sake!" There was, Justine recognized, a slight edge of hysteria in her own voice. She exhaled slowly. "Okay, Mother, you win. We'll see Tucker. I'll get Agnes and Judy Ann."

He answered his door on the second knock. His brows arched in surprise as his gaze swept over them, then he registered their strained and unhappy expressions. Alarmed, he tightened the sash on his short terry robe. "What's wrong? Your house on fire?"

He looked beyond them, saw no smoke, nothing out of the ordinary.

Justine shook her head. "No."

"One of you is hurt?" He stepped back and gestured them into his home.

"We're all fine."

What the hell? "Ah! Don't tell me. You want to borrow a cup of sugar. And you have so much pride, it takes the whole family to do it."

"We have sugar," said Pauline, moving to sit down as if her legs were of no account and unable to bear the burden of her weight. Agnes followed suit and pulled Judy Ann onto her lap. Pip hung back by the door.

"We have a slight problem," Justine began, the words dying in her throat. Now that she was in his house and facing him, she felt an utter fool.

She put off saying more by inspecting her surroundings.

Her first impression was one of space. The downstairs was one long rectangular room. Vaulted above their heads was a ceiling with thick cedar-beam struts. A set of stairs along one wall led to a sleeping loft under the slope of the roof. The loft projected out over the kitchen and became its ceiling. There were dishes in a drainer on the counter. The stove looked so clean and modern, she felt a twinge of envy.

Out of the corner of her eye, she noticed a small desk and typewriter. The furnishings were sparse and clean, a perfect blend of comfort and simplicity.

"You have a nice place," she said artfully. "Did you do all of it yourself?"

Tucker gave her his undivided attention. Justine's eyes seemed lit from within by a curious glowing flame so that all he saw of her face was their huge opaque splendor.

"You came over here at midnight to talk construction and Salvation Army chic?"

"It was a stupid idea. I'm sorry we disturbed you. C'mon, everybody, let's go home."

"Pooh on that!" said Pauline.

"A chair moved by itself," said Pip, drawing Tucker's attention. "We all saw it."

"I didn't," said Agnes, eyeing Pauline as if the entire affair were a conspiracy against herself.

"You most assuredly did!" Pauline responded. "You were in the hall the same as the rest of us!"

Agnes clamped her mouth shut in a thin line and shook her head vigorously.

"You'll forgive me," drawled Tucker, "if I tell you I'm not enlightened."

"A ghost lives in our house," Judy Ann said defiantly. "It made my doll drink tea and now it's moving furniture."

"A ghost?" It was all he could think of to say.

Judy Ann nodded. Tucker smiled down at her, then lifted his head. "You all saw this ghost." He made it a statement.

"We all saw a chair moving down the hall—by itself," said Pauline.

"Don't include me," said Agnes. "I was asleep."

Tucker looked at Justine. He was grinning. "You sure as heck picked a novel way to get a guy outta bed."

"The fiddle-backed chair did move," she said. "At least, we think it did. Now, I'm not so sure."

"Justine!" exclaimed Pauline. "We saw it with our very own eyes. I'm not blind, neither are Pip and Judy Ann. Agnes," she added snidely, "is another matter."

"I will never get in the car with you again," Agnes retorted.

"Mother, Agnes . . . please . . ."

"You're serious, aren't you?" Tucker said, floundering in unfamiliar territory and wondering how best to handle the situation.

He was out of his depth. A house full of females gone potty on mass hysteria. He sure as hell didn't believe in ghosts.

"What would you like me to do?" he asked for want of anything better. His robe gaped open, revealing a thick mat of hair on his chest. Justine's gaze traveled up to his lived-in face, admiring the mustache, the deep-set eyes. He looked a romantic criminal, far more dangerous than whatever was in her house—if anything.

Self-consciously she averted her face and in her mind's eye saw suddenly how they must appear to him. She cleared her throat.

"We don't want you to do anything. This is silly. We shouldn't have bothered you. It's an old house. We're not entirely used to it yet. We scared ourselves." She gestured to her mother, the children and Agnes.

Agnes clutched her cane, but made no move to rise. Judy Ann leaned against her shoulder.

"We do so want Tucker to do something," parried Pauline. "I'm not budging until he's been through the house from one end to the other. And be certain you look under my bed."

"Mine, too," said Judy Ann.

"We don't have a gun or anything," Pip said.

It was no use. Even Agnes, for all her stubborn denials, was holding her ground. Justine was boxed into a corner and knew it. She implored Tucker with her eyes. "Would you mind?"

"Hey, what are neighbors for? Ghost slayer to the rescue. Allow me a minute to put on some pants. I wouldn't want to meet any fairy folk bare of feet or... well, never mind. I'll only be a minute.''

When he returned, clad in jeans and pullover shirt, Pip put on a brave front. ''I'll go with you,'' he said.

''You'd better keep an eye on things here, sport. Keep the ladies quiet. Turn on the television, watch the late show, why don't you?''

Justine was not so easily dismissed. She insisted upon accompanying him.

''There's no ghost,'' she confessed, once outside.

''I didn't think there was,'' Tucker said and grabbed up a short sturdy piece of wood as they passed the chicken coop.

''Is that necessary?''

''Boy Scout motto. Be prepared. Could be you had a prowler, though we're so far off the beaten path, it'd be a fluke if a transient found us. This is a pretty safe area. I've never locked my doors myself.''

What he wasn't prepared for was her nearness. He had spent hours putting her out of his mind, trying to forget the way her lips had felt beneath his own, the fragrance of her hair. The scent she now wore brought it all back. There was the swish of her robe. He wondered what she had on under it and cast about for some reason to put his arm around her. But the moon and stars lighted their path and she was surefooted.

She hesitated on the back porch step. ''We left through the door in my bedroom.''

''You keep the back door locked?''

''No, because the bathroom's out here.''

''You ought to leave a night light burning.'' He reached around the screen and pushed open the thick wooden door. ''Where's the light switch?''

''The light hangs down on a wire above the table, you have to pull a string. And there's a lamp on the counter by the microwave.''

''Wait here.''

A moment later the kitchen lights went on. ''Okay. All clear.''

With Justine trailing a few cautious steps behind, they went through each room, switching on lights, checking under beds, in pantries, in chifforobes, behind furniture. In the living room Justine pointed out the fiddle-backed chair.

"There it is."

"Looks harmless."

"I know. But it wasn't there earlier."

He picked it up, inspected it, put it back down. "It's just an old chair. Well constructed, though."

Of course it is, said Lottie contrarily. *Elmer built things to last, as you ought to know, Tucker Highsmith. You're living in the barn he labored on for better'n six months.*

Justine paused. "Have you ever heard of kinetic energy?"

"Sure. You think it moved this chair?"

"I thought of it. But I don't suppose it's likely. It's just..."

"Just what?"

"They say kids can be conduits for unexplained movements. Especially if they're unhappy or going through puberty. Judy Ann and Pip haven't been...they're sort of lost way out here. They're not used to having to entertain themselves. Agnes and Mother don't get along as well as I'd hoped either.

"There has to be a logical explanation." She felt as if something in her chest had broken. "We should never have moved here," she whispered. "I had the mistaken idea that a new place, new faces...change—" She shook her head, going mute. If she said one more word, she'd start to cry. That was the last thing in the world she wanted to do in front of Tucker.

"C'mon now. You had a fright. Everybody got caught up in it and made it seem worse than it was. Now you're coming down. It's the adrenaline leaving. Everything will look better in the morning, after you've had a good night's sleep."

She looked so forlorn, he could not keep from touching her. He brushed stray hairs from her face with the back of his hand, then trailed his fingertips down her cheek until they were beneath her chin. "Damn! But you're lovely."

His touch on her face was electrifying. Not daring to move or respond, Justine was pinned helplessly beneath his gaze, breathing shallowly.

Lottie gaped. *Why, Tucker is courting Justine! What a hoot!* Still, it wasn't seemly to watch. Such goings on were a private matter. Leastways, she and Elmer had always found it so.

On the long side of it, her chair was safe for the moment. Anyhow, it was Pauline who was the mischief maker. Lottie felt bad now about frightening everyone else. She hadn't meant to and was sorely unhappy with herself. Howsomever, in spite of the hoopla it had caused, she had managed a fair night's work.

She flitted around the couple, who now had no interest whatsoever in anything but themselves, and made her silent way to the back of the house. She had in mind to investigate the fuse box in the bathroom.

"If we started something, I'm not sure where it would lead," Tucker murmured, talking more for himself than Justine.

"Nowhere," she replied, struggling to bring her emotions under control. She wanted to prolong the conversation but suddenly felt so awkward that she couldn't. She could feel the heat radiating from his body and smell the soap he'd used. She had to pull herself together.

Tucker put his hands on her shoulders and slid them down her arms. "So soft." He could feel his heartbeat in his ears. "Justine, I think I'm in love with you."

"Don't do this to me." Her voice was treacherous and thick. She wanted what his eyes, his mouth, his hands promised. And knew instinctively, sorrowfully, that anything serious, having to do with a man, was never going to be easy for her again.

"Don't do this to you? You moved into my space. What am I supposed to do? Ignore you? Sister, I can't stop thinking about you." His hands squeezed her wrists. "You know what I do at work all day? Daydream. Like some moonstruck kid, I make up all sorts of scenarios between us— Hell! I know it's too soon, but I feel like I've been hit over the head with a shovel.''

"Don't."

He gave her a grim smile. "I keep telling myself you've got more on your plate than you can handle. That you don't need me. I ask myself what I have to offer. And come up blank."

"You have a lot—"

"Name it."

"I don't know exactly. This is a stupid conversation, Tucker. We don't *know* each other."

"I know you." He wanted to say something romantic, something to fit the occasion, but the words that came to mind chafed with the good-old-boy image he had of himself. "When I saw you on the porch that first time, you switched something on inside me. I feel as if I've known you all my life. Something in my brain connected with you. You fit here, Justine. You do. Don't talk about it being a mistake. That scares me. Makes me think you'll just pack up and one day I'll come home and find you gone." Her expression was so dubious he knew he had to continue, convince her. He smiled the smile that made him seem so boyish.

"I know more about you than you think. I pick the kids' brains. They love to talk about you. I know about the time you baked a birthday cake for Pip and it slid off the plate onto the floor. Judy Ann has a picture in her shoebox of you when you were pregnant with her. She says it's a picture of her inside your tummy. Your hair was long then, almost down to your waist. I know about the time you were in the grocery store with her and accidently let one and blamed it on her—"

"What!"

Her face flamed, making her eyes seem like some warm and liquid sea, inviting him into their depths. He laughed and lost his momentum. "Yeah, she told me."

"I'll wring that girl's neck. I will." A second passed, two, then Justine cleared her throat, her emotions once more in check. "It's way past all our bedtimes...."

"Okay," he said, releasing her. "Look, I have to go out of town. My crew's been loaned to a site in Montgomery, but say you'll have dinner with me when I get back. Nothing fancy. I'm not a fancy guy. Burgers and beer. You'll see I don't pick my teeth in public, spit on sidewalks, dip snuff—the basics." He took her hand. "C'mon, we'll let your folks know the ghost has been banished to the cellar."

"We don't have a cellar."

"Don't have a ghost, either."

"Yes, I do," she replied very softly. "The ghost of a failed marriage."

"We'll talk about that, too. Hell, we'll talk about everything—raising kids, safe sex, mothers-in-law, paying bills, the price of eggs in China, even monks. Get it all out of the way." He might even tell her about the cookbook, he thought to himself. If she laughed him off the face of the earth, he'd pull in his horns, save face, cut his throat. Yeah, he thought. What she thought about the cookbook would be the bottom line. And his dad, too. The old man was as big a consideration as the book.

"You're going too fast."

"The hell I am! I'm holding back." All those old clichés about love were true, he thought. You fell into it, headlong, with no hope of stopping, and that was it.

"You're awfully sure of yourself," she said as they stepped onto the path between her house and his.

"I know. I surprise the heck out of myself sometimes. Don't dawdle. I'm fighting the urge to carry you off into the bushes."

"Crass, too."

"Only on the outside, inside I'm—"

"What? What are you on the inside?"

"Tenderhearted?"

"That just might be true."

"I should've kissed you when I had the chance. I want to now, bad. But there's Pip, standing on my stoop, playing lookout."

Against her will and better judgment, she suddenly wished he'd kissed her, too.

Pip showed up clearly in the light from the porch. He looked so like his father that Justine's heart wrenched. She withdrew her hand from Tucker's. Grow up, she told herself.

Wishes don't count.

Chapter Ten

Justine banged on the bathroom door. "Pip, what are you doing in there? I need to get cleaned up."

I'll tell you what he's doing, Lottie said with a snort of disgust. *He's counting the hairs under his arms. And when he's not doing that, he's flexing those skinny arms of his or mugging in front of the mirror.*

"Gee whiz, Mom," he said pushing past her. "A guy can't have any privacy around here."

"You can have all the privacy you want—in your bedroom."

"Without locks on the doors? Anybody who wants to just walks in."

"You weren't doing anything nasty in there, were you?" Justine teased.

His face went the color of beets. "You sure are dumb, Mom. I'm growing up. You're supposed to treat me with respect."

Justine did a double-take, thoughtful for a moment. "Respect? All right. But that works two ways. There are five of us who have to use one bathroom. Growing up means having consideration for others."

Including me, there's six what have to use the room, said Lottie. She had hardly had a turn. Why, each time she thought she was clear to finagle the fuse box, somebody else came prancing in as if a call to nature was on orders from God Almighty Himself—not that she was taking up blaspheming, but there was something to be said for an outdoor privy. Nobody stood in line for that!

Pip was glaring at his mother through narrowed eyes. "Yah, you're just nervous 'cause you got a date with Tucker. Don't take it out on me."

Justine opened her mouth, then closed it. There was truth in what he said, but she didn't like having it thrown into her face by an eleven-year-old. "I am nervous. I admit it. That only makes me human. Which doesn't give you the right to hog the bathroom. Got that?"

"Sure," he said, sauntering off. "You don't have to make a federal case out of it."

Lye soap, Justine. You spare it now and you'll regret it to your dying day, Lottie said.

Pip slammed the screen door and Justine slammed the bathroom door.

Lottie sank down on the stoop and wilted. There was ruin in the air. Things built themselves up and then tumbled back to nothing again so fast she couldn't keep up.

After the fiasco with the chair, she'd been ever so careful not to wander about after the sun went down. Agnes had got into the habit of investigating every little noise she couldn't put a name to. Not only that, but the fuse box was defeating her. Thus far, no matter how she poked and pried, no jolt of current whipped out to give her that wonderful sensation of being solid again. She was just as invisible as ever, a figment, a phantasm.

Lottie sniffed the air, then felt her mouth watering.

Agnes was making popcorn and using real butter from the smell of it. She made a big bowl of it every day and nibbled on it while she watched game shows.

Lottie issued a mournful sigh and spent the time waiting for Justine to vacate the bathroom daydreaming of the time when she could partake of sustenance without having to sneak to do it.

"WHAT DO YOU THINK, Mother? Am I overdressed or underdressed?" She had chosen a peach-colored sundress, fitted at the waist with a full swirling skirt, and tied her hair back with one of Judy Ann's ribbons.

"You look quite nice, dear. Refreshing."

Agnes chafed. "Suppose I get sick while you're out with that . . . that—"

Justine sighed heavily. "I'll only be gone a few hours." Agnes was heaping more guilt upon the guilt she already felt about leaving all of them at home while she anticipated an evening of fun—or if not fun, getting away. She was thinking of it as a mother's day out. Looking at it as an actual date made her stomach lurch.

At the exact moment he had promised to call for her, Tucker drove into the yard and tooted the horn. The kids raced outside to say hello.

Tucker had grown to immense proportions in their eyes by virtue of the fact that the night before he had left town he had "hired" them both. For the grand sum of one dollar each per day, Pip had watered and weeded Tucker's garden during his absence, and Judy Ann had fed and watered the chickens and gathered eggs. Tucker had graciously insisted that they bring home the eggs and whatever vegetables were harvested.

To Justine's surprise, the children had taken their "jobs" seriously. Not once did she have to remind them. And they had done such splendid work, Tucker had paid them each a ten-dollar bill.

"In my day a man would come up to the door to call for his date," said Agnes.

"In your day they still used horse and buggy," quipped Pauline.

Justine's guilt and tension restructured itself. "Look, if it's going to cause all this hassle, I'll just tell Tucker I've changed my mind."

"You will do no such thing," insisted Pauline. "You've earned a night out. If Agnes becomes ill, I'll take care of her."

"Be dead for certain then," the other woman muttered.

Pauline put down her needlepoint, shoved Justine's purse into her hands and ushered her out onto the front porch. "I can recall the times when you couldn't wait to get away."

"I'm older now."

"All right, if you don't want to go, ask Tucker if he'd mind a substitute. I'd like a night out myself."

Justine laughed. "Okay, Mother. Point taken."

He was leaning against the cab of his truck, chatting easily with the children. When he looked up at her, his smile was disarming and sexy. Justine knew he meant it to be. She suddenly had another dozen instructions for Pip and Judy Ann. Tucker shook his head, gently pried her away and handed her up into the cab. Her hands were so unsteady she could barely fasten the seat belt.

Once they were off, it seemed to Justine they were acknowledging each other only by a soft flurry of vibrations. She was doing her best to remain cool and detached, to deflect the wealth of emotions that threatened to swamp her.

A quarter mile down the road he said, "If you'd honestly rather not do this, we can turn around...."

"I'm nervous."

"All because of a hamburger and beer?"

"Because I haven't been on a date in fifteen years! I don't know what's in—how to act, what to say—"

"Calm down, be yourself. You mind riding in the truck?"

"No, why should I?"

"See? Now we have an ordinary conversation going here. Easy as pie." He looked at her out of the corner of his eye. "Did you miss me?"

She had counted the days and finally, the hours. "No."

"Nine days and you didn't think of me once!"

"Well, when you called."

"I've got to think about this. Watch the scenery."

She did, some, but more often her gaze slid to his profile, his hands on the wheel, or the jean-clad length of his legs. He'd had his hair cut, and he smelled of a seductive woodsy after-shave. There had to be something primitive in the olfactory nerves, she thought, else why did his after-shave cause sudden erotic images in her brain.

At the stop sign before they got onto the highway he looked at her, and Justine could feel the warmth of his eyes on her lips. He sensed that she was wholly unaware of her impact on him. The light scent she wore filled his nose, swirling around him like an aphrodisiac. It took all the control he could muster not to pull over onto the verge and take her in his arms.

"You had to think of me," he said, hoping the huskiness of his voice didn't betray his thoughts. "No way you couldn't. The chemistry between us is just cooking away. We're on the same wavelength. The way I see it is, you're lying. Shame on you."

Justine salvaged what she could. "Maybe I'm not at the same point in this relationship as you are—or think you are. I'm not even sure we have a relationship."

"Put any name on it you want. I know what's plaguing me." He was creeping up to the danger zone, decided to pull back. *God,* he thought, *I need her.* His entire life had been spent focusing on survival, keeping the wolves at bay. He had ignored and discounted the loneliness that ate at him, nagged him like a toothache. *No more,* he thought, then sighed. He was afraid to trust his feelings. Justine had undone his equanimity.

He had thought he'd get back on track while in Montgomery, but when neither the memory of the soft feel of her skin nor the smell of her hair had diminished in his thoughts, he had phoned her. When she'd come on the line, his heart had sunk. There was something intensely appealing in the sound of her voice, something that made him wish he was with her and had her in his arms. He muttered beneath his breath.

Justine wet her lips. "You said something?"

"Halfway thinking out loud."

"About what?"

She was beautiful, the expression in her eyes uncertain. Tucker knew that he'd have to give her time to catch up, to ripen with love and desire. "Now that's a leading question," he said, smiling. "What if I told you, dreams?"

"What kind of dreams?"

"Same as everybody else. A cross between fantasy and reality, speaking of which, tell me—what's with our old friend, the chair, these days?"

Justine accepted the shift in subject with relief. "Nothing now, but it ruled our lives for three days. Pip drew circles in chalk around the legs. It hasn't moved an inch. I'm not certain that it ever did—on its own, I mean. But convince Pip and Judy Ann of that! Mother deplores it, Agnes ignores it. I sit in it. It's comfortable."

"Brave woman."

"Hardly that. I don't believe in psychic phenomena. At least, I don't want to believe in it." Justine paused. "But if I had to swear on a Bible, I'd have to say it did walk down the hall on its own."

Tucker grinned. "Put it back outside and see if it trots in again."

Justine laughed. "I wouldn't dare."

"Too bad. I could make rescuing damsels a habit."

"No doubt you've done your share of that."

"Not nice, and here I am on my best behavior to impress you."

"If I were any more impressed, I'd have to stand up and applaud." She couldn't keep her eyes off him. He excited her in a way that no other man ever had, including Philip.

He laughed, pleased by her approval.

The tavern was a weathered building boasting a much-scuffed wooden floor. It was built on stilts overlooking the Tensaw River. A red neon sign advertised beer and bait, the bait shop being beneath the tavern. A boat ramp was nearby and from the number of trucks and cars and boat trailers, Justine surmised it was a popular local watering hole. Tucker guided her to a table near a bank of windows which gave her a view of the river and the rocky bulwarks upon which long-legged water birds perched. A jukebox gave out an old Elvis Presley tune. A middle-aged couple swayed to the music in the small area set aside for dancing.

A few men spoke to Tucker, and the waitress greeted him by name.

"Like it?" he asked.

"Actually, I do."

"It's more fish camp than beer joint. I bring my dad here sometimes. Gives him a chance to keep his fish tales up to snuff."

The waitress set frosted mugs before them. The beer was so cold it hurt Justine's teeth.

Tucker placed his hand lightly over hers. "Tell me every little thing that's happened while I was out of town."

"You'd be so bored you'd never ask me out again."

"I like the sound of your voice. I just want to hear you talk."

"You flatter me."

"So indulge me."

"I jogged every morning. After that I worked, or did laundry or pleaded with Milo to quit digging gopher holes and mow the grass. Mother and Agnes practiced their driving. We're all three studying for our Alabama licenses. Mother wants to find a job...." A shadow flitted across her face.

"And?" Tucker prompted.

"Mother and Agnes fight more than the kids do. I think Agnes is envious. Tucker, I'm listening to myself. You don't really want to hear this."

"I'll tell you when to stop."

Justine shook her head. "I just wish there was more harmony. I miss it."

"What about your ex-husband?" Tucker asked, stroking her hand. He hated bringing the man up. It felt as if he was hitting himself over the head with a club. But if there was a force in the way of Justine's feelings for him, he wanted it banished. "Do you miss him?"

Her face closed up. "That's a topic that's still a little raw."

"In what way?" he kept on, pushing to exorcise the man, erase him from Justine's mind.

"I miss what he represented. The three-bedroom ranch, the mother-in-law quarters, the security and safety of being married. I hate it that the children don't have a father, especially now. Pip needs a firmer hand these days, and Philip was always the disciplinarian. And...I miss...having somebody there for me..." She trailed off and took another sip of beer. "Enough. What about you? Any ex-wives out there?"

"Not a one."

"Girlfriends?"

"Now and again."

"Did you ever come close to getting married?"

"Once, but I had a project going that didn't appeal to her and there's the matter of my dad. She thought three's a crowd. She didn't like country living either."

Justine succumbed to a twinge of jealousy. "You lived together?"

"For about twenty minutes."

"What kind of project?" she asked, changing the subject.

The bottom line. Tucker decided it was still too early to risk it. "Just an old dream. I'll tell you about it sometime."

"Dreams can turn out to be nightmares," she said with feeling.

Tucker gently squeezed her hand. "He really hurt you bad, didn't he?"

"I was devastated."

"Wherever he is, I hope somebody rubs his nose in it. Some guys just don't know how lucky they are."

"It happens all the time. Mid-life crisis."

"Drivel."

Anger glared in her eyes, lighting them from behind. "It's not drivel. Men turn forty and, poof! they want out."

"Don't make the mistake of including me in that group. I had my mid-life crisis when my mother died."

Justine started.

"Ah. You *have* been including me—giving me black marks when I didn't deserve them. You can't go around dishonoring a Southern boy like that, Justine. It riles them no end. As it happens I know just how I want you to make it up to me. Let's put a quarter in the jukebox and take a twirl on the floor."

She straightened in alarm. "No! I haven't danced in years."

He moved around the table and bent to whisper in her ear. "It's like this. You either dance with me so I can hold you in my arms or we can go outside and get it on in the truck."

"I'll dance," she managed.

His grin was wicked. "Knew you'd see it my way."

He picked out a couple of old Ray Charles tunes and once he had the whole of her in his arms, thigh to thigh, chest to chest, he merely stood still. "Oh, Lord," he murmured. "I knew this was how you'd feel."

Justine, too, felt the current; her nerve endings pulsed. She moistened her lips. "We'd better dance."

He two-stepped them about the floor.

She was very much aware of every inch of him pressed against her. It was the music, Justine thought. It seemed to insinuate itself inside her body, making her respond to Tucker without her own volition. She was at once dismayed, but the sensation of having his arms about her left her with no will of her own. It felt wonderful to be in his arms—as if she were whole again. As if whatever essence of womanhood she had left was being forced into bloom. She rested her hand at the back of his neck. His arm tightened at her waist.

"This is unadulterated hell," he whispered in her ear. "Like making love with your clothes on."

"I know," she whispered back, then flushed deeply realizing she'd just confided something terribly intimate.

They danced two more sets. When the last tune faded, Tucker guided her back to the table, reluctantly relinquishing her to her chair. "Can't handle any more of that. Maybe another beer will cool me down. Then we'll eat."

After he gave the waitress their order, he looked at her and with a troubled laugh said, "Remind me, when we leave, to have you ride in the truck bed. If you sit next to me on the way home I won't be held responsible for what I might do."

His voice had a slight quaver and Justine understood that he was as shaken as she. Up until a few moments ago, it had been little more than words between them, the seriousness lightened with jokes. But now . . . the only thing left to her was to put a good face on it. She patted his hand, put a smile in her voice.

"Don't worry, you're safe with me."

He frowned. "You're not taking me seriously at all, are you?"

"I can't."

"Or won't?"

"I won't deny I feel something for you—"

"What do you feel?"

"But one of us has to be practical."

"Forget practical," he interrupted, intrigued by the possibility of what she might say. "What do you feel?"

Justine was hanging on to her resistance by a thread. "I—I'm probably in as deep as you."

Tucker was suddenly flushed by a dizzying uprush of emotion. "Let me just run down the list, to be sure."

"What list?"

"Just answer yes or no. Does your flesh feel restless?"

"Tucker . . ."

"I'm not asking you to jump in the sack. I'm just trying to find out if we're talking the same language. Restless or not?"

"Restless."

"Your gut feel airy?"

"A little."

"Only a little?"

She gave him a half smile. "All right, a lot."

"You feel intoxicated?"

"Yes, because I've had two beers on an empty stomach."

"You feel like laughing when nothing's funny?"

"Sometimes."

"Are you terrified?"

She laughed outright. "Unequivocally. Now stop."

"Last question," he said, his eyes radiating a sudden intensity. "Wanna dance until our food comes?"

"We might embarrass ourselves."

"We won't. I just want to hold you close some more."

There were several other couples on the floor. They moved among them for a few steps, then Tucker maneuvered her into the darkest corner. He nibbled on her ear, kissed her brow, trailed a kiss from one eyelid to the other.

Justine's inner response was so profoundly receptive that all at once she found it impossible to believe it was happening. She pushed him away. "Please, you've got to stop."

"You're right," he said, breathing shallowly. Then he kissed her. His lips tasted the softness of her mouth, he had to fight the giddiness that swept over him.

Justine forgot about being sane and sensible, forgot that she had vowed never to get involved again.

The waitress breezed past the dance floor holding up a tray. "Hey, Tucker, food's up."

ON THE RIDE HOME Justine felt the tension rising in her once again; apprehension about the note on which their evening would end. Over the hamburgers and fries, which were the best she had ever eaten and not done justice to, they had talked of everything under the sun: clothes and people and food, the new morality sweeping across the country, his job, her work, his dad, her parents, senior citizens, young people, street people, fishing, hunting and gardening.... Words had seemed to just rush back and forth of their own accord.

She had found herself confiding in Tucker as if he were a long-lost best friend. He had sympathized and encouraged, and all the while her feelings for him deepened. She discovered he was compassionate, stubborn, arrogant, witty and fun. Best of all he never seemed to take his eyes from her, as if he couldn't get enough of looking at her, or of touching her. It had been easy to reciprocate, yet she couldn't see how they might manage to end up a couple.

For her, simply keeping afloat from month to month was a major accomplishment. Looking down the long road, theirs would be an impossible household. No sane man would consider it. And the idea of having an affair scared her to death. Fantasizing was one thing, but actually getting undressed? Discussing condoms? It was out of the question.

She wanted someone to relax with, to laugh with, to love, and pleasantness, if that made sense. Or perhaps she was hungry for all the small courtesies of marriage. Tucker was very good at small courtesies.

The lights from the dash cast an eerie glow upon his features. He was as deep in contemplation as she had just been. She reached over and touched his arm.

"What are thoughts going for these days? Still a penny?"

"You'd have to pay through the nose for the ones I'm having right now."

"Give me a hint."

A smile played at the edge of his mouth. "I'm wondering how in hell I can give you a good-night kiss, deposit you on your front porch and then walk away like the nice guy I am." The smile widened, he glanced at her, then faced the dash again. "The animal in me is warring with my good intentions. The animal wants to drive up to my own front door, carry you upstairs and have its way with you. Does that give you your penny's worth?"

"I think," Justine said carefully, "I've just bought more than I bargained for."

He reached for her hand and brought it to his lips. "I like a woman who places a high premium on certain things."

The sweep of his mustache on the palm of her hand sent a lovely tingle down Justine's spine. "What's that supposed to mean?"

"Just warning you to save up your pennies. There'll come a time when you'll want to spend them. I promise to give value for value."

"You're driving on the wrong side of the road, Tucker."

"Cripes!"

Euphoria got the best of Justine. She extended her arm across his shoulder then let her fingers trail up his strong corded neck. "I like you."

He took a deep breath. Like! That was small change compared to what was going on inside of him. He felt slightly dizzy from her perfume; an interior warmth squeezed through his chest and belly. He'd been too long without a woman, and the thought of yet another cold shower to dispel the heat made him say a bit too sharply, "Well, that's a start."

Piqued, Justine drew her arm back, ready to challenge his words, but realized she didn't know which direction the challenge would take—start or finish. She had just wanted him to say that he liked her, too. But of course, he'd already made himself plain. He was beyond the beginning, it was she who was the laggard. But she had to be! One of them had to be practical.

He turned into her drive and the headlight beams illuminated the disconsolate trio sitting on the porch steps. Justine's heart leaped into her throat.

"Something's wrong!" she cried and exited the truck before Tucker could even bring it to a full stop.

Chapter Eleven

"Where's Mother?" Justine asked. "What's happened?"

"We thought you'd never get home, Mom." Pip was no longer the swaggering preteen, only a very relieved youngster.

"Grandma Gates is crying," said Judy Ann, sniffling herself. "She's been crying almost since you left and hasn't stopped."

"It wasn't my fault," said Agnes, rising painfully to her feet. "Pauline has locked herself in her room," she explained. "We couldn't coax her out."

Justine sagged against a porch pillar. She looked from the three pinched faces to Tucker, as he took the steps two at a time. "What's the problem?"

"Histrionics, I think." Justine knew that she had to shelve all thoughts of continuing the evening. Tucker might as well know her priorities now. Her hand fluttered toward him. "I'm afraid we'll have to say good-night." She tried to sound casual, but disappointment overrode her tone. "I had a wonderful time."

His expression exuded a disappointment as strong as her own. "Can I help," he said, adding hopefully, "I don't mind waiting."

"I don't think you'd better."

Tucker shrugged. Outside of pleading with her, the only option she gave him was to bow out. "If you need me..."

Her heart and soul were in her smile. "I know where you are." She touched his arm. "You're good company, Tucker. More—" She stopped, mindful of her audience.

He cleared his throat, turned and clamped a hand on Pip's shoulder. "Listen, sport, you want to drive with me to pick up my dad in the morning?"

"Sure! Can I, Mom?"

"He won't be in your way?"

"Not a bit." His gaze lingered on her hungrily for a moment, then he spun off the porch while murmuring goodnight.

Justine suddenly felt empty of all emotion. She ushered her clan into the house. "Okay," she asked wearily, "what started it?"

"I made meat loaf for dinner like you said," Agnes replied. "The lid to the pepper shaker came off in Pauline's hand. She put it down calm as you please. Then she burst into tears, got up from the table and ran into her room. She's been there ever since. Nobody *said* anything."

"I told her I'd be her best girl, but she wouldn't talk to me," said Judy Ann. "She said for me to get away from her door."

"It's been a terrible evening," added Agnes. "Pauline isn't stable. She scared the children."

A myriad of feelings swept through Justine—anger, remorse, love, hate. She wanted to sidestep a confrontation, curl up in her bed and let her imagination run wild with thoughts of Tucker. But it would seem that even dreams were to be denied her. The unfairness of it all swamped her and it took her a moment to harness the flood.

"All of you go to bed, quietly now," she said finally. "I'll deal with your grandmother. Shoo. You, too, Mother Hale. Tuck Judy Ann in for me, why don't you?"

Once alone in the hall, Justine pressed her ear to Pauline's door. She could hear her mother's sniffling. Tea, she thought, and went to make it. When she had it brewed and the tray ready, she tapped on Pauline's door.

"Mother? It's me. I'm home and I've made us a pot of tea."

"I don't want tea. Go away."

"Don't you want to hear how my date with Tucker went?" She waited. Nothing. "Mother, I'm not budging," she announced in the no-nonsense voice she used on the children when they were being stubborn. "I'll stand out here and bang on your door all night if I have to."

A moment later there came the sound of scuffling, a chair being moved away from the door. Pauline tugged the door open. Her eyes were puffed and watery; her bed a sea of used tissues.

Without meeting her daughter's eye she turned back and sat in the center of the bed.

Justine set the tray on the Pembroke table that served as a nightstand. She poured the tea, took a cup for herself and curled up leaning back against the bedpost, gathering strength for what lay ahead.

"I had a wonderful time with Tucker," she said and her mother's head jerked in Justine's direction. "Now, what are you so distressed about?"

Pauline buried her face in her hands and began to sob again. "It was the pepper..."

"So the lid came off," Justine said gently. "Mother, that's not anything to cry about."

Pauline wiped her nose. "You don't understand. The last meal I shared with your father was steak au poivre. When he made that noise in his throat, I thought, 'Cook's used too much pepper'... and then... and then—" She took a deep breath "—Evan just... slumped."

Justine set aside the tea and moved to put her arms around her mother. "Oh, Mom, I know it's been hard on you. I miss Dad, too."

Pauline hiccuped. "I'm so angry with him, Justine. The same way you're angry at Philip for leaving you. I feel abandoned and so *helpless*! First your father, then the house, the furnishings—I've misplaced my gray silk and now my last pair of silk stockings—all lost! Everything! I have nothing."

"You have yourself, me, your grandchildren. We're here for you. Even Agnes is here for you." She realized the assurances were almost word for word those she had urged upon her ex-mother-in-law weeks earlier. "Things will work out. And you probably forgot your dress at the cleaners. Send them a note."

"It's more than that. I know it wasn't your father's fault the market collapsed, or that a blood vessel burst in his brain before he could recoup all of his losses, but what am I going to do? What are we going to do? We've both been forsaken."

Justine opened her mother's hand and pressed the tea-cup into it. "Philip's gone and Dad's gone. Dad had no choice. Philip did. They were our anchors and we've been cut loose. We feel adrift. Let's accept that. We can't undo what's done. We have to learn to anchor ourselves to life, not depend entirely on anyone else. We're going to keep on doing the best we can. You're doing fine, Mother. Learning to drive and cook, helping with Pip and Judy Ann. I'm proud of you."

Pauline's eyes widened. "You are? You don't think I'm just a silly old twit?"

"Of course I don't. You're just a little rusty on how to use your smarts. You're adjusting fast."

Pauline took a long draught of tea. "Your father was proud of me, too, but now I think it was for the wrong reason. He appreciated that I was an extension of him. I see that now. But I liked it, I went along with it. He provided so much."

"And he would've kept on providing. He wouldn't have copped out like Philip."

"No, I'm sure he wouldn't. I guess life just conspired against him. You really think I'm learning to be my own person?"

"I believe it with all my heart."

Pauline glowed. "I feel so much better. You're a good daughter, Justine."

"Why don't you get some sleep?"

Her mother hesitated. "From all I've read, appearance is so important. I do so want to look nice when I go for job interviews, dear. I don't suppose you'd consider ordering me some stockings from Harrods?''

Justine gave a small laugh. "You supposed right. But I do have an extra pair or two of panty hose you can have.''

"Oh, but what shall I do with all of my garter belts?''

"Burn them! You're going to be a modern Millie now.''

Pauline's face fell. "So much left behind...''

"We're on our own, Mother. Financially, emotionally. Garter belts are the least of our worries. We'll do fine. I know we we will.'' She looked about the room. It was a hodge-podge of expensive bibelots, curios that Pauline could not bear to part with. "You know, I bet you could raise some cash if you'd put some of this stuff up for sale—that Tiffany lamp, for instance, and those ivory whatnots.'' Pauline looked stricken. Justine retreated. "Well, there's no harm in considering it.''

She took a last sip of tea, then replaced the cup on the tray. Pauline grabbed her hand.

"You're not going off to bed now?''

"I am. I'm tired.''

"Your evening with Tucker went well, you say?''

"It was magnificent.''

Pauline cleared her throat, a sure sign an unwarranted curiosity was on the rise. "Did the two of you...you know—''

"We ate, we danced, we talked,'' Justine said firmly, but Pauline's emotions were splintered and she didn't catch the warning.

"You will discuss safe sex with him, won't you, dear, before—''

Justine's face flamed. "Mother, for heaven's sake. Don't put me in bed with a man I hardly know.''

"Well, I was remiss in my parental duties once. And I distinctly recall that you said you'd known Philip only hours when you... You do have a tendency to make up your mind on the instant, Justine. I don't want you to make the same mistake twice.''

"Neither do I!''

"I don't think you will. Not with Tucker. There's more to that man than meets the eye."

Suddenly animated, Pauline shook the bedspread. Tissues went flying. Then she turned back the linen, crawled between the sheets and smiled beatifically at her daughter.

"Mother, do you know something about him that I don't?"

Pauline ignored the probe, fearing she might have overstepped boundaries, if not her daughter's, then Tucker's. "I have great faith in you, Justine. Great faith. You're right, misplacing a dress or a pair of stockings is a mere bagatelle compared to what I can do, if only I try. Now I almost have as much faith in myself as you do." From beneath her pillows she drew out a jar of astringent-soaked eye pads. "Get the lights, will you, dear? I think I can sleep now."

In her own room, in the soft glow of the night-light, Justine's bed loomed like a hole full of infinite nothingness. She threw herself across it and moaned.

Why was it, she wondered, that she couldn't be blessed with a single day without problems? Why couldn't she find the easy happiness others had? All she had ever wanted in life was to find her soul mate; someone to share her life with.

She regretted that she had not allowed Tucker to wait. Her whole life was one long series of regrets and wrong decisions!

She had made the wrong decision with Philip. Poor Philip. He was wrong for himself!

Now there was Tucker.

He attracted her like a magnet. He seemed so right for her; for all of them. In a single evening he had made her doubt her hypothesis that no man under the age of forty was reliable.

She turned over and gazed up at the ceiling, wondering what her life might be like with him if she gave up her mistrust and took him wholly into her heart.

How would it be if he were in bed with her this minute?

She laughed at the idea. With her luck, Agnes would barrel in...Judy Ann would require a glass of water...the roof would fall in.

TUCKER ADMITTED to himself that he was more in love with Justine than he had ever thought it possible for a man to love a woman.

He was trying to doze, but his mind refused to sleep. It kept filling with a picture of his hands moving across Justine's body, slowly and deliberately. He could see himself stroking her until she ached deep within, see his mouth following his hands, exploring her, touching her, exciting her to a point where even the feel of his breath would cause her to quiver.

He groaned and punched his pillow.

But it was more than sex that he wanted from Justine. She completed him, as if she filled in all of his emotional blanks. He wondered what her reaction would be if he told her that.

She'd tell you to drop dead, probably, said an interior voice.

And, what if he mentioned he was writing a cookbook?

Tell her, urged the voice. *She could use a good laugh.*

Chapter Twelve

The electricity failed for the second time that morning. Justine threw up her hands and yelped. "No! No! No-o-o-o!"

"I always seem to arrive hard on the heels of a crisis," said Tucker as he knocked on the doorjamb before stepping through the opened French doors.

Justine looked up and smiled. "It's not a crisis, exactly. It's just we can't use more than two appliances at the same time I'm using the computer. We keep blowing fuses."

"Maybe you have a ghost who wants to conserve energy."

"Very funny. The house probably needs new wiring."

"You're looking at the best handyman this side of the Mississippi. I've got a shed full of leftovers from renovating my place. If you like, I can separate the circuit you use for the computer from the rest of the house."

"You've got to stop doing things for us, Tucker. It makes me feel we're taking advantage of you."

"Is that bad?"

"There's so little I can do for you in return."

He grinned. "I can think of one or two things—my laundry, wash my truck or, better yet, read me a bedtime story..."

"Good try," she said airily and laughed. "But no thanks."

"You have a sexy laugh. It's enough to give any man salacious ideas."

Their eyes locked, and for a moment the intensity of his stare unnerved Justine, leaving her mute. He stood tall and exuded a maleness that made her recall every minute of the evening before. Pleasure rippled through her body in tiny waves. She was obliged to shift her gaze lest he read the longing in her eyes.

"You're just full of bad jokes this morning," she teased. "Was it something you ate?"

"Ah, food. That reminds me why I stopped in . . . to tell you we're back. Pip's helping my dad put away his things, then they're off to the fishing hole. I'm going to barbecue a slab of ribs this afternoon. I thought the rest of you could walk down, meet my dad, break bread . . ."

"I'd like that," she said, giving him the full benefit of her sultry green gaze.

"I have something for you." He drew his hand from behind his back and offered her a brown paper sack. "I didn't have it wrapped—"

"A gift?" she whispered, surprised and suddenly unable to find her normal voice.

"Look and see."

It was a small porcelain piggy bank, painted with delicate flowers.

Tucker grinned seductively. "For your pennies."

It was a dual moment of knowledge, words that echoed the past and thrust them into the future. Justine tried to be very very still and think carefully. Her eyes were luminous.

"You're crazy," she said, her smile overfull and heavy.

"I am. About you." He took her arm, drawing her to him so that they stood within an inch of each other. "We have some unfinished business."

"We do?"

"In my book when a guy takes his lady out, the least he can expect is a kiss good-night. I was cheated. You did want to kiss me last night?"

"I—" Quickly she catalogued the whereabouts of the other family members: Pauline was in her room, Agnes at her desk, Judy Ann outside pestering Milo to put up a swing for her. The moment was theirs alone. She went into his arms.

His lips brushed hers softly at first, as if waiting for a response. Every part of her came alive, tingling, pulsating, elevating her senses to a pitch that felt almost unbearable. She put her arms around his neck, pressed against him and tentatively returned his kiss.

"I knew I was right to be crazy about you," he murmured against her mouth, his voice deep and husky. "I want you Justine, more than I've ever wanted anybody or anything. In my fantasies I've already made love to you, *absorbed* you."

Justine found her own feelings both exciting and frightening. She had never been so affected by a man in her life. And he sounded so sincere, but didn't all men when they wanted something? It was too easy to be tempted by dreams that denied reality.

"I've heard that before, or at least variations of the line," she said, the words tumbling out.

A black shadow descended over his face. "Damn it! Don't make the mistake of comparing me to somebody else."

"I'm trying not to. But you know the old saying— If something is too good to be true, it is."

"I'm too good to be true?" Astonishment coated the words.

"My perception may be faulty," she observed with a smile. "You may have a Jekyll and Hyde personality."

"Not this old boy. What you see is what you get. And I'm trying to give you all of me."

A spike of shyness surged through Justine. "I know."

"Then what's the problem?"

He stiffened suddenly.

Justine followed his gaze over her shoulder. *One* of the problems stood behind her, stone-faced, frozen, standing still as a mannequin and glaring at them.

She disengaged herself from his encircling arms. "Mother Hale," she said, wondering how long the older woman had been observing them. "We didn't hear you."

"I could tell."

"Tucker just came over to invite us to a cookout."

"How nice," she said, imbuing the words with sarcasm. Before Justine had a chance to respond she made her exit. A moment later the television went on, volume high.

Embarrassment flared in Justine. "I'm sorry."

"Don't be. I'm used to old crabs. I own one myself."

"At least he doesn't live with you."

"He will eventually," he said, giving Justine food for thought and watching her face.

"I hope you handle it better than I do," she said consideringly. "I've got to check the fuse box."

"Did I lay that on you wrong?"

"No, not wrong. But lately I've thought how hard it is to have a relationship. There's so much baggage to drag into it."

His stomach somersaulted. "Does that mean you think we have a relationship?"

"Probably," she said lamely.

She looked so forlorn, he couldn't hold himself apart from her; he pulled her to him again and pressed his lips to her brow. She was flesh and soft and he wanted more than anything to feel her suppleness yield beneath his body. With a sigh, he held himself in check.

"How does four o'clock sound?"

"Four o'clock?" She sounded dazed.

"Barbecue, food. Four o'clock?"

"Oh. Perfect. Shall I bring something?"

"Your family..." He let his hands trail down her spine. "Your body, an appetite, kind words." His hands settled about her waist and he pushed her a few inches away. "I want to tell you something. Don't laugh."

"I won't."

"No woman has ever gotten me so erotically inclined at ten o'clock in the morning before."

"And I have never felt so shameless." Or powerful, she thought, flushing with a strange sense of pride. Philip had been such a prude. No amount of pleading on her part had ever convinced him to take her into his arms—unless they were behind a locked bedroom door. Woman power. It was heady emotional baggage. Without a doubt it was the kind of baggage she *could* learn to live with.

"WHY DO YOU KEEP taking pot shots at Tucker, Mother Hale? He's been nothing but kind to you, to all of us."

"You were kissing him."

"I may do it again!"

"It just doesn't seem right. Suppose Philip comes back?"

Justine blinked. "If he showed up on our doorstep five minutes from now, I wouldn't have him back—not as my husband. Ever."

"He's the father of your children."

"Biologically, yes, otherwise, he's proved himself not interested," she said, defending against the criticism she heard in the older woman's voice.

"You're becoming hard as nails, Justine. I don't like it."

"What you don't like is that I might find somebody to love and be loved in return. I'm still young, Agnes. I want some happiness and continuity for myself and for the children."

"You hope to find it with Tucker Highsmith?"

"I don't know yet. Please, couldn't you see your way clear to be nice to him?"

"If it means that much to you," she said on a note of aggrieved martyrdom. "I guess I know which side my bread is buttered on."

Justine took a deep breath. "Thank you."

THE HOUSE WAS SILENT and empty. Justine had herded her family together and trotted them down to the barn at Tucker's invitation. Lottie sat in her chair staring at nothing, her spirit wrapped in numbness. She thought her frustration level was about to break its limits, vexing beyond measure.

She had tried all that she could think of with the fuses and electricity. No wonderful arc had flowed into her. Each time she had loosened a fuse, the current had stopped altogether and each time Justine had come racing into the bath mouthing epithets that should never cross a decent woman's lips.

Life, Lottie thought sadly, was nothing more than a sleight of hand. Now you see it, now you don't. She wanted to be seen so badly the taste of want was acrid on her tongue. She laughed at herself. *As if she had a tongue.* But she must have—she could taste, couldn't she? And if she couldn't yet be seen, she at least wasn't blind. Dust motes floated in the patches of sunlight checkering the floor. She saw them easily; and the crystal arranged in the cabinet; the bottles and carafes of liquor were a symphony of color—browns and greens and yellows, prisms that caught the odd shaft of light.

She drifted over to the cabinet and read the labels; Absinthe, Sambuca, Drambuie, brandy of which there was cherry and Napoleon; vodka and rum. Rum. The tobacco buyer had always made her a gift of a small keg of Jamaican rum with which she had made cakes and puddings. And oh, the heady smell in the kitchen while raisins had soaked in the dark amber liquid!

She poured a small amount of rum into a glass and passed it beneath her nose. Ambrosia—she could smell. She took a small sip—and, taste... She filled the glass to its brim, and regally, as if playing to an audience, returned to her chair. The rum made her feel warm, also light-headed. It seemed to expand her world, put her in touch with herself. After a second glass, Lottie gazed around at the dusty splendor that was her home. She was disappointed with Justine's housekeeping and had to fight the urge to take up dustcloth and mop. Soon, she thought. Once she had mastered electricity, she'd see to it that the old house and all its contents sparkled. Justine would be glad of the help. Lottie was certain.

AGNES KEPT HER WORD, treating Tucker with a polite, stiff formality. She did not extend the same courtesy to Tucker's father. The two septuagenarians declared war almost from the moment they were introduced.

"Think you was born to the purple, do ye?" Wheeler said, looking Agnes up and down.

"Better born than out from under a rock," replied Agnes, stabbing her cane into the soft earth as if defining her territory.

Wheeler rocked on his heels and popped his suspenders. "You walkin' around brain dead, or you just appear that way?"

"I understand you're under court-ordered supervision," Agnes said, feigning sympathy. "It's so sad when one of our age has been declared incompetent."

Wheeler grinned and there was in the set of his mouth a youthful resemblance to his son. "What'd you have for breakfast, Purple Lady? Hemlock tea?"

Justine was mortified.

Tucker thrust a soft drink into her hand and pulled her away. "Come talk to me while I baste the ribs."

"We can't leave those two alone. They might kill each other."

"What do you suggest? That we make them stand in the corner until they promise to behave?"

There was a cluster of dogwood several yards from Tucker's back door and it was beneath this delicate shade that he had set out his kitchen table and chairs to accommodate his guests. A forty-gallon drum converted to a cooking grill held ribs, a pot of corn on the cob, another of pork 'n' beans. The savory smells hung in the air.

Pip was wandering the vegetable garden, Judy Ann scouring for a nest an old hen meant to keep secret. Pauline was off in a world of her own, settled in a lounge chair studying the driver's handbook.

With reluctance and a glance over her shoulder, Justine moved away from the oldsters.

"Let it go," Tucker said.

"What?"

"The weight of the world."

"Easier said than done," Justine replied.

Tucker expertly dealt with the food. He sliced off a small rib and handed the sample to Justine.

"It's delicious. Better than delicious. You ought to enter that sauce in a contest, Tucker. You'd win."

"You think so?" He turned away so that she couldn't see the pleased flush that seeped into his face, then he fortified himself with a swig of beer.

"I know so. What can I help you with?"

"I've left the salad until last. The makings are on the kitchen counter. Come on, I'll get you started."

The ingredients were all laid out—cherry tomatoes, radishes, spring onions, all from Tucker's garden; lettuce leaves, washed, black olives, feta cheese . . . "You've gone all out," Justine said.

Tucker leaned against the counter, one foot crossed over the other. "We have to talk."

"We are talking."

"About us."

Justine gripped the sink. "What about?"

"Merging our families? Solving our problems together?"

All the air seeped from Justine's lungs. "I'm not ready. *Our* families aren't either."

"That's because you're trying to make the decisions for all of us. Why don't we put it to a vote and see what everybody says?"

"No! I'm responsible. . . . That won't work."

"You're holding back."

"One of us needs to."

With a dawning clarity, Tucker surmised what he was up against, why she protested so. He had recognized a vulnerability in her, but it went further than that. Justine had never been deeply loved in marriage, as she should have been. Distanced now from those years and Philip, she must be wondering what was real, what was fantasy. The move to Alabama, the directing of Agnes's and Pauline's lives and those of the children, working at home, were all efforts to shore up her own lagging confidence.

It was beyond her to understand that what she had to offer was everything in the world he had ever dreamed of having for himself: stability, wife, children, an extended family. She thought herself a failure as a wife and a woman. Though he was well aware of his flaws, or thought he was, failure was a luxury he'd never allowed himself within the narrow confines of his life, for he'd had no one to fall back on. What needed doing he stuck with until it was done.

"The difference between us, Justine, is that I see all the ways a thing will work and you see all the ways it won't."

He searched her face. "Are we supposed to be falling in love by some rule that I don't know about? First we do this, then we do that.... I have never been so affected by any woman in my life. That tells me something."

Her eyes were huge and troubled and full of uncertainty. "It's not any of them that would have to sleep with you, it's me!"

"That doesn't appeal to you?"

Their eyes met. "You know it appeals to me! Oh, I must be crazy. I need a cigarette."

"You quite smoking."

"Yes." Now she couldn't look at him.

He stroked her hair, it was silky beneath his fingers. After a long, tense silence, he said, "I want to see you tonight. Leave the porch doors open in your bedroom."

Stunned, she shook her head. "With my children there? My mother? Agnes?"

"Dear heart, I won't arrive beating drums or tooting bagpipes."

"You're mad, completely out of your mind..."

"The salad dressing is in a cruet in the fridge," he said and sauntered out of the kitchen.

Shaken, Justine sagged against the sink.

She closed her eyes for a moment, concentrating. Had she agreed to bed the man? No, only if the doors were left open. She'd keep them closed and that would be the end of it.

Endings.

But she was weary of endings. She just wanted everything to be in the middle; no cautious, awkward beginnings, no harsh, unhappy endings. She dredged up a self-deprecating smile. Nicotine withdrawal. That's what she was suffering.

That, said an interior voice, *and Tucker Highsmith.*

IN THE LAST RAYS of sundown Wheeler and Agnes sat at the table, elbow to elbow, trading acerbic remarks like a pair of bullies, each trying to best the other.

Pip and Judy Ann hung on their every word, laughing, cheering them on.

Pauline nudged Justine. "You should speak to Agnes. She's making a fool of herself. Imagine! Flirting like an adolescent! At her age."

"Flirting? Be serious, Mother."

"Well, you and Tucker don't have a monopoly on it, you know."

"We haven't been flirting, either!"

"Pooh!"

The hens, which only moments earlier had been pecking at supper scraps thrown them, began to seek out their roosts.

Tucker struck a match, lighted the pair of citronella candles, then began gathering up dishes. Justine leaped to help.

"Sit," he ordered. "I'm just clearing these out so we have room for dessert and coffee."

"I don't think I can manage another bite," Justine told him.

"That's the appreciation I get after slaving over a hot stove?"

"I'll sample your dessert," Pauline put in. "You can't know how wonderful it is to eat someone else's cooking."

The coffee was Decaf Golden Pecan and the dessert was Mandarin zabaglione in sugared meringue cups.

Justine stared at her plate, then at Tucker. "You made this?"

His awareness of opportunity was outweighed by his desire to be casual. "It's just a way to use up egg whites," he said.

"Don't be so modest. I can't believe you concocted this."

He meant to say it was a recipe he had collected for his book, but his lungs fluttered and "It's just an old favorite of my mother's" came cowardly off his tongue. Bloody damn!

"Somehow I just can't quite picture you in the kitchen creating such elegance," Justine continued.

In the candlelight his expression was irresolute. "Why not? Lots of men cook."

"Not zabaglione, they don't."

"Oh, we had a chef once who created all sorts of wonderful delicacies," said Pauline. "But Evan let him go."

"Why?" Tucker asked, curious.

"Well, he was...limp-wristed, you know. Evan couldn't tolerate that sort of thing. Gave him the shudders."

Tucker wished he'd made ice cream instead. Cranking the handle would've been a far more masculine endeavor and more acceptable.

The way he saw it, he had narrowed the critical hurdles of his relationship with Justine down to two: cookbooks and condoms. He'd thought of the zabaglione as a way to insert writing cookbooks into conversation, get it over with that he was attempting one. He blew it.

Next, if he messed up discussing sex, Justine would no doubt suggest to him in precise terms the anatomically impossible things he could do to himself.

Maybe, he thought, he should've reversed the order of his priorities.

The zabaglione was consumed amid lavish compliments. On the one hand Tucker lapped up the praise, on the other, he felt condemned.

Pauline, being polite, offered to do dishes.

"Thanks," he agreed and escaped to clean the grill.

Pauline gaped.

Justine laughed. "Since you stuck your foot in your mouth, I'll help," she said.

"He wasn't supposed to take me up on it."

"You did sound sincere."

Pauline sighed. "Living with you has made me lose my touch."

Chapter Thirteen

She eyed the clock. It was already after eleven. Of course he wasn't coming. That business about needing to see her, merging families. It was just talk. Jaw-flapping, as Agnes would say.

He and Wheeler had walked them to the back door and uttered platonic good evenings before she and her family were well into the kitchen. No secret looks had been exchanged, no whispered reminder of their earlier conversation.

She had thought he was being circumspect. And so she had bathed, changed into a sundress, dabbed perfume behind her ears and in the hollows of her neck.

Perhaps he was waiting for his dad to be sound asleep. She had long since made certain that Pip and Judy Ann were in dreamland. Pauline and Agnes were another matter. After watching the antics of the *Golden Girls*, they had passed up the news and late-night television, saying they, too, were exhausted.

She must have said something that offended him. Or he had taken her at her word when she'd said she wasn't ready. Oh, foolish, lying tongue when she was so swollen with caring for him she felt she'd burst. And here she was all dressed up in the middle of the night, for nothing!

She cast off her clothes, trading the dress for pajamas, turned off the light, surrendered to the cool welcome of the bed and gazed ruefully into the shadows. At least she was saved from the humiliation of having an audience observe her make a choice fool of herself.

Lying there, sleepless, she couldn't slow down her thoughts. She wondered if he was as sexual as he appeared; wondered if he had decided she had no sex appeal whatsoever; wondered if she should have said something, given him a sign, been more aggressive. That was it, perhaps he liked aggressive women.

She was so involved in the turmoil of questions that when the light tapping came she discounted it as night sounds, the old house settling. It was only after the tapping became more insistent that she switched on the bedside lamp and sat up, her chest suddenly an inefficient bellows.

He whispered her name.

She opened the double doors and he was caught in the lamplight. He just stood there, his smile tentative, a shoe box held in his large hands, giving her time to absorb him. He was wearing a beige suit, a white shirt, a wide pink tie poorly knotted and sandals sans socks.

"Monumentally unfair!" she said with a righteousness and hint of hurt that camouflaged her relief at his arrival. And because relief brought anger, she was compelled to accommodate it. "I've already undressed. You could've at least—"

"Do I get to come in?"

She threw up her hands and moved aside. "What's that on your lapel?"

"A boutonniere."

"Looks like weeds."

"It's a sprig of blooms off a tomato plant. Kinda hard to find flowers this time of night, y'know."

"I know you want me to ask. Why're you dressed like that?"

"I've come a-courting, said the country bumpkin to the sophisticated lady."

"I'm hardly sophisticated."

"Well, you smell better than any woman I've ever met. And when we jog, you hardly sweat." He made a noise somewhere between a laugh and a groan. "I can see by the look on your face this explanation is getting nowhere. Suppose I told you I felt tonight might be special, that I ought to have on more clothes than a pair of shorts and shirt.'' It made perfect, if perverse sense to him. A pair of shorts and a shirt could be discarded in half a second. If he read her wrong, he'd be standing there buck naked while she told him to get out. What with suit, shirt, tie, et cetera, he'd have an inkling of where the evening was going long before he was entirely disrobed.

She walked away from him to the bed and sat in the middle. After a moment he followed and gingerly took a spot at the foot, one leg bent and the box cradled in his lap.

"Naturally I'm supposed to find you funny," she said.

"I just thought you'd like to know I can be presentable, even debonair, if need be."

"But not on time." Something was at stake here, Justine thought, but whatever it was escaped her.

"I didn't say a time, I said later. Besides, I had to wait until all the lights went out."

She stared at him, then let her tensed shoulders drop, offering him an uncertain look. "You're up to something."

"You have an excellent mind. Have I ever mentioned how much I admire your intelligence? I said to myself when I first saw you flapping your arms, 'Hey, this woman's something, good-looking, smart'...is this working?''

She looked up at the ceiling, her throat working. Finally she was able to direct her eyes to him and nod. "Are those really yellow suspenders I see under your jacket?"

She had adroitly backed and filled, shifting the direction in which he was trying to take them. He went with it. "They're Dad's. The pants have gotten a little too big since I wore them last. I always drop a few pounds in the summer—sweat it off. You don't approve?''

"I approve wholeheartedly of anything that keeps your pants up," she said too quickly.

Ah! Back on track. He managed to look pained.

"I walked into that one nice and snug."

"Yes, you did."

"Do you feel better now that you have all the vitriol out?"

"Much better, thank you. What's in the box?"

"Well, we're going to get to that. First, I have a little speech prepared."

"Gosh. I'm all ears."

His look was meant to chastise her. "I wish you'd let me get on with this."

"Forgive me," she said, not at all contrite.

"You're starting to make me mad. I get prickly when I get mad."

"How prickly? Do you flex your tattoo?"

A glower set his face like stone, crumbling only seconds later when a light dawned. "You really thought I wasn't coming?"

Her eyes picked a spot on the wall beyond his shoulder. "That may have crossed my mind twenty or thirty times."

"I'm eminently trustworthy. Which you should know by now. I'm trying to woo you, to confide in you. I'm trying to be sensitive and I'm also running out of pluck. No man in his right mind would put himself through this for more than five minutes. Maybe I ought to leave?" Now why did he say that? Testing the waters?

"Why? You're here now," she said shakily, fearful he might leave. "I'm listening."

"No more smart remarks?"

"I promise," she said, sitting cross-legged and folding her hands demurely in her lap.

He loosened his tie and drew in a good solid breath. "I thought we should discuss the nasty little details of carnal indulgences."

Justine's mouth fell open.

He dumped the contents of the box on the bedspread. "There's red and orange, clear...heart-shaped. How that one works is beyond me, but—"

"*What!*"

"Shhhh."

"I never said I was going to do it!" she expostulated, remaining motionless, determined not to make a visible signal.

"Entirely up to you. But you'd better button up your pajamas. All that flesh hanging out is getting me sorely excited."

She closed the wayward gap in her pajama top. "This isn't happening."

"It's a delicate situation. I admit it. I didn't want you to think me thoughtless. You don't do you?"

"Mindless, but not thoughtless."

"May I continue?"

She gestured with a trembling hand. "Be my guest. But do tell me when to applaud."

His brow furrowing, he gazed at her, mute.

"I'm sorry. Truly. It just slipped out."

"Well, these little gadgets come in all shapes and colors and flavors. Eckerd Drugs didn't have any flavored. But I thought—" He looked up suddenly. "You taking this okay? How'm I doing?"

She could barely speak. "A minus two with the Soviet judge abstaining?"

"Oh, my. In that case, pick three or four—performance is everything. Here's a pink—"

"Tucker, I think I'm going to start laughing."

"Don't do it. Think of my ego."

She wrapped her arms around herself. "I'm trying."

"You're not. You're grinning from ear to ear. Where was I?"

"Performance," she said, snickering.

"That was an aside. I was going to add—since sex is a necessary biological burden—"

She began laughing, quietly at first, and then more loudly. He reached for her and clamped a hand over her mouth. "For crying out loud!" he croaked. "You're gonna wake everybody between here and Mobile!" After a moment he cautiously moved his hand.

"Sorry."

"You should be. Laughing—"

"But a *biological* burden?"

"You start up again and I'll just go home and sulk. Anyway, it sounded good when I thought it up."

"At least you weren't bothered by reality."

"That was the hardest thing I've ever done in my life, and I've had to do some pretty tough things. And since I can tell right now I'll never be able to go through that again, I guess I'll grow old and lonely all by myself. Unless . . ."

"What?"

"Unless it worked."

"You're insane."

"Only when it comes to you." He ran his hand down her side, cupping the commendable curve of buttock. "I want to touch you all over, explore every inch, kiss you until you're dizzy. I want things to be so right between us that you wouldn't consider saying no except on pain of death. Can I take my tie off?"

The house slumbered in the grip of midnight's silence. For a flash of a moment, she drifted, picturing them together in bed, out of bed, at breakfast, going for walks, late nights on the sofa. But only for a moment because a different part of herself took command. She wet her lips. "Tucker—you're certain?"

"Dear heart, doubtful dalliances have never been my long suit."

She tilted her head to one side, thinking. She had the image of herself standing boldly on some ragged precipice, gazing down into endless reckless depths, but all she was looking into were Tucker's dark, smoky eyes. Same thing, she thought.

She loved him. The knowledge was the warm respite of joy. It was right. Perfectly right because it was beyond reason. He loved her. There was no question in her mind about that. And to add to the craziness of it all, she reached for the lamp switch and said in the softest of voice:

"Then yes—take off your tie."

Bearing a dozen fresh eggs as his contribution, and the Sunday papers under his arms, he came for breakfast the next morning. She served up scrambled eggs, bacon and toast on the side porch. The kids fought over the funny pages. Tucker took them and tore them down the middle. "When you're each finished . . . trade."

"A regular Solomon you're turning out to be," Pauline said approvingly. "Pass me the classifieds. I'm job hunting, though I'm having a dreadful time finding anything commensurate with my abilities."

"Maybe I can help," Tucker suggested. "What can you do?"

Agnes snickered, and said sotto voce "Nothing."

"Justine dear, if you'll just refill my cup, I'll go pore over these in my room."

Justine wished all of her family would scatter and leave Tucker to her alone. She wanted to demonstrate the pleasure she felt at being in his company in a tangible way—a kiss, a hug, soft words that would remind him of last night. Instead she sighed lightly and asked, "Is your dad joining us? Shall we save some eggs—"

"He'll be around in a bit, but coffee—"

"Excuse me," said Agnes, leaping up with more agility than she had shown in ten years. She disappeared into the house, purple robe trailing the floor.

"It seems your dad made an impression on Agnes," said Justine.

"She made one on him, too. He was shaving when I left the house."

"What's it mean, you think?"

He shrugged and rattled the paper. "What say we take in a movie this afternoon?"

Pip's head jerked up. "I say, yes!"

"Me, too," allowed Judy Ann.

"I don't know," said Justine.

"You can stay home," said Tucker, keeping his eyes on the entertainment page. "The kids and I will go."

"How dark is it in movie theaters these days?" she asked.

"In the back row? Very," he said.

"I'm sitting in the front row!" said Pip.

"I really need to get some work done. The electricity's been off so often, I've fallen behind."

"I understand," said Tucker. "I admire your dedication. Would it help if I took the kids out to supper, too? Say pizza? That'd give you a couple of extra hours."

She smiled sweetly. "What time would you like for us to be ready?"

He leaned over and gave her a chaste kiss on the cheek.

"What was that for?" she asked, distracted because the kids were watching them, wide-eyed.

"No reason," he said and crossed his legs to better control a certain wayward part of his anatomy.

As if she had antennae on alert, Agnes reappeared the moment Wheeler was seated and offered coffee. She wore her Sunday purple best, even adding a dash of matching lipstick.

"Don't sit across from me, woman," Wheeler started in. "You hurt my eyes."

"From the looks of you, you can't see beans," she said, commenting on his face full of shaving nicks.

"Cuttin' my throat ain't the same as lettin' purple smote me between the eyes." He sipped his coffee and with an air of disdain packed his pipe.

Justine was on the brink of saying something, but Tucker beat her to it with a discussion of movies.

Wheeler looked at him, trying to hide his alarm. "I suppose that means you'll be handing me back into the clutches of old Iron Bottom early. Save you another trip into town."

"Who's Iron Bottom?" asked Agnes.

"This nurse. She drives me crazy. Wants my body."

"That broken down old thing?" Agnes couldn't have had a clearer opportunity. She turned to Tucker and spoke in her kindest tone. "If you want, I'll keep an eye on Wheeler, see he doesn't get into mischief."

"By gar! I don't need a baby-sitter! If I wanted turmoil and insult, I'd've stayed home."

Agnes patted his gnarled old hand with her gnarled old hand. "Then make yourself useful. Help me learn to parallel park the station wagon. We're taking our driver's tests tomorrow."

Wheeler drew himself up to the moment. "I reckon I can do that."

Justine gathered up plates and carried them into the kitchen. Tucker followed.

"Out with it, what're you mad about?"

"I can't figure Agnes. She was almost sugary. That's not like her."

"Dad loves to bicker and I don't accommodate him. Agnes is a perfect target. Wouldn't you say it helps if she likes my dad?"

"I know what you're aiming at. I can't think that far ahead."

He leaned against the counter, watching her put the dishes to soak. "You know, Justine, you're one smart lady, one of the smartest I've ever met, but you don't read your men right."

"Me? What men? There's only Philip, and now you."

"Last night we talked about being together."

"That was in the heat of passion." It hadn't been like that at all. He had been gentle and caring and strong. Concerned not to do anything that made her feel awkward or embarrassed. And when they were lying in each other's arms, she was happy. "This is ten o'clock in the morning."

He reached around her and turned the water taps off. "Look at me."

"I'm looking."

"You're scared."

"If it was just us, I wouldn't be. You have to understand, I dated Philip for six years—I lived with him before we married."

"So what did that six years tell you? Where is he now?"

"That's low."

"Life is chancy."

"Next you'll be entering contests like Agnes does."

"Next you'll be saying I took advantage of you."

She dropped her eyes. "No. You didn't. I wanted the same thing you did."

He put his arms around her. "And still want?"

Her heart beat faster as she snuggled against him. "Yes. But find out from your dad what's going on between him and Agnes."

"I won't pry and neither will you."

"I don't like the way you said that. Like you're ordering me."

"I'm suggesting. They're adults and we're adults. Here's another suggestion from one adult to another. Come back to my place with me for an hour."

"In daylight?"

He sighed heavily and with knight-errant reluctance, released her. "You mean to make me walk the long road, don't you?"

"I don't even know what that means."

"I'll explain it to you when we're in that dark row at the movies. Meanwhile, I'm going home, get some puttering done. If I keep near you, the savage that lurks inside this good old boy will bust out, and no telling the damage he'd do."

"Do you go on like this all the time?"

"Only when there's somebody around who brings out the best in me."

"Best or beast?"

He brushed her cheek with his lips. "Same thing."

He walked home whistling and high of spirit, ready to do battle with his typewriter.

Justine stood at the sink with her hands in soapy dishwater, smiling.

"What's funny, Mommy?"

"Nothing, sweetie. What're you up to?"

"Wheeler says I can sit in the car while he teaches Grandma to park between some sticks on the road. Can I?"

"Sure," Justine agreed and made a mental note to casually question Judy Ann about the septuagenarians. Judy

Ann could repeat entire three-sided conversations when the spirit moved her.

LATER IN THE AFTERNOON while they were getting dressed for the movies and Justine was braiding her daughter's hair, Judy Ann, giggling, told her that Wheeler had asked Agnes if her teeth were her own or store bought.

"What did Grandma say?"

"She said it wasn't polite to discuss body parts in mixed company."

"Then what?"

"Then she told Wheeler about raising Daddy and about being the best waitress in Henrico County, Virginia, for thirty years."

"They didn't argue back and forth?"

"Only when she knocked down the mailbox. But Wheeler and Pip put it back up so you're not gonna get mad at them are you?"

"No."

"Wheeler's old enough to be my grampa."

Justine smiled. "Yes, he is." And that meant he was too old for anything beyond talk. A harmless old man. And she couldn't fault Agnes for enjoying Wheeler's attention. She got so little from the rest of them.

The problem with the elderly couple, and what made Justine so anxious, was that she didn't know what to be anxious about.

LOTTIE WAS DISCOVERING many things, the foremost being that she should never, ever, imbibe rum while in her present condition. She had the sense that it made her head swell up to the size of a ripe melon. And one little tap would've made it burst, so dreadful was the ache. The pain surprised her, for during the decades she had been betwixt and between, nothing had ever hurt, except the pain in her soul.

For the past few days she had been in pitiful repair, slinking downstairs only often enough to keep up with the family.

Pauline kept hard at planning a coup on the world, Agnes was making goo eyes at Wheeler Highsmith and Justine was behaving like a courtesan, allowing Tucker into her bedroom every night. The moral fiber of the modern world was in need of great repair or a good old-fashioned Christian revival, was Lottie's considered opinion. And she wanted desperately to voice it. She might be surrounded by people, but she was extremely lonely. It was no good being ignored.

And for all the attention anybody gave her chair anymore, that incident might never have happened. Agnes had even got into the habit of tossing her sweater across it.

This morning Tucker had no sooner sneaked out of Justine's bedroom than the entire household awakened, bathed, dressed and left the house to go get driver's licenses. They left wet towels scattered, coffee cups on nightstands and dishes on the kitchen table.

And not once since they'd moved in had a body sprinkled the floors and damp mopped to keep the dust down.

Howsomever, she had at least learned that unscrewing the fuses meant no electricity flowed. It had finally dawned on her that she needed to be on the opposite end, like the toaster, or the television or the light bulbs hanging at the end of the wires. The electricity flowed into them and made them work.

After much thought, Lottie deciphered she needed to somehow connect herself to an outlet where electricity was stored.

And so without knowing the technicalities of electricity, or that it was a natural phenomena, or anything about how subatomic particles freed themselves from association of any particular molecule or atom; without knowing about vacuum tubes, gases and semiconductors, positive particles or negative particles, Lottie Roberts understood electricity was energy and that it conducted itself upon those little wires, as if on tour, and was available to all and sundry who had the sense to flick a switch.

She deduced, too, that she herself must be some form of energy, for one could not see electricity, yet it existed, invisible.

It was an enormous discovery, she knew. She understood that no matter how forbiddingly awesome electricity might be, it was now quite reasonably possible for her to return. The problem as she now saw it, was to avail herself of that flow, soaking it up until her aura filled out with good, solid flesh.

The electrical impulses in Lottie's brain put everything into order the same way they had when she ruled the house and was the comfortable wife of Elmer. But instead of planning when to set bread to rising, when to churn butter, when to boil starch and what day in spring she would take up wool carpets against moth eggs and put down hooked rag rugs against summer's dust, Lottie planned her emergence into a world she found wanting, and one which she hadn't yet found a better replacement for, despite what the Good Book said. She wasn't blaspheming. She made a vow that she'd make things right with Himself the instant she was decipherable and got her voice back.

Meanwhile she dusted her bones, aired Pauline's gray silk, the stockings, Agnes's shoes, laid out undergarments, a hair brush and bone hairpins; her hair was long and she wore it knotted at the back of her head. She was probably tolerably gray by now. She wished she had her cameo and wedding ring, but those could be retrieved from hiding once she could direct Milo where to dig. Of course, her family Bible would have to be handy, else how could she prove who she was to Justine?

Since there was no electricity in the attic, all of these things would have to be moved downstairs for the event. The experience in the bathroom with that freeloader, Kessler, proved that. She couldn't tolerate the anxiety of wondering if she'd make it back to her bones in time or not. Best to have them on hand. Best to be sitting right on them when she plugged herself into the flow.

By the time she thought she had perfected her plan, down to the last detail but one, Justine and her family were noisily arriving home.

She went downstairs to join in the celebration. The two old biddies had passed their driver's tests! Unexpectedly envy tweaked her. Mayhap one day she could set aside her fear and could herself master the automobile. Leastways the machine was a lot less balky than a pair of mules.

There was a sly smile at the ends of Agnes's perennially downturned lips as she toasted Pauline. "Now the whole world knows how old you are. It's in a computer."

"You deplorable old nag! You were eavesdropping! At least I don't have any restrictions. I can drive at night."

Justine stepped in before there was a full-fledged fight. "Mothers dear," she said brightly, "have some more champagne." She was truly proud of their achievement. What scared her was that they were both making long verbal lists, trying to outdo one another, of the places they would go and errands they could run, while behind the wheel of the only vehicle among them. Of course, should there be a mishap, insurance would replace the car. But what of Mother and Agnes? The images of their maimed and broken bodies, lying in a ditch somewhere, blunted her gaiety.

Chapter Fourteen

A burst of panic made Justine's pulse fluctuate wildly. "Mother," she pleaded, "please reconsider."

Pauline clamped her mouth into a thin line as if she had been taking lessons from Agnes. "No. You promised if I passed my driver's test, which I did last week, I could use the car to job hunt. The State of Alabama says I'm equipped to drive. Here's proof." She waved her temporary license under Justine's nose with righteous indignation. "Nothing on this says I need a guide, or someone sitting next to me in the front seat. Especially that bully, Agnes."

"I'm only thinking of your safety."

"I will never get a job if I have to drag Agnes, wearing that ghastly purple, everywhere. In addition to which she's become positively mewly... Wheeler this and Wheeler that," Pauline mimicked Agnes perfectly. "You've put me off with one excuse or other, but now I have an interview. How do I look?"

"You look fine."

"Professional? This is a Coco Chanel suit, years old. You don't think it's overdone? I'll make a good impression, won't I?"

"I'm afraid you're going to impress yourself into another car or the pavement. Mother, please..."

Pauline drew herself up. "Justine, if I have to, I'll manage without any encouragement whatsoever from you.

And, I would remind you that you got your first license at aged sixteen. Not to mention your father bought you a car. Did I ever withhold your keys?"

Justine felt small for being anxious, and smaller still for refusing her mother the station wagon. The panic she felt was becoming weighed down further by guilt. Yet she had to try one more time. "Mother, if you could just wait a few minutes, I'll dress and drive you myself."

"I have an interview in less than an hour. It will take you that long just to do your hair. Then the children will want to come, and Agnes won't stay by herself lest something jump from behind the drapes and grab her. If I wait, it'll take up the time I've allowed for getting lost, which I won't because I took down the directions very carefully." Imperiously, she held out a perfectly manicured hand.

Justine tried to erase images from her mind; a fiery crash, the telephone call...the rush to the hospital. With the same reluctance with which she would approach a snake, which was not ever unless forced, she reached into her robe pocket. She put the car keys into her mother's hand, knowing there would be no redemption for her in her mother's eyes if she refused again.

"Call me if you have any problem, call me when you get to the interview. You'll have time. They always make you wait. And don't forget to give turn signals, don't tailgate, and remember to stay on your side of the road."

"I will, dear. All of those things. Now, which key goes in the ignition? The square or the round? I always forget."

"The square one," Justine said and bit the inside of her lip.

The morning sun was golden warm; the breeze rippled low making the webs of moss in the trees sway gently. Chickens came up to the back door hoping for a handout. Blackbirds swooped and woodpeckers pecked. Justine didn't notice.

The telephone was mute.

For the remainder of the morning she lived with growing apprehension and a self-recrimination that refused to allow her to concentrate on her own work.

Over a lunch of grilled cheese sandwiches she lectured the children. "Don't either of you *ever* consider asking me if you can drive the car until you're twenty-one, and then only after you've had years and years of driver's education."

"I'd rather have a motorbike anyway," said Pip.

"How old is twenty-one?" said Judy Ann. "As old as Grandma?"

The phone rang. Justine answered it before the first ring died. "You promised to call me as soon as you got there!" she hollered into the receiver.

"Ain't been nowheres," said Wheeler.

"I'm sorry," Justine said, deeply embarrassed. She called Agnes to the phone and hovered until the older woman put her hand over the speaker and said indignantly, "Justine, do you mind?"

A second phone call came at ten minutes after two. It was her contact at the insurance company wanting to know how she was progressing on the software. Fine, Justine told him, excellent. Glad to hear it, said the contact, to which Justine replied she had every intention of collecting the bonus they had promised if she brought the project in on time. The contact chuckled and said the company had just been licensed in two more states and the computer network was of utmost importance now and would it be possible for her to complete the software and instruction manual ahead of schedule? Say by the end of August instead of September. The company was prepared to up the bonus to five thousand dollars. And Justine heard herself agreeing because Pauline had no doubt had a crash and was at this moment in some hospital emergency room and she would need all the money she could lay her hands on to call in specialists to repair bones and do plastic surgery. Undoubtedly Pauline had gone through the windshield because, foolishly, Justine had forgotten to remind her to buckle the seat belt.

If Pauline had told her the name of the company for which she was to interview, Justine failed to recall it. At three-thirty she called all the area hospitals. No Pauline Gates, injured or applicant.

At five-thirty Justine was lying prostrate on the sofa with a cool cloth over her eyes.

Lottie sat in her chair, trying to console her. *Used to, it'd take Elmer two days to travel down to Mobile,* she said. *And up to a week there and back if rain had rutted the roads and bogged down the wagon. Why, Pauline's hardly had time to turn around.*

"Maybe she missed the turnoff from the highway," suggested Agnes.

"If she did," said Pip, "she's all the way to Florida by now."

"Disney World is in Florida," said Judy Ann. "Grandma wouldn't go there without taking us, would she?"

A car door slammed.

As one the family raced to the front porch.

One foot on the bottom step, Tucker looked up, startled, and in a very few seconds his brain had catalogued their expressions; the same as those that had greeted him the night he'd found them all on his doorstep. "Let me guess," he said. "The chair did a two-step in broad daylight."

"No. Mother's lost." The scope and shape of Justine's eyes were exaggerated, filled with anxiety. "She took off in the car this morning and hasn't come home, or called. She was supposed to call."

"She went to get a job," said Judy Ann.

"She did?" Tucker looked at Justine from beneath his brows. "And that's what has you so upset?"

"She's not an experienced driver. She's not experienced at anything!"

"Yes, she is," said Agnes. "Sarcasm."

Justine whipped around. "You'll be sorry you said that if she's dead!"

Mumbling, Agnes retreated into the house.

"Hey," Tucker said, taking the steps two at a time and enclosing Justine in his arms. "Calm down. Here, sit on the steps."

"I don't know what to do. I don't know where she went. When she gets home, I'm going to kill her, I swear I will."

Tucker signaled to the kids. "Come on. I've got something for each of you in the truck." To Judy Ann he presented a very small, very thin, gray-striped kitten. "Somebody dumped her on the job site. Think you can take care of her?"

"Ooooo, she's so cute. Oh, Mommy, can I keep her?"

Another mouth to feed, Justine thought, but she agreed. "She looks hungry and scared, maybe you can fix her a dish of milk."

For Pip, Tucker went to the bed of the truck and hauled out a huge cardboard box. He spread some of the contents out on the flattened tailgate; an ancient thirty-five-millimeter camera, film spools, developing equipment, a film editor. "One of the guys on my crew bought a house. This stuff was in the attic. They were going to toss it out, I thought you might like it. Some of the chemicals are dangerous, so be careful. There're instruction books in there, read them first. Got it?"

"Oh man, this is great! Mom! Look at this stuff."

Justine was hard-pressed to raise any enthusiasm for inanimate objects. Tucker shooed him into the house. "Clean it up and show it off later, sport."

Tucker plopped down next to Justine. "Now, listen to me. There's a good three or four hours of daylight left. If your mother isn't home by dusk, we'll go look for her."

"If anything goes wrong, she can't cope."

"Sweetheart, believe me, your mother can cope. She had me rearranging furniture before you'd been in the county twenty minutes, and by the time the last bed was in place, she knew my life history."

Justine couldn't let it go. "But she was supposed to call!"

"I'm sure she'll have a perfectly reasonable explanation."

"If she can find her way home."

Tucker chuckled. "I'm going home to eat and bathe. I'll see you later, but let me leave you with a nickel's worth of thought. You are one smart lady. Genetically speaking, some of your smarts had to come from Pauline. So why do you discount that she has any?"

"You don't understand. She has never had to do anything in her entire life—it was always done for her. My dad treated her like fragile porcelain. She's never had to think for herself. I've been truly on my own for almost a year now. I know how hard it is."

"Justine, you cannot protect her from life. You can't take your dad's place. You can't be all things to everybody."

"Since when have you suddenly become the world's greatest philosopher?" she said, anger rising because he had touched a nerve.

"Since my mother died," he said with a twinge of worry that he was revealing too much, "and I tried to take her place in my dad's affections. I thought I could be good to him and for him and he wouldn't miss her so much. It was an impossible task. He coped his way and I coped mine."

She propped her chin in her hands and gazed off into space. "I hate people who are right all the time."

He stood up and then bent down quickly to kiss her atop her head. Her hair was fine and smelled wonderful. "Lordy, lordy," he said. "You sure do smell good."

"And you stink." In truth it was a man smell that wasn't entirely unpleasant; the muskiness a combination of earth, sun and sweat.

"Gee whiz. To think I was going to ask you to trim my mustache tonight."

"You would trust me to do that?"

"Why not? I've trusted you with other parts . . . my big toe, my earlobe, my—"

She laughed.

"Ah! Now, I can run along home."

She put out a hand but didn't touch him. "Thank you."

She watched him walk back to his truck. He had a kind of hip-shot walk that was very sexy.

For the next ten minutes Pauline didn't enter her thoughts once—until she wheeled into the drive, grazed the mailbox and braked halfway up the stone walk.

Justine stood up. Relief flooded through her. She could hear herself breathing, a kind of rushing noise inside her head. And way, way back in her brain she was cautioning herself to remain calm: a thing she managed to do until her mother was ensconced on the sofa, shoes off, sipping a glass of iced tea.

She remained calm while Pauline admired the newly acquired kitten and camera and acknowledged Agnes with barely a nod.

She remained calm while Pauline adjusted a pillow behind her back and said, "My day was more tiring than a marathon bridge game. But I feel so up. I achieved something! I never really understood when Evan got all excited about a business deal. Now, I do. I even understand what you mean about being independent, Justine. It's exciting! I had a wonderful, wonderful day."

That was when Justine felt the calm sliding away. "And just how did your day go, Mother?"

"Well, straightaway I got the job. A lovely hotel, dear."

"Oh? Why didn't you call me?"

"Well . . . that was the problem, you see. They explained the PBX—that stands for Private Branch Exchange—a telephone system. It was all computerized. You'd have understood it in a flash."

"You were hired as a telephone operator?"

"PBX operator," Pauline corrected. "Then at lunch— we had to buy our own at a discount—I spent my money. I only had the three dollars."

"Mother," Justine oozed between clenched teeth. "You worked on a phone exchange with outside lines and you didn't take one minute to call me? You let me go bonkers worrying myself crazy about you—"

"Don't yell, dear. I'm trying to explain. Had I been able to master the PBX, I'd still have the job, wouldn't I? After they told me I wouldn't work out, I'd already spent my money. Then they gave me a check for sixteen dollars, but I couldn't get it cashed at the bank because I don't have an account, and the grocers refused, too, because you have to have a driver's license with your picture on it, not the temporary, plus a credit card. I could hardly borrow the cost of a phone call from a stranger. How would that look? So I thought, why waste the entire day? I went to the second place on my list and I have another interview in the morning, at a lovely, lovely restaurant. They need a hostess. And so, that's why I didn't call. Dear me, Justine, you're looking at me the same way your father used to when he was dreadfully unhappy."

"You drove Daddy crazy, didn't you?"

Pauline's hand fluttered. "I got the first job I ever had in my life today and all you can say is something shameful?"

Agnes cackled. "You mean you got hired and fired, all in the same day!"

"And paid for it," Pauline reminded proudly, displaying the check.

"But fired!" Agnes pushed.

"That was a business decision, Agnes. My goodness. No wonder you were only ever a waitress." She passed the check to Justine. "Could you make me a loan against this, dear? Oh, I'm so happy! My very first paycheck!"

Justine felt suddenly enervated, as if whatever it was that held together her bones and joints had dissolved. It was the aftereffects of the fear she had borne all day, she knew. "You did well, Mother," she said, meaning it.

"I didn't mean to worry you, dear. Next time, I'll call. I promise."

"Next time." Justine closed her eyes. Another day of fear like today and she would shut down completely. "Mother Hale, can you manage supper? I need to lie down."

"All by myself? What about Miss Cosmopolitan?" she exclaimed, flouncing out of the room. "I suppose I'm going to be the slave around here from now on."

Lottie had a remark ready, but held it steady on her tongue. She was counting on good luck to make her life right. It was bad luck to say certain things aloud, even if she was the only one who could hear them.

For years and years, she hadn't been afraid. But today, she had caught fear from Justine. It had been a physical element in the air and attached itself to her, reminding her what fear was like. How it insinuated itself somewhere deep inside, how hard it was to get around and beyond it. She had everything planned. But suppose there was a barrier she knew nothing about? She didn't remember one whit about arriving on this side of things. Suppose she didn't really exist? Suppose she was just lost in her own mind? She moved past Judy Ann. The kitten arched her back and hissed.

That answers that, Lottie thought. The cat knew she was here. The cat would leave fleas and cat hair. Lottie sighed. More mess.

Still, the business of fear worried her. Fear caused doubt. Fear, Lottie decided, was treacherous. Fear was making her wonder if the family was going to accept her.

And how, she wondered glumly, was she going to explain where she had been all this time? Suppose she returned only to be cast out? She doubted she had a relative left in the world—outside of Milo Roberts, and he was only a distant cousin by marriage. She most assuredly did not want to take up housekeeping with the likes of him!

Pondering the problem, she left it too late to slip unnoticed into the pantry, for unexpectedly Justine and Tucker occupied the kitchen. They were too swift of ear and eye to miss the secret door opening. She settled herself on a stool in the corner and passed the time pleasantly—eavesdropping.

They sat at the kitchen table facing each other. Justine had set out cold drinks. Disconsolately, she stirred hers with a fingertip.

"C'mon," Tucker coaxed. "Let's go for a walk. The stars are out by the millions tonight. It'll make you feel better."

"I can't. I have to do the dishes, sort dirty clothes, try to get in a couple hours of work and, before I get in bed, commit hara-kiri."

He laughed. "Dear heart, your mother got home safe and sound. It's over. Stop worrying."

"That's not it. The insurance company called today when my brain was nonfunctioning. I agreed to contract completion a month early."

"Can you do it?"

"I have to. They upped the bonus to five thousand dollars if I bring it in by the end of August."

"Very nice. I'm impressed."

"Don't be. The whole contract is only worth twelve thousand, and that's with the bonus. It may be all the money I'll ever earn in my life." She looked at him, her expression intense. "See, what I hoped was to use that money to buy this house. Then I wouldn't keep having to dip into what I got out of the divorce for mortgage payments. That money has to last until I'm established."

"What's in the way of your getting the work done early?"

"Mother, Agnes, the children, laundry, not to mention you're keeping me up nights."

"Whoops. Let me ask another way. Is there anything that can be done to increase your productivity?"

"If I tied in a second computer, I could write sections of the program, then immediately write out that portion of the instruction manual. Make sure the bugs are out. And, I'd have hard copy as I go along. Sort of like editing as I went. But the wiring in this old house won't carry the extra pull. If the television and the computer are on, and somebody uses the microwave, poof! Another fuse blown."

Lottie leaned forward, agitated. Not enough electricity? What did that mean? Mayhap there wouldn't be enough for her. She hadn't thought of that.

"I'll rewire the office circuits for you this weekend," Tucker was saying.

"You're too much in our lives as it is. I'd just be more obligated."

"Too much in your life?" he repeated, genuinely astonished. "In my mind I am your life and you're mine. Are you telling me that's not clear to you?" He went on, provoked to the point of anger. "What do you want in a man, Justine? Another gutless wonder like your ex?"

She reeled from his sudden attack. "That's not fair."

"Suppose you tell me—what's fair?"

"For one thing, taking on my family isn't fair... to you. You don't know what you're letting yourself in for, emotionally, financially—"

"Wait a sec! I'm not going to let you make that kind of decision for me. I know what I want. I may not have it blueprinted, but I can handle anything that comes my way." Dark as slate with sudden knowledge, his eyes fixed on her. "I got it. You want absolute control. You want to control your mother, Agnes, the kids, me. That's not how life is, or relationships. I decide for me, you decide for you. Right or wrong we all have the right to make decisions for ourselves."

"That's not true! I'm trying to hold us together!"

"That's what you're telling yourself. Think about it. Or perhaps you don't want a man who came up through the school of hard knocks."

"That's not true, either. You're the best thing that's ever happened to me. But, it can't last. I know it can't."

He made a sound in his throat. "I'm getting out of here. If I stay another minute, I'd be tempted to shake you until your brain rattled. And since so little of it seems to be functional right now, we can't risk that, can we?"

"Wait! Please."

"Nope. I'll start work on the wiring Saturday morning after I pick up my dad. Maybe by then, you'll have come to your senses."

"You're saying you won't... we won't... that's five days!" She was devastated.

"I have things to do."

"Like what?" she shot back, lashing out with sarcasm because she knew he was right about her, right about wanting, needing control, that it was central to her sense of well-being; her protection against pain and hurt. Yet, she was hurting now.

"Well, I'll tell you like what. Like writing a cookbook. I was ashamed to tell you, afraid you'd think me a limp-wristed nitwit. But listening to you just now I realized it was my own shame I was hiding behind. I had myself whacked out thinking it wasn't a manly thing to do. Somebody might laugh. You know what? I don't care if anybody laughs. I like writing the damned thing. I like cooking, too. And, I'm good at it." He paused and almost smiled. "The look on your face is priceless."

Beautiful, vulnerable, lovable face, he thought, behind which was a brain that was deluding her into believing that control was the foundation of life. There would be trust between them, he decided, or nothing at all.

He left. Justine got out of the chair, went into the bathroom, looked at herself in the mirror and cried.

LOTTIE WAS EMBARRASSED. She wished she had not stayed to witness the raw emotions that spewed between the two. Safely in the attic, she sat on her bed and gazed out at the starlit sky. A tremor started at a point very low in her spirit and moved rapidly upward so that it seemed to touch her very soul. Tucker was going to do something to the electricity. She would watch him and learn precisely how to use it for herself.

On Saturday.

Chapter Fifteen

After three mornings of watching her mother drive jauntily off for yet another interview, Justine began to take it in stride. By the fifth morning she could see the humor in the situation. Pauline wore three-hundred-dollar suits, hundred-dollar-an-ounce perfume and two-dollar panty hose to interview for jobs that would pay three dollars and thirty-five cents an hour. She invariably got hired in the morning and terminated in the afternoon, an event to which she attached no social stigma whatsoever.

She also kept a list of all the people she met and soon counted among her acquaintances the president of the local garden club, the secretary of a chapter of the Daughters of the American Revolution, a vice-president of First Alabama Bank, the members of two bridge clubs who had invited her to join and the chairwoman of the auxiliary of The Order of Inca that sponsored a Mardi Gras ball every year. Pauline's professional life died at the end of each day, but her social life was becoming a whirlwind of telephone calls and invitations.

Agnes spent less and less time pursuing contests and more and more time on the telephone with Wheeler Highsmith. If Justine was within hearing, Agnes's end of the conversation came to a dead halt.

They're plotting something, Justine thought. Harmless as it might be, she would've liked to have discussed it with Tucker. But, true to his word, he had kept his distance from her. She had not seen him all week. The children saw him every afternoon and sensed nothing amiss.

During the day she focused on her work, but her nights were inept attempts at sleep. Too often she had gotten up and sat on the porch, staring into the midnight sky. To her dismay and guilt, she had smoked a half pack of stale cigarettes.

Every time she recalled Tucker's accusation, she felt a drowning sensation. She recognized that Philip's defection had caused her to develop a strong defense against hope. It kept her from marching down to Tucker and telling him that she had come to her senses, lest she discover another dream crushed. She was afraid she had lost him.

On Saturday morning she arose at dawn, soaked in the tub, shampooed her hair, shaved her legs, applied cosmetics and donned her most flattering sundress. She was sitting at the kitchen table polishing her nails when Pip wandered in, pajama-clad and still half asleep.

"Go back to bed, sweetie," she told him.

"Can't. I'm goin' with Tucker to pick up Wheeler." He made himself a bowl of cereal. This time of morning there was none of the defensive, hostile preteen in his demeanor. His favorite topic all week had been the photo equipment. She asked him about it.

"I'm ready to load film and take some pictures. Tucker's takin' me to get some."

"Remind me, I'll give you some money before you go."

"I've got money. I earned it, remember."

"I just thought—"

"I want to use my own money, Mom. I don't want you doin' everything for me. I'm not a baby. If I get to be any good, I might even earn money with photographs. There are contests all the time. I could even get to be class photographer when I'm in high school."

"You've really been thinking about this, haven't you?"

"It's exciting, you have to know all about composition and shadows and framing. It's brain work as much as skill and I figure I'm pretty smart. At least Tucker thinks I am."

"He's right. You are."

"You never said so."

"There are a lot of things I haven't said that I should be saying every day. One of which is that you are very, very smart and handsome, too."

"Oh, yuk!"

Justine bent her head and smiled. Pip finished his cereal and put the bowl in the sink.

"Mom, can I ask you something?"

"Ask away."

"Is Dad ever coming back?"

Her lungs deflated. Very carefully she inhaled. "I don't think so. I don't want to hurt you, or Judy Ann, or your grandmother, but I don't want your dad back, not as a husband. We might, some day in the future, be friends again. That would be all right with me. And I would never stand in your way if you wanted to write to him or see him."

"I don't like what Dad did," he said with no anger, only a kind of sadness.

"None of us do."

"Dad was selfish. And he ran away from responsibility."

"I would say so, yes," she said, wondering if Pip were parroting her own words or had come to that conclusion himself.

"Wheeler did, too, once. He told me."

So that's where all this was coming from. "What else did he say?"

"He said there's some little part in each of us that nobody else can ever know. He said sometimes the part is there and we don't even know it ourselves, and that it makes us do odd things, even hurt people we love. Wheeler did it. He said that's what Dad did. And that one day, Dad will be sorry."

"Wheeler is probably right."

"But I might be all grown up by then."

Justine sensed her son had come to a decision; that a milestone had been reached. Pip was severing himself from a past over which he had no control. It was a very adult thing for him to do—more than she had accomplished. She was both envious and proud of him. "How did you feel about that?"

He shrugged. "I'm gonna grow up anyway and be the best person I can—" he paused "—but I still might have fights in school."

Justine smiled. "Well, we'll deal with that when it happens."

"Wheeler says Tucker is so responsible he squeaks with it, and that I'll most likely be the same way. Are you gonna marry Tucker, Mom?"

Justine floundered for a full ten seconds. "I don't know," she said finally.

"He's all right," he said, which was Pip's highest accolade. "Judy Ann likes him, too."

"Has . . . has Tucker said anything about me?"

"I gotta get ready or he'll leave without me."

"Hold on. He has, hasn't he? What'd he say?"

Pip sighed, reduced to looking every inch the very much put upon eleven-year-old. "He said you were the smartest woman he ever met."

"Well, that's nice."

"And, the dumbest."

That finished her. "Go brush your teeth."

Agnes drank her morning coffee on the fly. On Wheeler's account she was determined to look her purple best. She hogged the bath until both Judy Ann and Pauline were taking turns pounding on the door. Justine coaxed her out by saying Tucker was due back in less than fifteen minutes.

When the men arrived, Tucker admired Justine up and down then suggested she get into a pair of jeans if she was planning to be any help to him.

Wheeler, snide as ever, ordered Agnes out of her purple. He wanted to hook fish, not blind them. And Agnes, who seldom took a step outside fearing she'd break an ankle in one of the holes Milo was forever leaving behind, and who complained of how difficult it was to negotiate the long aisles in grocery stores, donned an old pair of pants, covered her hair with a scarf, dragged on a pair of galoshes, tucked her cane under her arm and marched the quarter mile with Wheeler to the fishing hole. Pip went along to fish and photograph the event. Judy Ann was generously allowed to tag along, provided she carried the bait bucket.

Pauline, dressed to the nines, also escaped. "You don't mind, do you, dear? Mrs. Ellison has invited me to brunch and to make a fourth at bridge this afternoon. Now that I'm solvent, I can play penny-a-point. And I can put gas in the car."

Pauline had collected the grand sum of ninety-six dollars from her various jobs, which could hardly be regarded as solvent, but Justine knew Tucker was listening. "How late will you be?"

"I should be home before dark, but if I'm not, don't worry, I do know how to turn on the car lights. And, I've left Mrs. Ellison's number on the pad by the phone."

"Have a good time," Justine said, and walked her mother to the door.

After Pauline drove away, Justine turned back and was aware of the awesome quiet of the house. Arms folded, Tucker was leaning against the doorjamb of her office, watching, waiting for her return.

"Well done," he said softly.

"I'm improving."

"Yes, you are. And I think every little bit of improvement deserves a reward." His tone was light, but his eyes burned dark and promising.

"You have something specific in mind?" she asked, voice hollow and her eyes fixed on a spot beyond Tucker.

"Actually, I do."

Oh, hooey! Lottie groaned as Tucker took Justine into his arms and began to nuzzle her neck. How could they stop to spoon on the most important day of her life in a hundred years! She took herself off to the side porch where she could watch for their return to Justine's office.

"NOT THAT I THINK sex is the be-all, end-all answer to every spat we might have," he said much later.

"But it's your first choice?" she said, stretching languidly. The sheet was pulled taut, outlining her breasts, hips and the length of her legs. He opened one eye and watched her appreciatively. Justine had a contented look on her face that made him feel good. His arm tightened about her waist.

"It was my choice of the moment. Truth is, I cut my nose off to spite my face by staying away from you all week. I was miserable."

She turned in his arms and ran her fingers through the hair on his chest. "Tell me about your cookbook. I want to see it. I'll even try some of the recipes. If I can do them, then anybody can."

"I don't want to talk recipes," he said lazily, letting his hand trail down her hip and up again.

"I think it's exciting. You could become famous. Women would go crazy over you...on second thought, I don't think I'd like that."

"Nobody's gonna go crazy over me because I'm not gonna get famous. I just want to make a few extra bucks to get my dad out of the old folk's home."

"I'm crazy about you."

"You're supposed to be. Look at all the nice things I do for you."

"What nice things?"

"This, for instance," he said, moving a fingertip down the valley between her breasts and lower.

She shivered. "Hadn't we better get started?"

"We are."

"I meant on the rewiring."

"Seems like I'm generating a bit of electricity right now." The inside of her leg felt like satin against his muscular thigh. Words galloped in his brain, soothing words, words of love, words that said how much she meant to him. He couldn't say them because she pressed her lips to his, whispering, "Yes, you are..."

Gently he shifted her body entirely atop his own.

She lowered herself upon him then, and he forgot everything else but his need to bury himself in her.

JUSTINE FUMED. "Do you bark orders like this to your crew all day? It's a wonder one of them hasn't stabbed you in the back. Or hit you over the head with a crowbar," she said, hefting the one Tucker had instructed her to use to pull baseboards away from the wall.

All the furniture and equipment in the office had been shoved to the middle of the room to give them work space. Not a breeze stirred. It was hot, dirty work. Sweat trickled down her back and between her breasts.

Her nice, neat office was a wreck. The ceiling fixture dangled. Tucker planned to rewire it and the one in the kitchen so that they could bear ceiling fans. The disorder frightened her, for the office had been her haven, the one place where she felt she knew what she was doing at all times. Now it was chaos. It made her feel unsettled and cranky. She knew she was taking her fright out on Tucker unjustly. She just couldn't seem to help it.

Too, something had happened between them in the bedroom. There had been more sharing, playing, talk and questions than ever before. He knew everything about her. What she liked, disliked, how scared she'd been when Philip left, how safe she felt now, with him. She had no protective defenses left. She felt naked without them.

"I just said, be careful with the trim so I can put it back after I run the wires. Now, get moving or I won't be able to jury-rig anything before nightfall. You want to spend the night in the dark?"

"But I don't know what I'm doing! Suppose the baseboards break?"

"That's why I'm telling you. Just work the beveled end down between the wall and the trim and pull away gently. They'll give."

He was installing outlets midway up the wall and enclosing the open wires with piping down to the baseboards, then drilling holes through the walls at floor level to repeat the process in the next room. A fine film of drill dust lay over everything.

"I hope you know what you're doing."

He ripped an old wire from the wall and insisted she inspect it. "It's been painted over, but see that? The covering has cracked clear down to the live wires. You're lucky this place hasn't burned down around your ears every time a fuse blew. Now, stop nagging. I'm happy. Why can't you be happy?"

"I'm happy. I'm gloriously happy. And, I'm properly meek and in awe of your ability."

"Good! Go make us something cool to drink. I'm thirsty."

"How about a nice cool glass of arsenic?"

"Ice water will do."

"I can't get water, the electricity is off, which means the pump doesn't work and all the ice has melted in the fridge."

"Step down to my place and get some."

"So now I'm a gofer."

Curtailing his impatience, Tucker wiped sweat from his face with the tail of his shirt. "If I weren't so fond of you, dear heart, I'd turn you over to Milo. He knows how to handle gophers."

"Very funny."

"Okay. That's it. We're two hours into this. You mind telling me what the problem is? Did I say or do something wrong earlier? Act like a savage in bed? Hurt your feelings? What? for crying out loud."

"Nothing's wrong," she said, her voice seeping through clenched teeth.

"The understatement of the century. You'll have to do better than that. There may be times in our life that I'll be able to read your mind, but right now is not one of them, so out with it."

Justine swiped at a rivulet of sweat on her chin. "Suppose you can't get all this back together? Suppose afterward, nothing works or it goes haywire?"

"I know what I'm doing."

"A lot of people say they know what they're doing. They don't."

"I'm not one of those people, but you'll just have to take that on trust. Uh-oh. Trust and control. We're back to your pets, are we?"

"We just don't seem organized, is all." There was a beseeching light in her eyes that he could not ignore.

"I think," he drawled slowly, "that we have a conversation going on two levels here. You know, before we make love, everything is fine...while we're making love, everything is fine...after we make love, the doubts start. This is plainly and unequivocally unfair.

"I'm not going to run out on you, Justine. Only I can't prove it except by living with you for forty or fifty years, by which time you will have no doubt driven me so loony, I'll be like poor old Milo, thinking the world is flat and spending my days digging for imaginary gophers. You got that, or shall I chisel it in stone?"

Justine got more than he realized. She was trying to put their relationship within the narrow confines that she had known growing up and later, with Philip; boundaries beyond which she'd never been allowed to stray until Philip himself had left, and then there were none.

Tucker was a man with such a strong, healthy sense of self that no boundaries were necessary. He loved, and that was it, simply and steadfastly. He saw no need to analyze it or force it into a mold. It would take her a lifetime to gain that kind of confidence. With his strength beside her, she could do it.

"You've made yourself clear. I'll go get that water now."

"Good."

"You don't want to kiss me or anything before I go?"

"No, I don't want to touch you. If I do, I won't finish this wiring and if I don't finish the wiring, we'll be right back where we started."

"I understand."

"I'm not sure you do. Hold up your left hand. See that little finger? That's me twisted around it. That is severe entanglement. That is the end of all the miserable nights I've ever spent alone." He scowled at her. "That's happiness."

Justine clasped her hands behind her back. "You're a very special and wonderful man, Tucker."

His heart seemed to swell to bursting within his chest. "Stop batting your lashes at me like that."

Mush and piffle! exclaimed Lottie from her perch atop the stepladder. She determined if those two didn't stop jawing and hugging and kissing and get on with the business of electricity, she was going to do something drastic. Fortunately Justine left on her errand and Tucker began measuring and cutting wires and stripping the ends again, a procedure Lottie watched with keen interest.

LATE SUNDAY AFTERNOON Justine looked up from the dual computer screens and smiled exuberantly at Tucker. "Mother said there was more to you than met the eye—she was right."

"Somebody had to tell you that? You didn't figure it for yourself?"

"It was hard for me to be objective." She wanted very much to start working again at that very minute. But Tucker had put in two long days and she had promised him supper tonight. He had even installed a second fuse box and wired up the clothes dryer, for which Agnes had unabashedly thanked him in front of everybody.

"Mom," said Pip, careening into the room. "The grill is ready. Are we gonna cook burgers or what? I'm starving."

Justine shut down the computer. "I was just coming."

"All that work and my supper is hamburgers?" Tucker asked.

"My only other accomplishments in the kitchen are pork chops and meat loaf. I can't compete with you."

"I'll do the salad."

"You can't. I promised that chore to Judy Ann. She's showing an interest in cooking and I'm encouraging her. I was twenty-four before I learned to boil an egg, and still can't do it without the shell cracking. I don't want her to suffer from the same lack of skill."

"I'll show you how to boil an egg properly."

"If you feel you just have to do something . . . make dessert."

"Justine? May I interrupt?"

"I know, Mother. You're starving, too."

"No, I nibbled a cracker. I was just wondering if Tucker would mind loading those Japanese sculptures into the station wagon for me."

"Load them?"

"Well, yes dear, you've never liked them and Pip is just using them as hat racks and . . ."

"Back up, Mother. Start from the beginning. Load them to take where? I may not like them, but they are museum pieces."

"That's the whole point. Yesterday one of the women I played bridge with noticed the pin on my lapel, the jade one that your father bought on one of his trips to Asia, and we started talking and it seems her husband is an avid collector of Japanese art. A dilettante, I'm sure, not nearly as expert as your father was. But the upshot is, he would like to see the sculpture . . . perhaps buy it."

"Wait a minute, Mother."

"Control," Tucker said, sotto voce.

She gave him a dark look and went on. "Those pieces are priceless, you don't know enough about—"

"According to your father, everything has a price. He often said 'priceless' was a label applied when nobody wants to buy, or can't. I've agreed I'd sell the man an option to purchase. And once your father's estate is settled, I'll get an appraisal from Christie's or Sotheby's. If my buyer wants to meet that price, fine. If not...well...Evan used to buy and sell options all the time. You don't get your money back on options. Options only give one the right of first refusal. It's astonishing what I remember about your father's business when even I thought I wasn't listening, isn't it? Meanwhile, I've decided to loan the pieces to the museum. That way they'll sort of be in escrow and safe."

"And you're going to take them to the museum tonight? Mother, it's one thing to have all your ducks in a row, quite another to drive around after dark with priceless *objets d'art* to tempt a mugger or thief."

Pauline looked hurt. "I've an appointment with the director in the morning. Evelyn Ellison is going with me. I was only trying to organize efficiently, make use of Tucker while he's available. I have lots of common sense, Justine. It may have more of an aristocratic bent than most, but I can't help that, can I?"

"I was only thinking of what was best."

"I'm sure you were, dear. Only...I want to do my own thinking from here on out."

"I can't quarrel with that."

Pauline eyed her daughter with a modicum of mistrust. "You're sure? There's so much of your father in you, dear. Now that I look back on it, he was a dreadful busybody."

"You'll be pleased to know Tucker has been giving me lessons on how *not* to be a busybody."

"Really? I had the impression that the two of you were..."

"I'll load those things for you now," said Tucker.

"You're such a dear man. I don't know how we would've managed without you all these weeks. Which reminds me. I have something that might interest you. Wait here."

Tucker tossed a questioning look at Justine.

"Don't ask me. She's her own woman now."

Pauline returned with a large, square, paper-wrapped parcel. "It's my scrapbook. I thought you'd like to have it."

"Pictures?" He aimed a boyish smile at Justine. "Hah! Now I'll know what you were really like when you were a kid."

"Oh no, it's not that kind of scrapbook. That's my book of menus of all the important luncheons and dinners Evan and I gave through the years. My grandmother started it. I thought the recipes might be of interest to you, some have been in my family for generations."

"Recipes?" Mortification ignited anger. He turned on Justine "You told!"

"I haven't said a word!"

"Of course you haven't dear. I'm afraid I snooped. That night we had that touch of hysteria. I didn't mean to snoop, but there were several pages out of your cookbook lying under the coffee table. Of course, I recognized them for what they were right away. I used to proof Evan's articles for financial magazines. He always said that if I could understand the words he used, the magazine's readership should have no problem."

Tucker's face was slowly turning a rich shade of pink.

With gamine relish, Justine spoke. "Unless you knew it for a fact, it's almost impossible to believe Mother's only recently learned to be independent. Isn't she marvelous?"

"That's a lovely thing to say about me, dear. I meant to mention the scrapbook that night Tucker had us to supper, but we got off on something else. Dishes, I think, and it slipped my mind."

She took Tucker's arm, propelling him into the hall. "You're a real find, Tucker. You really are, you can work with your hands, you're intelligent. Imagine! Writing a cookbook. You'll be sure to have your photograph on the back cover. When it's published, we'll have to arrange an autograph party. We'll invite all of my new friends and of course, all of yours."

He glanced back over his shoulder at Justine and mouthed the word, "Help."

The grin she gave him was one of friendly malice. "How would you like your hamburger cooked?"

"Bloody hell!"

"I think he means rare, dear," Pauline said, and patted his arm that she had tucked into her own.

Chapter Sixteen

"You're not being fair, Justine! I got my driver's license, the same as Pauline."

"It has nothing to do with being fair, Agnes. Mother has an appointment this morning."

"She's used the car every day! Now I ask to use it and you say no. I'm all dressed and so is Judy Ann. Besides, Wheeler's waiting for us."

"I knew you two were up to something."

"My check came, I'm going to open an account at the bank. Wheeler's just going along for the ride."

"Why not wait until tomorrow?"

"The banks are closed. Tomorrow is a holiday."

"What holiday?"

"The Fourth of July."

"It's July already!"

"Time flies when you keep your nose in your office all day and your nights occupied, doesn't it?"

"That was uncalled for."

"Fact is fact," Agnes said, stubbornly refusing to give an inch.

Justine tried another tack. "You know you can't check Wheeler out of the nursing home. They won't let you. You have to be on their list."

"He's at Tucker's. He doesn't have to go back until Wednesday morning. Tucker lets him do anything he wants except smoke in bed. You don't let me do anything—except the laundry,'' she said, her voice rising. "I'm more of a prisoner than Wheeler.''

Justine held up her hand. "Let me think about this a minute so I don't say the wrong thing.'' She stared down into her coffee. "Neither you nor Wheeler are prisoners,'' she said, looking up. "All of us, at some time or another, are victims of circumstances. That's you, me, Mother, Wheeler. You got your driver's license only because Mother did. For years you haven't wanted to get five minutes away from the house.''

"People change. And anyway, I can do anything that namby-pamby can.''

"Please don't talk about Mother that way.''

"She makes fun of my purple. I like purple.''

"Okay, I'll give you that. Why didn't you mention your plans to me sooner?''

"When? We only decided last night and you had already gone into your office and said not to disturb you on pain of death. That's what you said.''

"Mother Hale, this is so unlike you.''

"Pauline is taking charge of her life. You don't say that to her. But when I try to—''

"Did I hear my name being maligned?'' asked Pauline, breezing into the kitchen. She bent over and kissed Judy Ann. "You look so sweet. Even your hair is brushed this morning.''

"I'm goin' with Grandma.''

"That's nice.''

"Agnes wants to use the car this morning, Mother.''

"Well, she can't. I'm using it.''

"Selfish. You've always been selfish, Pauline. You only think of yourself.''

"That's not true.''

"I've had it.'' Justine took the car keys off the hook by the cabinet and put them in her pocket. "We'll solve this diplomatically. Mother, you and Agnes sit at the table, have coffee and work it out between yourselves. Until then, neither of you get the keys. Judy Ann, come with me. You're too young to view carnage.''

Pip came barreling out of his room. "Why didn't you wake me, Mom? Now I'm late."

"Late for what?"

"I'm gonna try to get some closeups of a tomato worm in Tucker's garden. They're ferocious looking, like prehistoric monsters. Once the sun dries the dew, they hide."

"Eat some cereal first and wear your tennis shoes."

"I gotta catch the light!"

"Not in bare feet and on an empty stomach."

"You just wanna ruin my career!"

"Heaven forbid. Okay, go."

"You're all right, Mom!"

What I am is permissive, Justine thought. She'd pay for it later. She just knew it.

While she dressed, Judy Ann sat on the floor and played with the kitten. "Grandma said she'd take me to Mc-Donald's."

"If not today, then another day, sweetie."

"Mommy, do you think there's magic in our house?"

"Magic? Like what?"

"You know. The sounds an' things. Grandma hears noises at night."

Me and Tucker, Justine thought, abashed. "If there is, it's good magic."

"Grandma told Wheeler our house is full of cold spots."

"Grandma Hale's circulation isn't as good as it used to be. She gets chilled easily, that's all. What else do Grandma and Wheeler talk about?"

"It's a secret."

Justine turned away and began brushing her hair. "Besides the secret," she said casually.

"My lips are zipped."

"Can you tell me if the secret is good?"

Judy Ann hesitated, then shook her head. "My lips are zipped." She looked up at her mother and smiled. "You're pretty, Mommy. Tucker says when I grow up I'm going to be as pretty as you, maybe even prettier."

Eight years old and already she could shift topics with the adroitness of a politician. "Did Tucker say anything about how clever you are?"

Agnes appeared in the doorway. "We've worked it out," she announced stiffly.

"Where's Mother?"

"Here," Pauline said. "I was just speaking to Mrs. Ellison. Agnes can drop me off at the museum. Evelyn is going to meet me there after I've conducted my business and I'll spend the afternoon with her."

Justine handed the keys to Agnes. "Drive very, very safely." It was on her tongue to say Judy Ann couldn't go, but the child was squirming with anticipation at the prospect of being treated to McDonald's. "Make sure Judy Ann keeps her seat belt buckled. I suppose you don't want to tell me what mischief you and Wheeler are up to?"

Agnes exhaled tremulously. "I told you. I'm going to open an account at the bank with my social security check. He's just going along for the ride." She gestured past Justine to her granddaughter. "Run tell Wheeler we're ready to go."

"I suppose that means I'll have to ride in the back seat," said Pauline.

"Either that or walk behind the car," snipped Agnes.

Justine stepped between them and put a comradely arm around each. "If the two of you aren't cheerfully on your way by the time I count to ten, I'm letting all the air out of the tires. Now, who wants to be the first to kiss and make up?"

It was incredibly peaceful after they left. Barefooted, Justine walked through the house absorbing the silence. It was this kind of lovely quiet she had imagined when she had decided to work at home. Perhaps after school started she'd have more mornings like this one.

Dust, dishes and unmade beds tugged at her, but for the moment work had to come first. She made a fresh pot of coffee, ignored the urge for a cigarette and started work.

She couldn't pinpoint when the queer feeling began. She was alone in the house, yet she felt odd, as if she were not alone, as if someone were peering over her shoulder. Pip, sneaking photographs of her maybe. She walked through the house, then made a pass of the wraparound porch. No Pip.

She went into the living room and stared at The Chair. Then she sat in it. Cold spots, Judy Ann had said. Did she feel cooler sitting here? No. But the entire house was cool, considering there was no air-conditioning and it was deep into summer. Still, she had an eerie sense of something spiritual, as if some mystical sense was touched in her.

Certainly no murderous lunatic was going to come vaulting out of a closet. There were no closets.

But there was Milo.

She found him out behind one of the backyard sheds, digging around the foundation.

"Yes'um?" he said, leaning on his shovel when she approached.

"Milo, have you ever actually found a gopher?"

"Yes'um."

"They burrow under buildings, too?"

His eyes narrowed. "Seems like."

"Have you been working up near the house this morning?"

"No'um."

She shook her head, and told an outright lie. "I thought I saw you."

"'Twasn't me."

"Must of been my imagination."

"Must've."

"Well, you can take the clotheslines down now. Tucker wired the dryer for us."

"Yes'um."

She could feel his eyes following her all the way back to the house and the feeling didn't stop until she was inside again. It was the same feeling that had driven her outside to begin with.

Maybe the house was too quiet. She turned the television on at a low volume and went back to the computers,

losing herself in her work until Tucker rapped on the door
and made her jump.

"Take a break for a late lunch," he said.

"You scared the daylights out of me! And, what're you
doing home in the middle of the day?" His jaws were
darkened with two-day-old beard stubble, his eyes looking
at her in a peculiar, searching way.

"Got today and tomorrow off for the Fourth. You look
pale. Did I really frighten you?"

"Nobody's home but me. The house feels odd. Or, it
did."

"That sounds almost like an invitation to ravish you."

"Pip could wander in any minute."

"I'll settle for lunch."

"Chicken noodle soup and sliced tomatoes?"

"Anything. I never taste food when I'm around you."

Smiling, she saved the text she'd written and shut off the
computer. In the kitchen she opened soup, heated it in the
microwave and served it in cups along with crackers and
tomatoes on a side dish.

"You know your dad and Agnes are up to something."

"Can't be much at their age. Now at ours—"

"Eat your soup."

"Too hot." He pushed the cup away and leaned on his
elbows. "My crew and their families are coming out tomorrow. It's sort of an annual thing. We barbecue, play a
game of softball, set off a few bottle rockets. That sound
okay to you?"

Her heart fluttered. "You mean, meet your friends?"

"They know you exist."

"You talked about me?"

"Sort of." He opened his mouth to say more, then closed
it.

"I'm getting a bad feeling, Tucker. Sort of—how?"

"You're not getting mad, are you?"

"No," she said airily. "Just curious."

"I've been working with this crew a long time. I've
hauled 'em home when they've had too much to drink, let

one or two stay over when they were having problems at home, been best man at their weddings—"

"What have you said about me?"

"I'm even godfather to..." Losing courage, his voice trailed off. The rings felt as if they were burning a hole in his pocket. Now just wasn't the time, he decided. Not in a noon-day kitchen with a sink full of dishes for a backdrop.

He wanted atmosphere, romance. He was only going to do this once in his entire lifetime. Hell! If he didn't do it right, she might say no.

"You're beating around the bush, Tucker."

"I was only going to say they might razz you a little, being the boss's girl and all."

"You told your crew I was your girl?"

"Don't worry, I can keep them in line."

"You're not telling me everything."

"Sure I am. Would I lie to you?"

"I don't know, would you?"

"Tell you what, let's talk about this over dinner tonight. We'll go someplace fancy." He came around the table and kissed her hard on the mouth.

The screen door slammed. "Yuk! Do y'all have to do that all the time?"

Not the least bit self-conscious, Tucker raised his head and grinned. "Listen sport, you want to drive over to the county line with me to buy fireworks?"

"I'll say!"

"Then wash up and be quick about it." To Justine, he said, "Ride with us, we'll stop for a Coke somewhere."

"I think I'll work some more. Anyway, one of us needs to stay by the phone. With Mother, Agnes and your dad loose in the world, anything could happen. They have my daughter, you know."

"Look at me," he said, with his hand on her chin, tilting her head. "Worry about Judy Ann if you must, but let the grown-ups do it for themselves."

"You're not at all worried about your dad?"

"Not as long as he doesn't smoke in bed, or spend an evening alone with a bottle, which he is prone to do if nobody's looking. Otherwise he's as capable as any man his age. He just got himself caught up in the system, is all.''

"You're not concerned that he's off with Agnes?''

He laughed. "His taste in female companions seems to have deteriorated over the years, but he's having a great time with Agnes. Sits up at night racking his brains for purple jokes. Now, lighten up. Better yet, think about me.''

She smiled at him through her thick fringe of lashes. "I do enough of that already.''

After he and Pip left, she continued to sit at the table.

The dark hole that was the pantry caught her eye. A shadow seemed to dissolve out of the wall. She blinked and looked again. Nothing. A case of nerves, she thought. What woman wouldn't have them on a day like this?

LOTTIE WANDERED the house unable to sit still. There was a kind of jagged wedge of anxiety inside her chest. She had everything ready. Her clothes, her bones, her Bible, the piece of copper wire she had pinched from Tucker. All she needed now was the opportunity to extend herself.

When Pauline and Agnes had driven away with Judy Ann and Wheeler, and Pip had taken off for the barn, she had thought the opportunity was upon her. She had only to wait for Justine to begin work. It seemed the computers mesmerized her for hours.

But today Justine herself seemed to be in a perpetual state of flux; unable to concentrate. She kept leaving her office to poke about the house so that Lottie could find no room or dark corner in which she'd be safe enough to unravel her destiny.

Then a curious thing had happened. Justine behaved as if she sensed her existence. Once she had even stared right at her. Lottie had watched her face, saw Justine's eyes widen, then saw the expression that said Justine had dismissed the possibility. Lottie didn't know if that would stand her in good stead or not. Agitated, the moment she could, she got back behind the secret door and perched on the step above her bones and the neatly folded garments.

She fingered the gray silk longingly, which only served to increase her impatience.

Law! She had been awaiting this event for more decades than she could rightly recall. She supposed she could manage a few more hours.

"WE CAN'T JUST GO and leave Pip home alone," Justine protested to Tucker. "The others should be along any minute now."

"Aw, Mom, I can take care of myself."

"Of course, you can, sport," agreed Tucker. "I made reservations, Justine. If we're not there..."

"You don't understand—"

"Sure I do. Stop coddling the boy. He's got a good head on his shoulders, let him use it."

"I won't get into any trouble, Mom. Really. What could I do? I don't mind staying by myself. I want to. I'm just gonna read my camera books and watch TV."

Faced with the combined force of their argument, and the fact they were right, Justine allowed herself to be persuaded. But all the way into Mobile, she kept watching oncoming cars in the hope of spotting her own station wagon on its way home.

The restaurant had all of the romantic ambiance that Tucker wished for. They were seated at a table overlooking the bay. The moon shone unimpeded in a cloudless night sky and the path it made on the water seemed to come right up and join the candle-lit tables.

Champagne was not Tucker's drink of choice. But tonight he ordered it and sipped it because he wanted everything to be special for Justine. He couldn't take his eyes off her. She wore a very simple beige shift and had pinned her golden hair loosely atop her head so that the elegant length of her neck seemed extraordinary. He felt quite drunken with a profound sense of loving and possession. But her lovely brow was furrowed and he knew he'd have to deal with that before he could broach the subject hard on his mind.

"Stop worrying," he said. "You've done a good job with Pip. It shows. He won't disappoint you. Now, relax. I want you to enjoy yourself tonight."

Warmth filled Justine's gaze. "You do, don't you? You genuinely want me to have a good time."

"It may sound trite, but if you're happy, I'm happy."

She put her hand on his. "You're a rare man, Tucker. You make me feel as if I can do anything, be anything. I was a basket case when I arrived here. We all were. Pip was hostility incarnate. Judy Ann seldom let me out of her sight.

"You've helped to change all that. You exude confidence, it flows into those around you, even Mother and Agnes. You're right. I *should* trust Pip. I should also trust myself more. I'm sure everything is fine."

"You make me sound like a wonder man or something," he returned, pleased and yet slightly embarrassed.

"Don't you want me to speak from the heart?"

He leaned toward her. "I want you always to speak from the heart." His own heart beat wildly. He could ask her now.

The waitress brought their food, breaking the illusion of privacy.

After dinner, then, Tucker told himself.

"WE'VE DONE NOTHING but talk about me all evening," Justine said, laying her silverware aside. "Tell me more about your cookbook. You promised."

He rolled his eyes heavenward. "Right now, I'd just as soon trash the thing."

"Oh, no! You can't! I won't let you."

"I don't have a publisher, Justine. I think the book is just a diversion to keep me from feeling guilty about Dad. I did a side job a couple of weeks ago for a man who owns a small press in Mobile. He said there are fifty-five hundred cookbooks in *Books in Print*. That's a hell of a lot of competition. I'd need a gimmick if I hope to publish. I don't have a gimmick."

"But if you did?"

"He said he'd look at it."

"Then we'll have to find you a gimmick."

"We'll see. In the meantime let's just keep this to ourselves."

"Meantime? As in tomorrow, when all of your friends are over?"

He grinned. "Something like that." The champagne had made a fine start for the evening and the food had been superb.

Now, he thought, when coffee and after-dinner drinks had been set before them. He patted his coat pocket. The box wasn't there. He searched all of his pockets. Hell!

"Don't tell me," Justine laughed. "You forgot your wallet."

"Something else," he said morosely and signaled the waitress for the check. "Let's go home. I'm kind of worried about Pip and the old folks myself."

"What!"

"You talked me into it."

There were certain glaring flaws in that statement and Justine saw each of them. "Tucker, what's wrong?"

"Not a damned thing."

"In that case . . ." she searched for the right words, puzzled, but unwilling to push and spoil a lovely evening. After a pause she continued, saying, "Dinner was wonderful. Let's go." And those were the last words spoken between them until he pulled up in front of her house.

"Whose car is that?" she wondered aloud, looking at the late model Ford parked behind her own station wagon.

He helped her step down from the cab of the truck.

"Well, they seem to have made it home. Are you coming in?"

"Just for a few minutes. Big day tomorrow, you know."

"You are going to tell me what your crazy behavior is all about, aren't you?"

He took her elbow, almost propelling her up the steps. "Eventually."

The entire house was alight. The soft rise and fall of conversation wafted from the great room.

"Is that you, dear?" Pauline moved into Justine's line of vision.

"Mother? Is everything all right? Everybody?"

"Do come meet, Evelyn. She's staying the night. She brought me home."

Justine's heart lurched. "What happened? Where's Judy Ann . . . and Agnes? Why—"

"And, my dad?" said Tucker.

"In Agnes's room, which is just as well. See," Pauline exclaimed, turning to her friend. "Didn't I tell you they make a handsome couple."

"Nice to meet you," Justine said, smiling at Evelyn Ellison. "But something's afoot here. I can smell it."

"I do want to have a word with you, Justine. In private."

Tucker sank down on the sofa to wait for an answer.

The door opened across the hall and Agnes peeped out. Wheeler urged her out and across the hall. Judy Ann and Pip, wearing pajamas, trailed behind.

"Hello, Son."

Tucker nodded. "Dad."

Agnes and Wheeler just stood there.

Justine noted their stance. "You wrecked the car."

"No, we didn't." Agnes poked Wheeler. "You tell them."

"No, you do it."

Tucker came to full alert. "Tell us what?"

"Could I get a word in, please," said Pauline. "Justine—"

"In a minute, Mother."

"I'll tell 'em," said Judy Ann, grinning.

"I better just go along home, now," said Wheeler. Agnes hooked his arm with her cane. "You'll stay right where you are. We agreed."

Worried, Tucker sprang to his feet. "What's going on here?"

Agnes cleared her throat. "We didn't do anything wrong."

Justine glanced at Tucker. His expression was black. "Maybe we'd all better sit down and talk," she suggested.

To Agnes and Wheeler, sitting seemed a good idea. They skirted Tucker, who'd ignored the suggestion, and seated themselves on the sofa farthest from him.

In an effort to regain center stage, Pauline issued an elegant sniff. She was ignored.

Wheeler clapped his hands. "Well, Son. I'm outta the clutches of old Iron Bottom for good."

"You're what!"

Justine put her hand on Tucker's arm. "Don't yell."

"How?" Tucker growled.

"We . . . we saw the judge . . . a hearing . . ."

"You didn't." Justine flashed Agnes a reproachful glance. "Did you?"

"Agnes got custody of me," said Wheeler.

"I didn't. I just signed an affidavit swearing that I'd be looking after him. That's all that was necessary."

The cords on Tucker's neck stood out. "You went behind my back!"

"An' I told the judge that my grampa already died and I wanted Wheeler for a grampa, now," said Judy Ann.

Tucker registered betrayal. "You, too?"

Gently, Justine rose and guided Tucker to a corner of the sofa. He sat down heavily. She sat on the sofa arm near him.

"There's more," Agnes said timidly. "We've registered for college."

Justine stared at the elderly couple. "You're kidding!"

"You think we're brainless nobodies, but we're not. Senior citizens go for free, so we signed up for fall classes. Me and Wheeler. He's going to audit, but I'm going for credit."

"You had no right—" Tucker began.

"Yes, they do," Justine said. "They have the right to make their own decisions, the same as you or me. They're adults." Tucker was shaking his head. "It's all about control, and trust," she added in dulcet tones, giving him back his own words.

Tucker didn't move for a full minute, then he nodded.

"You're right." He reached across the coffee table and shook his father's hand. "Okay. You outsmarted me."

"Didn't. It's just that the purple parrot," he gestured toward Agnes, "and I see eye to eye on things."

"I'm glad that's settled," inserted Pauline. "Now, Justine, if I could just have a word with you."

"Later, Mother, why don't you see Evelyn settled in your room? Off to bed, kids. It's way past your bedtime."

"Aw, Mom . . . I wanna wait to see if Grandma is gonna marry Wheeler."

"No," said Agnes, face flaring pink.

"Might," said Wheeler.

"We've had enough excitement for one night," Justine declared in a voice that brooked no protests. "Everybody to your own room, now." The children went, albeit reluctantly.

Pauline exchanged a look with Evelyn, then shrugged. "I do believe we're all tired. Come along, Evelyn. Justine, I'll share your room tonight?"

"That's fine."

Wheeler looked at Tucker. "I reckon I'll see you at home," he said. Agnes walked him to the back door, then disappeared into her own room.

When they were alone, Justine turned out lights until just a lamp near the sofa cast a soft glow over Tucker.

She kicked off her heels, sat beside him and pulled his arm around her. "I suppose after all that, you have indigestion. Did you suspect what they were up to? Is that why we left the restaurant in such a hurry?"

He laughed and the deep sound of his laughter carried with it yet a measure of stunned acceptance. "I had no idea. The old goat . . ."

"Agnes helped."

"Or hindered, depending how you look at it."

"I'm glad they like each other. Aren't you?" She didn't dare say another word. But she was thinking how it would make things easier all around in the event . . . that she and Tucker . . .

She sighed beneath her breath.

"I'd better go along home," he said. "Big day coming up tomorrow. We'll need an early start."

She couldn't keep the disappointment from her voice. "Always the practical one, aren't you?"

"I'm crazy about you, Justine, but it just isn't my day. Can we call it a night?"

"Of course."

Her tone was somewhat stiff. This wasn't the way he'd planned for today to end. Served him right, he thought ruefully, for forgetting the rings on his dresser.

His smile was crooked beneath his mustache. He wasn't going to let the evening end this badly. "On the other hand," he suggested softly, "could we try a little modest necking on the sofa?"

"Your behavior is strange tonight, you know. I can't keep up."

He pulled her onto his lap and nuzzled her earlobe. "Just answer the question."

A lovely shiver raced up her spine and she relaxed into his embrace. "A little modest necking? Why yes, I believe we could."

Chapter Seventeen

"I really must talk to you, dear."

"Taste this potato salad first, Mother."

Pauline took a step back. "Am I being punished for something?"

"Don't be that way. It has to be perfect. It's my debut in front of Tucker's friends."

"All right. But only one teensy spoonful." She scooped up a minuscule portion. "It's ... better than last time. The potatoes are soft."

"Too salty?"

"No. It needs a smidgen more," she said, standing at Justine's elbow while the salt was added. "You know dear, having Fourth of July with Tucker is so unexpected."

Justine picked up on her mother's cue. "Are you backing out? You can't do that. He wants to introduce you to his friends. Anyway, I need your moral support."

Pauline frowned. "It's just that with Evelyn here... She's a widow like me. Her only son lives in Atlanta—"

"Mother, she'll be as welcome at Tucker's as you are. I don't see the problem. Look, I'm running a little behind, could you check on Judy Ann for me? And tell her to put on a pair of clean shorts."

"But—" Pauline said despairingly.

Justine leaned over and kissed Pauline on the cheek. "Don't worry, Mother, I'm sure Evelyn will have a wonderful time. Now, please. Be a dear and get Judy Ann ready. Agnes and Pip have gone ahead already, and I still have to do my hair.''

"It's going to be a madhouse. All those people. The cars have already started arriving.''

"We'll have fun.'' Justine finished wrapping the salad bowl in plastic wrap.

Pip slammed into the kitchen. "Mom, Tucker says you better get down there, now!''

"I'm coming. Take this salad when you go back.''

Pauline threw up her hands in surrender. "I'd better see to Judy Ann while Evelyn is dressing.''

LOTTIE WAS TRYING not to feed her hopes, but when the house finally emptied she took it as a good omen.

There was one problem she had not been able to solve entirely and that was her sense of Time. The framework of minutes and hours still defeated her. She had no idea how long it would take or how fast electricity flowed. Thinking back, it had seemed only an instant and a single jolt that had given her unextended self some substance. And at that, she considered, the jolt had been diluted, passing first as it had through Jim Kessler.

She had listened to Tucker explain electricity to Justine, but he spoke of it in numbers, one-ten and two-twenty. The dryer had electricity called two-twenty, which sounded more powerful to her, but she could hardly expect to extend herself in the open on the back porch.

She needed privacy without interruption. So she decided to use the bathroom, for it was the only room in the house with all the proper elements. It had curtains on all the windows, a door that locked, and the essential electrical outlet. But as she was coming out of the pantry carrying her clothes, she spied a young mother with a baby heading across the back porch toward the bathroom door. And soon after, there seemed to be a steady run on the facilities by the impatient crowd partying down at the barn.

Then Pip came racing back into the house to get his camera; Justine ducked in for a jar of mayonnaise; Judy Ann, with a new playmate in tow, came for her kitten.

The only room that seemed off limits to all for the day was Justine's office. Those doors all stayed closed.

Heart palpitating and breathing as if she'd been running up a hill, Lottie moved first her clothes and, when the way was clear, her bones.

Footsteps on the side porch startled her.

She looked up to see a little boy with his nose pressed against a pane of the uncurtained French doors.

BY FOUR O'CLOCK that afternoon Tucker's yard over-flowed with guests and good cheer. There were more than twenty-five children and about the same number of adults, as some had arrived with entire families in tow, from grandmothers to babies only months old. Justine was hav-ing a hard time keeping track of who belonged to whom and finally gave it up.

A good half dozen or so of the boys were Pip's age and he seemed to take delight in leading them into all kinds of mischief, from chasing chickens to climbing trees. But it warmed her heart watching both her children enjoy the company of others their own age again. She made a men-tal note to get the names and phone numbers of the chil-dren's parents from Tucker.

"Those hens are never going to lay another egg," said the young woman who was helping Justine turn ground beef into hamburger patties at one of the makeshift tables.

Justine smiled. "Probably not. I'm sorry, but I've met so many people today I've forgotten your name."

"Janie. That's my husband up to bat now," she added, pointing to the field where the men had a softball game going.

Wheeler had been tagged as umpire and Agnes, who knew not the first thing about softball, was scorekeeper. It was making for a lot of noisy catcalling from the sidelines as she contradicted every one of Wheeler's calls. Janie's husband hit a pop fly. Tucker caught it in left field, which signaled the end of that inning, and the teams broke ranks for refreshments.

"Mama!"

"And that's our boy, Jimmie," Janie said, as a six-year-old raced up to them.

"Mama!" he said, breathless. "I just seen a skel'ton."

Janie gave a small embarrassed laugh. "Jimmie's long on right-brain hemisphere—he's got an imagination that won't quit."

He tugged on her arm. "I'm not 'maging, Mama. It was moving and then it sat in a chair and then it started dressing itself! I seen it!"

Janie laughed again and bent down to kiss the top of his head. "That's a wonderful story. You can tell me the whole thing later." To Justine, she said, "His teachers said for us to encourage him—that imagination helps in defining cognitive skills. I hope it's so."

Justine paused and looked toward her house. "Maybe he saw something he misinterpreted."

Janie shook her head. "I don't think so. This morning he had a long tale about a herd of dinosaurs wearing saddles. He stabled them in his room last night."

Tucker came up on Justine from behind and put his arms around her. "You holding up okay?"

She felt his breath on her neck and sighed happily. "Everybody seems to know my name, but I can't remember theirs. You should've warned me. Or we should've had name tags or something."

"You'll know all of us real good by Christmas," Janie put in. "We get together on Labor Day too, and sometimes at Thanksgiving—"

"Here?" Justine said, shocked, thinking of all the preparations, the cleanup.

"Be quiet, Janie," Tucker said. "You're scaring the daylights out of my best girl."

"One good turn deserves another," she retorted easily. "Remember that the next time my darlin' hits a fly ball and you think to put him out."

"Mama!" cried Jimmie, pulling on her shirt.

"Hush. How many times have I told you, don't interrupt when grown-ups are talking." She wiped her hands on a wet cloth. "Y'all excuse me. I got to turn this kid loose on his father for a few minutes."

Tucker tightened his arms about Justine. "That's what I'd like to do with you," he murmured. "Haul you off into the bushes somewhere..."

"Before or after we feed this horde?" she joked.

A very attractive, long-legged brunette, wearing a revealing knit shirt and very short shorts, touched Tucker on the arm. "Can I talk to you a minute?" she said, ignoring Justine.

"Later, Christie. I'm busy."

"When, later?" she cooed.

Justine went on full alert. She tried to move out of Tucker's embrace, but he locked his fingers over her abdomen and held her where she was.

"Later," he said. "As in tomorrow at work." He stared the girl down until she flounced off, buttocks jouncing.

Justine turned, still within the circle of Tucker's arms and looked up at him. "Tomorrow? At work?"

"The telephone company doesn't discriminate."

"You mean that... that creature works for you?"

"You're right on the money."

Justine's heart sank. "But, she's gorgeous."

"She keeps her warts covered up."

"What about when you go out of town on jobs?"

"She still keeps them covered up. Say, are you jealous?"

"I'm green!"

"Christie's not my type."

"Has she ever been?"

"Nope."

"Lucky for you," she said with feeling.

"If all these people weren't around I'd show you just how lucky I think I am."

"Tucker, do you have to manhandle my daughter in public that way?"

He stepped back, but not before he planted a swift kiss on Justine's lips. "Actually, Pauline, I do. Can't help myself."

Evelyn hovered behind Pauline. Justine thought the woman was a plump, polyester version of Pauline. But Evelyn was pleasant enough, and she appeared thoroughly taken with Pauline and content in Pauline's shadow. Both had done volunteer hostess duties, fetching and carrying, but after an hour or so they had moved a pair of chairs under a distant tree and kept to themselves.

"One of you needs to speak to Agnes. She's making a spectacle of herself."

"Oh, Mother, she's just having a good time."

"Good time, my foot. She's inebriated."

Justine had just the tiniest suspicion that her mother was trying to show off for Evelyn's benefit.

"I'll check on her," she said.

"I thought I'd mention that Evelyn is staying the night with us again. It's getting much too late for her to make the trip back into the city in holiday traffic."

"She's welcome, Mother, you know that." Justine smiled at the woman over her mother's shoulder.

"I'll bunk in with you again, too," Pauline said pointedly.

There was a slight moan from Tucker. "Two nights in a row?" he muttered into Justine's ear.

"That'll be fine," Justine said.

"Won't," said Tucker.

"Sex maniac," Pauline aimed at him in a disdainful whisper, then she and her new friend retreated to their chairs.

Tucker shook his head. "You get the feeling your mother was trying to pick a fight with me?"

"She was just putting on an act for her new acquaintance."

Then a mass of hungry youngsters descended upon them, mothers rushed over to lend Justine a hand with the food, and the men yelled to Tucker that it was his turn at bat.

LOTTIE WAS STUPEFIED to see that scalawag's face pressed against the window. She expected that within moments of his running away his parents or Justine would come rush-

ing into the office and discover her bones. Yet no one had
come. She reacted to that with utter disbelief.

Fearful that her sense of Time was betraying her, she hid
her bones inside the deep well beneath Justine's desk and
sat in the kitchen watching the minute hand move on the
clock that was a part of the microwave oven.

Ten minutes marched by and seemed more of an eternity to Lottie than all the previous years she had spent in
her condition.

There was a clamor on the back porch. She heard two
women's voices. She braced herself for discovery—an end
to her dream, the single hope that had sustained her. One
of the women stuck her head into the kitchen. Lottie froze.

"Christie, you'd better not snoop. Tucker will have your
head on a platter if he catches you."

"The men are using the bathroom at his place. Why
would he come up here?"

Christie stepped into the kitchen. "Look at that table,"
she said. "I bet it cost a fortune. Maybe he's interested in
her for her money."

"Whatever the reason, it's none of your business." The
other woman grabbed the girl's arm and pulled her outside. "Let's go! I value my husband's job even if you don't
value yours."

The screen door slammed.

Lottie hurried back into Justine's office. She checked the
side porch. Empty.

She pulled her bones out from beneath the desk, checked
the grey silk for wrinkles, smoothed out the pleats and arranged all in the desk chair.

She sat down upon the silk-clad bones and uncoiled the
ribbon of wire.

She debated praying, but pushed that notion aside. She
was still betwixt and between. If He answered, no telling
which side of the coin He'd come down on. Better to wait
and offer up hosannas once the deed was accomplished.

Then she leaned forward and thrust the copper wire into
the outlet above the desk.

Nothing happened.

She jiggled the wire.

A sudden whooshing noise inside her head caught her by surprise. It grew to thunderous proportions until her ears ached with it. Her fingertips were buzzing, her scalp tingled, her spine felt exposed. She was suspended, then sucked through a gurgling wash of warmth. Her limbs jerked in every direction. Her tongue floundered inside her mouth. She was on a journey... moving so fast she feared her soul couldn't keep up. Now she was tumbling, now sprinting forward, now sliding, now rocking. Oh! She couldn't see! She had the sensation of being at sea and she was convinced she was going to be violently sick.

Something snapped and she felt herself being hurled across the room. The chair crashed against the opposite wall with a thud. She banged her head. Law! She was being shot straight into the deepest hereafter! She saw stars. Millions of them, a kaleidoscope of colors like nothing she'd ever seen before. Especially with her eyes closed.

Fear held her immobile, transfixed. The heat she felt was incredible. She cried. Law! She had done it wrong. Had been cast into the deepest reaches of a place she never thought to be.

She fought to open her eyes and, at last succeeded, only to discover that her eyes refused to focus. With lives of their own they went round and round, in tempo with the ceiling fan. Ceiling fan? *Ceiling fan!*

She wished the roaring in her ears would subside. It interfered with her concentration. She closed her eyes. She was again suspended, but without the rocking sea this time. The sense of dreadful heat leveled off into a warmth more bearable and, when she once again opened her eyes, her vision was clear. The ceiling fan was clearly that. She recognized it. Tucker had installed it. Justine had argued with him. Argued that if it fell it would destroy her computers, not to mention her own head.

With hope and trepidation Lottie looked down and surveyed her immediate self and gasped.

She took a breath. Then another. She held her hands before her face. She had blunt, worker's hands. They were freckled and had blue veins. She turned the palms toward her eyes. Last time she looked she'd had calluses galore. Now she had none.

She touched her face, her arms, her abdomen, her legs. Her heart beat with a steadiness she could feel with her hand.

She stood up and took a step. After so many years of weightlessness, her limbs felt leaden. Gravity pulled at her. The floor beneath her was cool.

She was scared to think, scared to admit she had extended herself. But she had! She had! She tugged on the borrowed stockings and shoes and, walking with a motion cats spend years trying to perfect, she took herself into the bathroom to stare for long minutes at her reflection in the mirror.

A few minutes later she placed her hands on her Bible. She let Him know her whereabouts. She wanted as much of His attention and help as He could spare now, seeing as the next step would be to present herself to Justine and the family.

She had not met another human being face to face in more than a hundred years.

A chill swept up her spine. Suppose they refused to accept her?

She stepped out onto the back porch. Sound and smell crashed over her. The sound of a myriad voices came up from the barn, no single word clear. She heard chickens squawk, birds at evening song, crickets. The aroma of good, rich food being cooked over an open fire made her mouth water. She could smell the grass, the very earth itself.

She was back. Really back. She'd rest for now and introduce herself when there weren't so many strangers around.

She smoothed the gray silk over her hips, treasuring the feel of it.

They just have to accept me, she thought again. And this time the thought was as much a plea as prayer.

Chapter Eighteen

Pip shook Justine awake. "Mom! Get up!"

She opened one eye and glared at the bedside clock. Eight-ten. "Too early. Give me another hour," she murmured drowsily.

"Mom, darn it! Get *up*!"

His frantic tone was edged with an undercurrent of insistence. She turned her head and focused on her son. "What is it?"

"We've got company in the kitchen."

Justine reached behind her and poked Pauline. "Get up Mother, Evelyn must be wanting breakfast."

"Surely not," Pauline murmured and dragged a pillow over her head.

"It's not Mrs. Ellison," said Pip, dancing across the room. "You're in for a surprise, Mom. Wait'll you see!"

Still partially in the grip of sleep, Justine sat up. "Who?" she asked, but Pip was already out the bedroom door. She could hear his bare feet slapping down the hall.

A surprise visitor in the kitchen? In the middle of a stretch Justine froze. Her pulse rate accelerated. The only surprise visitor that could excite Pip like that was Philip! Her belly tightened with a cold sick dread. Dear God, why now? When she finally had her life back on track. Why would he show up now to undo what she'd built for herself, for the children? A life that promised more happiness and security than she had ever known.

"Mother! Get up. Now! We've got problems. Philip's here!"

"You handle him, dear. I'm not up to a scene this morning."

"What kind of mother are you?"

"A sleepy one."

"But I may need moral support!"

"You don't," Pauline muttered. "You have the backbone of a mule."

Justine frantically shoved her arms into her robe and finger-combed her hair.

In the kitchen Pip was sitting at the great old dining table—alone.

"Where is he?"

"It's not a he, Mom, it's—"

Wearing Agnes's apron over Pauline's dress, Lottie stepped from the pantry with a jar of Coffeemate. She smiled at Justine. "Mornin'."

"—a she," Pip finished.

Justine took a breath and gathered her wits. "Your father's not here?"

"Why would Dad be here?"

Legs suddenly rubbery, Justine slid into a chair. Lottie poured coffee and put the cup in front of her.

Trying to make the mental adjustment, Justine looked over at Pip, down at the coffee, then up at the plump, white-haired woman. "Who are you?"

"Lottie Roberts."

The coffee aroma penetrated Justine's brain. Absently she took a sip. "Roberts? Are you any kin to Milo?"

"By marriage."

Justine smiled slightly. Lottie Roberts was somewhere not far from sixty, with very white hair that was pinned into a bun at the back of her neck. She had a round face and eyes so faded they seemed almost colorless. Her mouth lifted at the corners as if ready to break into smile. Yet there was something else, and Justine tried to peg it. The woman looked so grandmotherly and old-fashioned she seemed of another age. Milo, she knew, was a certifiable eccentric, probably his wife was too. Had to be, Justine mused, if she was capable of walking into a neighbor's home uninvited. Not to mention perking coffee and serving it as if she were the lady of the manor.

"Did Milo send you over here for something?" she asked tactfully.

Lottie scoffed. "No."

"Does he know you're here?"

Lottie thought that over. "Like as not, he suspects, I reckon."

Justine noted the apron. Milo put a price on everything she asked him to do. Maybe he was hoping to put his wife to work. "Are you looking for a job?"

"Ask her where she lives, Mom."

Lottie shot him a withering glance. "Pipe down, you." Pip put his hand over his mouth and watched his mother. His eyes gleamed with Machiavellian delight.

Baffled, Justine pursed her lips. "I'm being tricked into something, right? Okay," she said to Lottie. "Consider the question asked."

"Here," came the firm reply.

"Here? You mean here, as in Alabama?"

"Here, as in this house. This is my house. Elmer built it for me."

Justine took a long draught of coffee. It was too early in the morning for her intuition to be on alert. She must've missed the clue to enlightenment. She just didn't get it. "So, who's Elmer?"

"My husband. He got hisself kilt in the Red River Campaign."

"That's a Civil War battle," Pip said. "She told me."

"I'm game. What's the joke?"

"No joke, Mom." Pip was grinning.

"Go back to square one. You just said you were married to Milo," Justine put to Lottie.

"I said kin by marriage. Milo's a distant cousin to Elmer—real distant by now, I reckon. I ain't one to marry the likes of Milo."

"I've rented this house with an option to buy it, and the price has been set," Justine said in case the woman's reason for dropping by was to up the price.

"Suits me," Lottie replied.

Pauline ambled in with a towel over her arm and cosmetic bag in hand. She stopped in mid-step and stared at Lottie who stiffened perceptibly. Then Pauline's breath caught audibly in her throat. "That's my gray silk!" She turned to Justine. "That woman is wearing my dress. And . . . those are my silk stockings from Harrod's. Look! There's the trademark on the heel."

"They're mine now," Lottie said.

"Thief!" said Pauline.

"Mother!"

"And those are my yard shoes," said Agnes, clutching her robe at the neck and watching from the doorway.

"I needed shoes to accommodate my bunions," Lottie replied with dignity.

Justine stood up. "Mrs. Roberts. You admit you stole those things? But how did you . . . ? When? Why?"

"While I was betwixt and between my own clothes fair rotted away."

"Betwixt and between?"

"She means while she was cruising the ozone, Mom."

"She means . . ." Goose bumps erupted along Justine's arms and legs. She sat back down with a thud.

"This ain't goin' a bit like I planned," Lottie told them all.

"Because you got caught!" Pauline cried. "Justine, call the police. Your father always, but always, had the servants checked out."

"Wait a minute, Mother," she said shakily. "There's more here than meets the eye."

"That's how it used to be," said Lottie. "Now you can see me, hear me . . ."

The adult faces were wearing expressions ranging from skepticism to outrage. Lottie sighed. She retrieved her Bible from a shelf in the pantry and laid it on the table in front of Justine, then quickly leafed the pages. "That's me and Elmer," she said pointing to Elmer B. Roberts wed Lottie Mae Wilks. The date, February 2, 1844, was written in an elegant spidery script. "We never had no issue and Elmer was kilt ninth of April, eighteen hundred and sixty-four. Howsomever, you'll note there ain't no buryin' date fer me."

"She's escaped from some lunatic asylum," said Agnes.

"I'm as sound of mind as you. More. I ain't the one with unnatural purple hair."

"Or jail," insisted Pauline. "She's probably a klepto-maniac."

Lottie had no idea what a kleptomaniac was, but it didn't sound nice. "As soon as I can get me some clothes, you can have these back. They're too immodest fer my taste anyhow. Don't cover up near enough leg."

"Don't you get it?" Pip said. "Lottie's our ghost. She's been here all the time. She moved the chair, she—"

Lottie was insulted. "I weren't never no ghost."

"Of course you weren't," Justine said and shot a warning glance at her son. Thief or not, the woman was sweet-faced and seemed harmless enough, but you could never tell. They were arresting grandmothers these days for dealing drugs and child molesting. She didn't want anything said that might turn Lottie Roberts's pleasant demeanor into one of pathological rage.

"Good morning," said Evelyn Ellison. "Am I interrupting a family conference or something?" She gave Pauline a pointed look.

"Sit," said Lottie. "I'll git your coffee."

Justine jumped up. "No, no. I'll get it. Mrs. Roberts, why don't you sit down while we thrash this out."

"It don't appear seemly fer me to be a guest in my own home."

"Just for today," Justine suggested, pasting on a smile. The queer old thing was unglued, suffering from dementia or Alzheimer's disease, she thought. As soon as the opportunity presented itself, she was going to send Pip to find Milo to collect his wife, or cousin or whatever.

Evelyn sugared her coffee. "Is everything set, then?" she asked Pauline.

Pauline cleared her throat. "Justine, dear, you can handle all this on your own can't you? It's not like you have the problem you thought you did when you so rudely pushed me out of bed. Which would be far worse than..." She gestured toward Lottie. "However, I do expect that my dress will be cleaned and returned to me."

"I ain't walking around naked," said Lottie.

"I'm sure we can find you a dress or two," Justine said soothingly. "Now, what were you driving at, Mother?"

"Evelyn's invited me and I've decided to accept. I'm moving in with her."

"What!"

"I've been trying to tell you for days, but you've had your head in the clouds."

"You can't just move out!"

"I can."

"But how will you live? What will you do for—"

Lottie got up and started breakfast. Fried bacon and toad in the hole, she decided, taking the fixings out of the fridge. She pinched the centers out of bread slices, cracked eggs into the holes and set them to toasting nicely in a skillet while bacon sizzled in the microwave. Modern inventions were wonderful, she thought. 'Course, store-bought bread was fair lacking. Come Thursday, she'd set her own to rising.

"Now don't upset yourself on my account, Justine. Everything is worked out. Evelyn has this lovely old home on Government Street and she just rattles around in it by herself."

"Pauline will be so much company for me," beamed Evelyn. "And, she's just vicious at cards."

"Remember the man who wants to buy the Japanese sculpture? He's agreed to five hundred dollars for the privilege of first refusal."

"Mother, that won't last you around a corner."

"I have a job, too."

"Your jobs are like one-a-day vitamins," snickered Agnes. "You have to have one every day."

"Oh, go break a hip, Agnes. Now, where was I? Oh. My job. I'm going to be working in the gift shop at the museum. The director was thrilled to get the sculpture on loan." She suddenly turned on Pip. "But you, young man, have no appreciation for the finer things in life. We found bubble gum stuck behind the ears."

Justine frowned. "Pip, you didn't."

"You said it was disgusting to keep it in the fridge."

Judy Ann wandered in and was ignored. While the conversation rose and fell around the table, Lottie scooped her up and put her on a stool by the sink. "How's my little darlin' today?"

"I'm hungry. Are you a friend of Grandma's too?"

"I'm a friend of yours."

"I've never seen you before."

"That's because you couldn't. Now you have special eyes and you can."

"I do?"

"We played dolls one day, but you got scart."

Judy Ann gasped. "You made Mrs. Pratt drink tea all by herself!"

"And now I'm makin' you toad in the hole."

Judy Ann giggled. "Little girls don't eat frogs."

"Piffle!" Lottie laughed. "You're too smart fer me. Later on you git me some eggs outta Tucker's henhouse an' I'll make you some little puddin's fer supper."

Evelyn gushed with delight at the food Lottie set before her. "I haven't had toad in the hole since I was a little girl! My grandmother's cook used to make it."

Lottie beamed and refilled coffee cups all around.

Wheeler showed up at the back door. "Tucker left for work 'afor I got up," he said. "I ain't been fed."

Lottie put him in the chair next to Pip. "Mind yore manners, we got company from town," she admonished Wheeler.

Justine watched Wheeler exchange glances with Agnes, and Agnes shook her head. Before she could decipher what more could possibly be going on between those two, her attention was drawn to the opposite end of the table. Lottie sat down and Judy Ann climbed onto her lap, allowing the woman to feed her.

"You're not hearing a word I'm saying, dear," Pauline said.

Justine sighed. "I was just wishing I was an embryo again."

"I'm going to finish packing. I do hope Mrs. Roberts works out because you need the help, Justine. However, you shouldn't allow servants at table. And keep the liquor cabinet locked. Come along, Evelyn, keep me company."

"I haven't hired—oh, never mind. Agnes, if you don't have any plans for the day, perhaps you can run into town and pick up a few things for me."

"We need some meat, some nutmeg and some orange flower water," said Lottie. "I'm of a mind to dobe a rump of beef and make some snow cream. And apples, don't fergit apples. I been aching fer some snow cream." She smiled sweetly at Justine. "It was fair hard to come on sugar during the war and after'ards."

"You said little puddin's," accused Judy Ann.

"I got the makin's fer puddin'," Lottie told her. "You run along an' git dressed now, little darlin'." She pointed at Pip. "First chance you git, which is after you clean your room, you run yonder an' find Milo and tell him to be up hereabouts when shadows is longest, and to bring his shovel."

"Why?"

"You'll see why," she promised mysteriously. The sun wasn't going to set another day without she had retrieved her money, silver and wedding ring. "Law! I recollect I can keep busy till then," she muttered aloud.

Busy doing what? Justine wondered. "Mrs. Roberts, thank you for cooking breakfast. I shouldn't have let you."

"You couldn'ta stopped me, an' that's a fact."

"I...think I'll get dressed," Justine said and made a beeline for the telephone in her office. Mr. Kessler came on the line at once. She hurried through greetings.

"Everyone's fine, thank you." She inhaled deeply. "I know this sounds silly, but has there ever been any comment about the house, other tenants complaining about noises that go bump in the night, that sort of thing?"

There was dead silence on the other end of the line.

"Mr. Kessler?"

"You movin', then?"

"No!"

"Waal, there's always talk."

"Like what?"

"Ghosts, hauntings and such like in houses as old as the one you're in."

"You ever hear of an Elmer Roberts?"

"You been talking to Milo? I told him! I sure told him. I ain't never gonna git that place sold if'n he keeps running off at the mouth and digging the place up. I imagine if you want to buy the place now, you're gonna want to knock a couple thousand off the price we talked about?"

"I..." Opportunity knocked. Justine had learned to open the door. "Well, yes, if we have to put up with a ghost," she said, to see what response that would get.

"Figured so," said a disappointed-sounding Mr. Kessler.

"What's the story on our ghost, Mr. Kessler?"

"It ain't documented or anythin', but the tale that traveled down the years mostly just had carpetbaggers cleaning out the house and carrying the woman off to parts unknown. Some say she just up and died, but nobody ever found her... y'know what I mean?"

Justine was afraid she did. "What's her name?"

"Lotus, or Lottie, some such."

She gripped the phone until her knuckles were bloodless. "I see. Well, thank you."

"Not gonna let her run you off are you?"

"Not if she can cook," she said lightly.

"Har, har! Ain't you somethin'!"

Justine cradled the phone. Okay, she told herself, it was a bizarre situation, but nothing she couldn't handle if she just kept an open mind and didn't panic. The main thing was to make certain that the children were safe.

She hurried Agnes and Wheeler on their way and insisted that Pip and Judy Ann accompany them.

"We're supposed to clean up Tucker's yard from yesterday," Pip argued. "He said so. Besides we want to stay and talk to Lottie."

"Well, you can't."

"But she might disappear!" Pip cried.

Justine had high hopes of exactly that.

"Go with your grandmother!"

No amount of coaxing could stop Lottie from doing dishes and later clearing up the debris Pauline had left behind in her room. Justine sighed and watched her for a moment from the threshold. The woman looked as much of flesh and blood as she herself.

"Please, Mrs. Roberts, can we sit down and talk over a cup of coffee?"

"Reckon you ought to call me Lottie."

"Lottie, then."

Reheating the coffee, Justine found her hands trembling. The idea of a ghost that cooked and cleaned was so preposterous, so alien a thought, that she had an intellectual skirmish with herself before she could raise the first question.

"Lottie...I want you to know that I don't believe in voodoo, the occult or anything supernatural."

"Me, either. I'm a Christian an' don't hold with heathen ways."

"But you expect me to believe that you have somehow returned from the dead?" Just saying the words made Justine shiver.

"I don't recollect I died. I jus' woke up an' I was betwixt and between. I weren't of this world or the next. I could see myself—"

"An out-of-body experience?" Justine didn't comprehend it, but she remembered an article on it in *Reader's Digest* and some people who professed to have experienced such things had been on a couple of talk shows. "How long did it last?"

"Best I can figure, better'n a hundred years."

Justine closed her eyes. Lottie Roberts was a real nut case. "You have a social security card?"

"Don't recollect as I do. I knowed I was gonna have a hard time convincin' you, Justine. I don't know where I'll go if you don't let me stay here. Sure as shootin' I ain't got a relative left. None that I know anyways. You wanna see where I been keepin' all these years?"

Now we're getting somewhere, Justine thought. "Can you show me?"

Lottie led her into the pantry. "Elmer built this secret door up to the attic after the war started. Then, once he was called up, an' I had ter be here alone, we put all our good stuff up in the attic. Them Union soldiers were fierce about lootin'. It's all here, 'cept fer our silver and such. That's buried." She demonstrated the wood panel that pushed in and released the latch. Then she swung the door open to reveal a steep, narrow flight of stairs.

Cautiously Justine followed her up the stairs.

Sunlight streamed through a dusty dormer window, casting light and shadow over an attic crowded with beds and tables, wooden boxes of dishes, crystal and oil lamps. Feather mattresses and quilts were rolled into heaps. Bedslats were of rope. An old trunk was open and overflowing with fabric. Justine lifted out a dress, it crumbled in her hand.

"Like I said, rotted through and through," said Lottie.

"You lived up here?"

"I liked to be around my things. 'Course, my chair was downstairs. I used ter sit in it and mull things over."

"Your chair." Disbelief and presentiment warred in Justine's mind.

"Elmer built it. It was the first piece of furniture he carved out fer me. It's special like."

Justine felt the low roof and walls closing in on her. She hurried back down to the kitchen, out onto the porch and sucked in great gulps of warm summer air.

"There's no logic to this at all," she said when Lottie followed her out. "Not one bit! You're asking me to believe in some kind of magic!"

Lottie scoffed "Magic!" She grabbed Justine's arm and pulled her over to the washer. "This is magic," she cried. And still holding Justine's arm pulled her into the kitchen and through the house. "That microwave is magic, and your computers! Computers. Law! I never heard of such. An' television that brings pictures right into the parlor, an' electricity. Why, I didn't extend myself on magic. I don't know magic. I used electricity!"

Justine slumped onto the sofa. Lottie moved to sit in her chair.

"How?"

Lottie shrugged. "I just plugged me in. Settin' right there at your desk."

Justine gasped. "The skeleton, a little boy named Jimmie—"

"My bones," Lottie agreed. "Nobody ever came to collect 'em so I figured I could use 'em over again. My plan was to extend myself an' live out my life." She straightened the apron she was wearing. "Which I *done* and which I *aim* to do. This is the only home I know, but I reckon if you cast me out, I'll manage. Howsomever, I been countin' on you to be my friend. An' you need my help, Justine. Why you can't hardly run this house and work, too. I seen that fer myself. Agnes ain't no help. And now she's goin' off to college or some such. Just lookit how she's neglected Judy Ann since Wheeler come into her life. That child needs me. I recollect you show me how to use that iron of your'n and you won't never see her wearing wrinkled clothes. Shameful, that's what that is.

"An' lookit my house! Why, I could grow peas under the beds, dust is so thick."

Justine held up her hand. "Enough."

Lottie eyed the dust balls under the liquor cabinet. She itched to set the house to rights, but her future rested with Justine, so she sat there, hands folded in her lap.

"I do need help," Justine mused aloud, but she was talking to herself. "But I'd be worried all the time about the children." She turned her head and gazed at Lottie. "The thing is, you don't look dangerous."

Lottie gaped. "Why I ain't. I ain't never hurt nothin' past flies an' mice . . . except . . ."

Justine's heart lurched. "Except what?"

"Well, once, I don't rightly recollect the exact night, but a passel of Union scouts was camped up the river a piece and one sneaked down to my henhouse. I hit him a powerful blow with the hoe. He fell like a sack of rocks. I left him a-lying there, but next mornin' he was gone. Don't rightly know if I kilt him or not."

"But that was a long time ago." The comment ran through Justine's mind a second time. Even to her own ears it sounded as if she was accepting a cosmic impossibility. It made her scalp tingle.

Lottie chuckled. "I reckon it was. You wanna show me how ter use that washing machine? I'm fair itching to wash a load of sheets. After'ards, I spec I'll sprinkle down the floors, then I got to git them little puddin's bakin' fer Judy Ann. I promised."

Against all odds Justine felt herself giving in to the impossible. No way could she put an old woman out on the street to fend for herself. "You like doing housework and cooking?"

"Law, I ain't hardly done nothin' else. 'Cept when I helped in the fields or in the curing barn. 'Course, back then, we had cows to milk, hogs to slop, an' I kept a mess of fowls—chickens, ducks and geese like. Don't spec you'd be needing butter churned or water boiled fer washin', howsomever, I do aim to bake my own bread, sweet cakes an' such."

"Home-baked bread?"

The kitten strolled into the room and leaped into Lottie's lap. "Flea catcher," she said, but she stroked it until it purred contentedly, knowing that all the while Justine was watching her like a ferret. She didn't think there was much more she could say. It was all up to Justine now.

They sat together in silence for over a minute.

The lure of help won out. Hiring Lottie would free her of much of the burden of housework and leave her free to press on with her computer project. "I couldn't pay you much," Justine said finally. "And I would be keeping an eye on you."

Lottie's face was suddenly so flushed she had to dump the cat and fan herself with the apron. "Law!" she exclaimed, feeling good all over, and before the feeling had a chance to run its course, she said, "Pauline's room use ter be mine and Elmer's. I reckon I'd be satisfied with it again, seein' as she's moved out an' all."

Justine nodded. "Well, for the time being." There was nothing more to be said. She felt unsure of what she was doing—hiring a self-proclaimed ghost! Despite a natural cynicism, she halfway believed Lottie. And if she tried to justify the story, she would probably talk herself out of hiring her. She stared at Lottie for a long second. "There is one more thing. Do you come and go, I mean disappear—"

"No, I'm here to stay. Only thing, when I die, you got to be certain, certain, y'hear, that I'm buried proper like, prayers an' all. With a preacher, if'n you can git one. I figure that was my problem last time."

"Listen," Justine said, voice intense, "you can't ever again talk about extending yourself. Okay? As it is, I'm never going to be able to explain you."

Lottie huffed. "I don't see why not. Seems like you got nothin' but old women traipsing in an' outta this house. One more ain't likely to fetch attention."

Chapter Nineteen

After they returned from town that afternoon, Agnes and Wheeler put their heads together at her desk. Pip and Judy Ann made short work of the yard debris left from the July Fourth picnic so they could hang around Lottie and listen to her tales of farm life in the 1800s. On the one hand, Justine wanted to caution Lottie about loose talk. On the other, the children were enthralled. Justine told herself it was educational.

When the sun began to drift deeply west, Lottie called Justine.

"Milo's coming up the path. Reckon you can witness fer me?"

"Witness what?"

"I got to git him to dig up my things. It's fittin'. He's been a huntin' them fer years."

"What things?"

"My silver, an' wedding ring, money—"

"Buried treasure, Mom!" said Pip. "Elmer hid it so the Union soldiers wouldn't loot it."

Milo stopped at the foot of the back porch steps.

Lottie fanned her face with the tail of the apron. But something, tension, an arc of knowledge or intuition passed between them.

Justine made the introductions anyway.

Milo's lean, rangy jaw dropped open.

"Knowed you was here!" he accused Lottie.

"You been misrepresentin' yourself," she told him. "Tellin' folks you're diggin' fer gophers and snakes an' such."

He cut a glance at the children, at Justine. "I aim to have what's rightfully mine. I'm a rightful descendant."

"I can tell you where to dig," Lottie said. "I can show you the exact spot. An' you ain't never come close afore, not once."

Milo's eyes went hard and glinty. "Show me."

Justine put a cautionary hand on Lottie's arm. "Whatever is buried belongs to Lottie," she warned Milo.

"You takin' up fer a ghost, missus?"

"She's no more ghost than you or me."

"Then the treasure ain't hers, is it?"

A rock and a hard place, Justine thought. Milo was trying to put her between them. "She wants her wedding ring—"

"An' my silver," Lottie declared.

"That leaves the money. Agree to halve it, Milo," Justine put to him. "That's fair. Otherwise, Lottie won't show you where to dig, now or ever. I'm buying the house. I've got a lease-purchase. Owner or not, you really aren't even supposed to be on the property—it has to do with privacy laws. Lottie can wait until I sign the papers on the house, can't you Lottie?"

"Sure can." She eyed the outbuildings, the way the shadows were lengthening. In only a few minutes more they would be at their zenith. She felt flushed and fidgety and tried not to show it.

Milo's greed won out.

"The money is in gold coin?" he asked.

"Elmer never said."

"Only half," Justine said.

Milo nodded.

Lottie walked to the corner of the porch, stood straight and ordered Milo to pace off her shadow.

"That's it," she said.

He stared at the ground. It was the center of a path that went round the house. Lottie grinned. "Elmer was fair smart, weren't he? He knowed anybody lootin' would be huntin' under trees an' barns and sheds, like."

Pip offered to help dig. Milo refused. It took almost an hour before scraps of a rotted leather trunk were revealed.

"Law," Lottie exclaimed. "Elmer oiled that good 'n fair. Now look!"

Milo went down on his bony knees. Lottie cried when he handed out the silver plates. They were black as smut.

"Don't cry," Judy Ann consoled. "We can polish them, can't we, Mommy?"

"It's worth a try."

A small stiff leather pouch came up on the shovel. Lottie snatched it, tore it apart. Inside was her wedding band. She slipped it on her finger. "Now then," she said holding up the dull filigreed gold for all to admire.

"It's lovely," Justine agreed.

Milo lifted out a rusted iron box, hit the padlock on it with the shovel and peered eagerly inside.

"That's the money!" Lottie said.

In the deepening shadows, Justine looked over Milo's shoulder. She stifled a laugh.

The money was Confederate scrip, rotted and worthless.

"WHERE IS SHE!" Tucker yelled as he came barreling into her office.

"Who told you?" Justine asked.

His eyes were blazing. "Damn it! Just where is she?"

"In the kitchen, dobing a roast, whatever that means."

Tucker turned on his heel.

"Wait!" Justine pleaded, racing after him. "She's not dangerous, she's just a sweet old lady..."

He pulled up short in the kitchen, glaring at Lottie. "Where's Agnes? Who the heck are you?"

"The new housekeeper?" said Lottie, looking past his shoulder for assurance from Justine.

"I needed some help, Tucker. You just can't imagine the day we've had."

"Sure I can!"

"Why are you yelling? Everything is fine. Really."

Agnes hurried into the kitchen, halting two feet from Tucker. "You're looking for me, I suppose."

Justine spun about. "Oh, Agnes, what have you done now?"

"Let me tell you," Tucker said between clenched teeth. "Agnes and Dad have been playing house. Rooting through my closets, my kitchen cabinets, changing everything around, even in the fridge."

Agnes puffed up. "I'm left-handed. I only rearranged them for convenience."

Wheeler moved in behind Agnes. "Hello, Son."

The yelling brought Judy Ann and Pip down from the attic where they'd been exploring. Lottie passed a damp cloth to each. "Wipe those hands afore you sit to table."

Meek as newborn lambs, they complied.

Lottie moved around people setting the table. "Look's like we're all here," she said. "Y'all sit to supper."

"Tucker," Justine pressed. "Calm down and sit down. Have supper with us. I was going to send Pip to invite you anyway."

"I don't know why you're so mad, Son. You been saying you was gonna rent the house out. I figured with my pension restored and Agnes's check, we could rent it ourselves."

"If you make it cheap enough," said Agnes.

Heart sinking, Justine turned to Tucker. "Rent out your place? Are you moving?"

Lottie served him a plate of sliced beef and vegetables and another of homemade biscuits.

"That smells good," he said, thinking fast. Lottie beamed.

Justine sat in the chair across from him. "Don't change the subject, Tucker."

"I'm not."

Nobody said the blessing. Nobody even thought of it. Lottie decided from here on out she'd say blessing while the food was in the pot. That way, they could all stay on the right side of Himself.

"And now that Justine has some household help," Agnes put forth. "She won't need me."

Household help? Justine bit down on her lip. Up until the moment Lottie had appeared, Agnes had been certain there was an unnamed force in the house. Now, faced with Lottie, she refused to accept her as such. It was the old cliché, Justine thought. We fear what we cannot see. Lottie was as visible as Justine herself, hence it was beyond Agnes's comprehension that Lottie possibly was, or ever had been the source of her fear.

"I've had all the suspense I can bear for a lifetime, Tucker. Get back to this business of renting out your place."

"Where's your mother?"

"Moved out."

He gazed at Lottie. "You hired a cook."

"That's a whole other story. I'll tell you later. That is, if I'm still speaking to you, which I won't be if you don't answer my question about your house."

"Let's talk about it later, privately."

"No, Tucker, now."

His cheeks went faintly pink. "Later."

"Now."

"The atmosphere isn't right." He cut into his meat and turned back to Lottie. "Magnificent."

Justine leaned across the table. "How would you like to *wear* that magnificent meat?"

"Are y'all fighting?" asked Judy Ann.

"Nope," said Tucker.

"Yes!" said Justine.

Tucker put down his knife and fork and reached into his pocket. Then he stood and leaned across the table to plop a box into the middle of Justine's plate. He sat back down saying, "How would you like to wear *that*?"

She opened it. Her hands flew to her cheeks. "Oh!"

"What is it, Mommy?"

"A wedding band," Justine answered, voice barely audible. Eyes wide and liquid, she gazed at Tucker.

"Well?"

She nodded.

He grinned. "In that case, I'm moving. Here. Satisfied?"

She was trying to hold back the tears. "Yes."

"I warned you the atmosphere wasn't right."

"It is. It's perfect."

"Law!" prattled Lottie. "Let me see."

Justine passed her the ring.

"There's some writin' on the inside," Lottie observed.

"It's in French," Tucker said, locking eyes with Justine. "*A jamais*. It means, forever."

"You'll be my step-dad, then," said Pip.

"That's right. What do you say?"

"Great!"

He turned to Judy Ann. "What do you say? You mind having me for a dad?"

"Do you spank little girls?"

"I wouldn't think of it," he said with exaggerated horror.

"Okay."

"I have some more news, too," announced Agnes.

"The straw that broke the camel's back," murmured Justine, but nothing Agnes said or did now could ruin the swelling happiness she felt.

"I won a contest. The confirmation came today." She looked at Pip and Judy Ann. "An all expense-paid family vacation . . . to Disney World in Florida! We can go before school starts."

After the squeals and hurrays and hugs abated, Lottie said, "What's Disney World?"

"OF COURSE I DON'T BELIEVE her tale for a minute," Justine said. She and Tucker were on his bed, leaning back upon a cushion of pillows. It was quieter here than at her house where the excitement of the upcoming trip to Disney World still prevailed. "But she's wonderful with the children and went through the house cleaning like a hurricane. She's related to Milo by marriage, you know."

"He probably put her up to it," Tucker mused. "He probably wanted to make sure there wasn't anything in the attic left to salvage before we put the down payment on the house. The old coot."

"It could be true, though. In terms of simple physics, our bodies are nothing more than physical collections of electrically charged particles."

"Did you talk to her about salary?"

"Of course."

"There's your truth," he said dryly. "Ever hear of a ghost who needed money?"

"As it happens, no." And that closed the subject. After a heartbeat, she said, "By the way, I think I've found a gimmick for the cookbook. Mother's menu scrapbook gave me the idea. Remember, she said it goes back to her grandmother's time. That's over a hundred years, Tucker! They kept guest lists for balls and buffets and soirees. There are any number of famous writers and actors and politicians on those guests lists! Plus comments about who liked what. Just think! You could—"

He sighed and pulled her into his arms. "I don't want to talk about gimmicks, or ghosts, or kids, or computers, or doing a honeymoon at Disney World. Disney World, for crying out loud," he moaned glumly.

Justine turned over and began unbuttoning his shirt. "Poor baby. So much has been happening, I've neglected you. I'm sorry. Have I told you lately how much I love you?"

"I don't believe so." He smiled into her eyes. "Are you by any chance in the mood for showing me?"

"Will you flex your tattoo for me?"

He nuzzled her neck. "Dear heart, I'll flex anything you ask."

Much later Justine lay content within the circle of his arms. She could ask for no more than this, she thought, his presence at her side, the years before them, laughter and talk, her children growing strong and happily and...Lottie.

She smiled drowsily. What most people think is the truth, is what they believe. Who was to say that there was not a spiritual dimension that had been overlooked?

Lottie had already made herself a member of the family.

Pip and Judy Ann were thrilled with her. They were not yet old enough to be skeptics. If Lottie said she manifested herself into the real world again after having been between and betwixt, they were willing to accept the tale. Pauline had not even considered that Lottie could be other than hired help. And years from now, who would even question it?

Outside the window a breeze rippled, moss swayed and the dark was seamless.

An owl hooted. Whooo, whooo, whooo...

My point exactly, Justine thought, and slept.